ENCHANTED DESIRE

She felt his lips kiss the hollow created by her collar bone, as if he were tasting her skin. Her lids sprang open. "I must warn you," she murmured, her breathing shallow, light. "There is a legend about this place."

He eased her to her knees and sank to the soft grassy bed opposite her. "That it is enchanted?"

She reached over and began to loose his doublet, saying, "That if you meet a fairy by the waterfall—"

"Are you truly a fairy, what the French call *fée?*" His voice was deep, stressed with the passion he constrained.

"—and drink its water, you will fall in love with her."

His dark eyes never left her face as she divested him of his clothing. "I do not believe in superstitions, mistress."

ACKNOWLEDGMENTS

Several years ago, I read Joseph Campbell's *The Power of Myth* and was captivated by its theme. From one of its messages, that of "following one's bliss," I was inspired to read other books that delved into the metaphysical. *Time is an Illusion* and *Ecstasy*, both by Chris Griscom, *Lovelight* by Julia A. Bondi, as well as *The Tao of Physics* by Fritjof Capra, were particularly enlightening, and I relied on these in fashioning my own story of *Sweet Enchantress*.

PARRIS AFTON BONDS

Sweet Enchantress

LEISURE BOOKS ▐▌ NEW YORK CITY

For Evan Marshall: Your guidance and support have meant more than you can ever imagine; and for Jacque D'Aponti, Jerry Jackson, Susan Karlovich, Sandy Zahasky, and the late Rick Baughman, the seeds of the rose.

A LEISURE BOOK®

November 1991

Published by

Dorchester Publishing Co., Inc.
276 Fifth Avenue
New York, NY 10001

Sweet Enchantress

"In the heaven of Indra, there is said to be a network of pearls, so arranged that if you look at one you see all the others reflected in it. The same way each object in the world is not merely itself but involves every other object and, in fact, is everything else."

Sir Charles Eliot

CHAPTER I

A sorceress?

A seductress?

The beggar stared hard at Montlimoux's chatelaine. Her skin was unbecoming, browned by the sun like that of a peasant woman's. Dirt smeared one sun-baked cheek. Her fingernails were encrusted with the earth in which she dug. By his troth, seduction by a wharfside wench would be more pleasurable!

From his viewpoint just beneath the vaulted inner ward, the chatelaine was within a lance span of his hands. He watched while she tended the courtyard garden. The pungent odor of sage, mint, and other herbs that had been winter-dead floated up from the soil tilled by her spade.

Corps Dieu, if she wasn't talking to herself. Her tone was clear, as resonant as a bell's virgin ring, a quality that doubtless was not attributable to her maidenhood, though she wore her hair loose as became a maiden.

A brown wren lit on a nearby stone bench, and she exclaimed in a mirthful voice, "Ah, my friend, you have come to greet me."

She raised her hand, one finger outstretched, he supposed for the bird to perch, but it took flight in a wild flapping of wings. A small cry of disappointment escaped her.

A sorceress? The beggar's lips pulled into a thin smile. The chatelaine was no sorceress— or seductress, God knows—but merely a simple-minded drudge!

Mayhaps, the farrier had made a mistake when directing him to the Countess Dominique de Bar. But, no, she was the only woman in this part of the inner ward. His gaze moved past her to search the domestic buildings and maze of hedge holly, possible places for concealment on a moonless night. He had noted earlier that no soldiers guarded the chateau's battlements. More telling, the chateau's iron portcullis was rusted.

Had no jealous army ever challenged its barbicans? Or loyal paladins charged out to defend those twin gatehouses? Yet the graceful chateau had been admirably constructed so that at one time it could have been made impregnable, if need be.

Admittedly, the once rich and cultured province of Languedoc had been known for the promiment role its women played. The delicacy and refinement of Languedoc was said to have been the creation of a society dominated by women.

Nevertheless, he scarcely believed that a woman, much less this madwoman, could rule an entire county singlehandedly. Surely, some man exercised authority in this far-flung principality between the province of Languedoc and the Duchy of Aquitaine. Surely, a garrison existed to defend the chateau and its glistening white town of Montlimoux, capital of the county of the same name.

Yet he had seen neither mercenaries nor local knights as he had climbed the cobbled road that corkscrewed upward through the hilltop town.

His mind's eye recalled that river-ribboned village with its limewashed, closely built guild shops and its steeply gabled homes with overhanging bay windows. Its countryside had once been a veritable symbol of stability. Thousands of acres of well-tended vineyards, dense woods, and allodial land had girdled it.

Casual questioning of the inhabitants had revealed that holy wars, the Albigensian Crusade in particular, had decimated it half a century before, but signs of the land's potential were evident. Silver mining in the area had long been profitable and had long been responsible for tales of Albigensian treasures.

Incredibly, this strategically located county was obviously undefended.

Although he had made no revealing movement, the chatelaine sprang to her feet and whirled to face him. For a prolonged moment, she studied him as intently as he had her. "Remove your hood."

More than her imperiousness, her direct gaze bothered him. It was merely her eyes, he reassured himself. Their bold, hazel color was too pale against her dark skin. Mayhaps, she had Saracen blood to explain her duskiness.

Just then February's brisk wind curvetted through her hair. He had judged it a nondescript brown color, but now it came to life in reddish flame. Like the fires of hell, maybe, but most certainly not the tresses of a Saracen offspring.

He blinked and the devilish red hue of her hair was gone. He would do well to remember that this land's strange sunlight played tricks on the eyesight. Languedoc lacked the pale, gentle sunlight and fine mists of England.

For a moment, he was tempted to seize her. He curbed his impatience. Slowly, he lowered the filthy hood, as ragged as his cloak. "God speed, my lady." His native Anglo-Norman French was not the language of Languedoc, which was closer to Latin than Castilian and northern French whose vocabulary was partly Teutonic. But his fluency in Latin aided him.

Beneath arrow-straight brows, her gaze inspected him as closely as a burgher's wife does bedclothing for fleas. Apparently, he proved unsatisfactory, because her eyes narrowed in a frown.

While he realized that she was by no means a hag, the severity of the strong nose, the square jaw, the broad forehead all bespoke a vexing intelligence that detracted from ideal comeliness. She might not be insane after all, but neither was she a seductress. Not unless she changed into one by use of her reputed sorcery.

"You do not mean well, villein," she said at last.

He blinked again. Had she read his thoughts? No, he did not believe in such foolery. "I seek only food, my lady Countess. I am hungry. By the law of your land I am permitted to enter and solicit leftovers from your board, am I not?"

"You do not mean well," she repeated. "However, the chatelaine of Montlimoux never turns away a soul seeking succor. We do not dine until the vesper bells. Until then you may assist in the stables. After you have eaten, you will be given alms. Then you will go on your way."

Old incidents exploded in his mind. Of his subservience. Of noblemen's condescension. And noblewomen's. His hands fisted into battering rams. His jaws tensed.

Before he could lose all control, a Goliath of

13

a man loomed before him, seeming to appear as if summoned by magic, though no doubt his presence had been concealed by the shadows of nearby statuary. The giant wore the white robe with the red cross of the banned Knights Templar. He was old, well into his late fifties. His complexion was ravaged, and he lacked brows and lashes. "I will conduct him there, my lady."

The beggar recovered himself and touched his forelock in a servile gesture that galled him because it came so readily, even after all these years. Rather than follow the ox-like Knight Templar, he strode alongside him, easily keeping pace with the man's lengthy strides. He himself was by no means of average height, was at least a head above most men. And while he was solid of sinew and bone, this giant would have thrashed him had their ages been more equal.

"You have traveled far?" the Knight Templar inquired.

"Aye."

"The lord to whom you owe allegiance?"

"My Lord God Almighty," he muttered.

The Knight Templar grinned down at him, then nodded meaningfully at his hood. "As the peasant says, 'The cowl does not the monk make.'"

The vagrant was struck by the gravelly timbre of the giant's voice and by his grin. A startlingly pleasant one in the visage of a gargoyle. "I earn my bread not by the cross but by the coin."

The Templar grinned again, his sparkling eyes like black peppercorns. "As the peasant says, 'A gambler's purse has no latch.' Ahh, here is our smithy. Bertrand will set your hands to earning honest coins."

The blacksmith was short with pipe-stemmed legs and powerful shoulders. "It will not be coins but manure your hands are working with, knave," he chuckled.

He put him to work with a tow-headed stable lad, Hugh, who was mute. While the vagrant swept the stables clean of manure, he pried the smithy with questions about Montlimoux. "Who is the Templar? A relative of the Countess de Bar?"

"Her steward." Bertand swung his hammer with a mightly blow to the red-hot steel he forged. "The Templar has leprosy, you know."

The beggar halted to stare at the smithy's soot-blackened face. "And the Knight walks freely among the villagers?"

Steam from the forge hissed and hazed. "Baldwyn Rainbaut's leprosy does not seem to be passed along."

"Oh?" He began spreading fresh rushes Hugh had fetched, noting that the horses in their stalls were blood stock. "Why is that?"

"Our chatelaine, Countess Dominique." The man fanned the red coals' flames with leather bellows. "She is fey. She has the healing hands."

He prompted Bertrand by commenting, "I am told they say other things about her. That her chateau walls are the color of a faded rose because she had the mortar mixed with the blood of beasts."

The smithy shrugged and fastened the glowing lump he held in his tongs on an anvil mounted on an oak stump. "They say a lot of things about Montlimoux."

The vagrant was interested in specifics, but Hugh passed him the fodder bag, and he had to wait until he had fed the horses before trying to elicit any more informaiton.

Finished with that task, he nodded toward Hugh, trudging toward the last stall with a bucket of water. "The mute stable boy there, the leperous Knight Templar—it would appear the chateau is a castle of outcasts."

The smith revealed missing teeth. "Myself included." He pulled on the laces of his leather tunic and almost proudly displayed the fleurs-de-lis that branded his sweat-sheened chest. "For poaching."

"At Montlimoux?"

"No, in Champagne." With iron tongs, he picked up the glowing andiron he had newly fashioned and held it aloft, examining it this way and that. "A fetching piece of work, eh?"

"You forge no armor, no helmets, no swords?"

From the town below, the vesper bells tolled the evening hour of six. Bertrand laid aside his work with a simple reply. "No need for such."

Along with him and Hugh, the beggar made his way across the bailey to the keep's great hall. Within, his practiced eye assessed all that it encountered. No rushes here, impregnated with grease from food and droppings from favorite dogs. The high-ceilinged room's flagstones were clean enough to reflect the candlelight. The candles were of beeswax, not the smoky, acrid tallow of rush torches.

But no tapestries heavy with gold and silver warmed the walls. Nor did ornamented chests and buffets display silver wine cups, brass *écuelles* or finely glazed pottery. The chatelaine's coffers reflected the impoverished state of the countryside. Compared to this small, seignural court, King Edward's royal one at Windsor, however bleak, coarse and militaristic, was lavish.

At least, entertainment was provided. From the galleries above, minstrels entertained on viéle, lute, and tabor. The lords and ladies of the chateau, numbering a dozen or so that evening, were already seated at one side of a long trestle table on a dais. He noted that the wash-worn table cloth, which doubled as the communal napkin, looked to be of the finest woven linen. Obviously, the county had once been a source of wealth.

His gaze located among the damosels the chatelaine seated in the center. By now he knew she was four and twenty and unmarried. She appeared to have washed, and her hair was, at least, restrained at her nape in a net seeded with pearls. She had donned fresh clothing, a long-sleeved silk tunic under a faded velvet surcoat embroidered with gold thread, now barely discernible.

The inevitable lap dog of every noblewoman was missing. Instead, perched on the back of her heavy chair was a falcon—sleek, hooded, and murderous.

A damoiseau, wearing her heraldic badge of the unicorn, hovered near her. The servant was waiting to carve for her a civet of hare. She ignored her food. Her full concentration was focused on the young man at her left. He wore a peacock-plumed beaver with a turned-up brim. Beneath it were lively eyes and a masterful jaw.

The beggar studied the young man more closely. His hands, strong yet graceful, made gestures, as if describing something to the countess. Though the beggar strained to overhear the animated conversation, the clatter of wooden platters and tinware along with the noise of guests chattering and the music of a plucked lute masked their intimate talk.

Was this man the power behind the chatelaine? Or the old Knight Templar, Baldwyn Rainbaut, on her right?

"Your turn," Bertrand prompted.

Hugh nudged him, and he recollected himself, moving forward to the copper basin on a low hutch. Fine soap, such as he rarely had the opportunity to use, lay at the side of the basin and pitcher. It was not the caliber of Windsor's Castillan soap, but neither was it that of meat fat and wood ash. Perfumed with herbs, it had an olive oil base that suggested a lot of preparation had gone into its making.

He left off his inventorying and washed his hands and face, then went to find an empty place on one of the benches.

The food being served was leftovers from the course just finished by the nobility and better than the thin gruel served at the Earl of Pembroke's board. Comradely conversation was exchanged by those gathered at the lower tables. Next to the beggar, a woman smiled coyly—or tried to. Her upper lip had been cut off. The fate of a harlot, most likely chased from the dark corners of a castle, doubtlessly to the regret of its sex-starved grooms and archers.

Repelled, he took up the communal tin cup, still greasy from the lips of the man to his other side, the chandler, and swallowed a draught. After he replaced the cup between them, his gaze sought the chatelaine again.

As he had been told, she was heralded as the patroness of the troubadours, and at the moment one was composing flowery verses in praise of her. However, she was not heeding the coxcomb's impassioned voice. She was

19

staring straight into his own eyes. Her green-
ish gaze was spellbinding. He did not stir. It
was as if she were stealing away his breath.

Laughing, Dominique de Bar plucked off
Denys's beaver cap and ruffled his shock of
jaw-length golden hair. "I have been wanting
to do that all evening, Denys Bontemps! And
now that we are alone, I may."

He grabbed her wrist and kissed its under-
side. "And I have been wanting to do this all
evening."

She saw the longing gaze cast by Jacotte, a
farm girl who had hired out as one of her
ladies-in-waiting, and quickly tugged her hand
away. "Enough. Iolande, tell the dolt to mind
his manners."

The old Jewess, domestic steward of
Montlimoux, sniffed her disapproval. She replaced in a chest the second of a two-volume,
gilt-bound *Tristan*, which her mistress had
been reading in the library. "You two were
never mindful children."

Dominique's childhood ally had matched
her bravado and outstripped even her impetuousness. Ignoring Iolande's remark, she said,
"Show me your sketches, Denys. 'Tis impatient I am to begin the construction."

She watched as his hands, powerful from
years of stone cutting, smoothed out the
scrolled parchments. "This is the shell of the
hospital."

"But the vault is so high."

"The higher the vault the more space for the windows you plan."

"Yes, we need windows. Scores of them." Her eyes marveled at the cross-ribbing, the piers and flying buttresses. Denys was a master mason with a knowledge so esoteric that it remained a professional secret. "Your skill, Denys, is superb." She glanced from the sketches to him. "You are much in demand in Paris and Troyes and Avignon. Yet you return here. I am grateful, friend." She adored him, had always thought him a bold, bright and beautiful creation.

"'Tis you who sent me away to Montpellier." Bantering reproach and yearning, always the yearning, colored his voice.

Denys Bontemps was baseborn, but it was not his low birth that had stood in the way of marriage with him. Courtly love might be based on grace, but married love was based on duty—and her duty was to Montlimoux first and foremost. Why marry when her life was already full, if not with happiness, then with a harmony that she had made her own?

"And you came back from the university there an architect and engineer of renown. For this you owe me a hospital, after which I shall release you to the French king and his grandiose plans for cathedrals."

"But 'tis the Great Architect I work for, Dominique."

"You and I both agree on . . ." She paused and smiled. Denys's thoughts were already

21

moving ahead, making preparations for the next phase of construction.

"A great deal of traveling will be necessary, at first," he was saying. "I expect to acquire our marble from Carrera. The Venetians have the best glassmakers. And, Dominque, I shall need the largest windlass—"

She laughed. "Enough, dolt, or you will surely bankrupt our meager coffers! As it is I charge you while on your travels to go to Cologne and purchase manuscripts." Her library contained already a large number ranging from philosophy and law to travel and medicine. "I shall give you a list of—"

"My lady Dominique?" Baldwyn stood in the library's arched doorway. Just behind him loomed the shadowy and imposing figure of the beggar. " 'Tis the alms you promised."

The same uneasiness she had felt earlier in the garden nudged the recesses of her mind, but she refused to identify its origin. She did not wish to ruin this evening with Denys. She only wanted the beggar gone at once. "Give him a handful of *deniers* from the strong-box."

She turned her back but was tensely aware of the beggar with every nerve of her body. She could almost feel the heat of his gaze. A violent man, she was sure.

Before daylight, the beggar rose from his place on the bench against the wall, where he had slept. His cloak had served as a covering.

The cock had not yet crowed, and snores still punctuated the great hall. The chill of predawn permeated the vast room. Remnants of last night's roaring fire flickered dimly in the fireplace at the other end of the darkened room. The fire would not be allowed to die; soon servants would be scurrying to tend it.

He stretched, wondering where he might find the chapel, as it was his custom to go first to Mass. A sleepy-eyed Hugh, barely stirring, pointed the way to the Bishop's Tower.

He passed through the guard room with its cavernous fireplace, feeling at ease in this setting but somewhat dismayed by its lack of soldiers. Only a few painted shields and a rack of blunted lances and maces girded the walls. Not enough to offer any sustained defense.

A tightly spiraling staircase led to the chapel. Candlelight from the chapel fluttered like a moth in the sculpture gallery outside. Reverently, he entered. Incense, sweet and heavy, pervaded the small, circular oratory. Where he had hoped to find a chancellor, he encountered the Countess de Bar.

Her back was to him. She sat cross-legged on a pillow in the center of the floor. Her unbound hair cascaded about her hips to sweep the colored tiles. From beneath the hem of her tunic, one bare foot peeked. With odd fascination, he stared at the soft exposed flesh, paler than her face or hands.

The incense . . . He felt heady. His gaze pulled free of her, seeking an altar or a wooden cross and found none. Instead of austere walls, the stones were plastered with a frieze of green scintillated with gold. The ceilings were adorned with metal stars—and a wheel of fortune, *par Dieu!*

Then he heard her voice: Soft, repetitive, unintelligible words. The hair at his nape bristled. She was unaware of his presence, and he quickly backed away. He was a soldier serving God and, thus, feared nothing. But whom did the chatelaine serve?

Troubled, he returned to the great hall, where a spartan meal was being served. With a murmured blessing, he quickly consumed a hunk of bread and a pot of cider. By now, the last members of the household had roused themselves to their duties. He, however, lingered behind to mix with the newcomers arriving to enter the Justice Room. From the shadows of a window embrasure, he watched with interest as the Knight Templar moved among the countess's vassals, questioning and sometimes lending advice.

The beggar had just about decided that it was, after all, Baldwyn Rainbaut who actually tended to administrative matters, when the Countess de Bar entered. She had dressed in a tight-fitting bodice over which was a lavender surcoat that was girded at her waist with a tortoiseshell brooch. Her hair had been brushed and bound once more in a net at her nape. Next to the Templar, she appeared fragile, no taller than a child. On her gloved fist rode the soft-breasted falcon, hooded.

She seated herself in the justice chair: a heavy chair covered with vermillion morocco and studded with nails. Its canopy was emblazoned with her cloth of estate, the same unicorn in full gallop.

The Templar passed her a sheet of parchment. Her eyes barely consulted the script as she enunciated in that cool, crystal voice the amount of acres that were to be ploughed that spring by boon custom and how many by desmesne ploughs; discussed what stock was to be kept and improved at each manor; and, finally, granted a communal charter to one of Montlimoux's villages.

Once that business was transacted, supplicants came forward. The beggar listened as she dealt with a cottar's respectful complaint about a neighbor's theft of his pig; a weavers' guild that desired to settle there if exempted from bridge tolls; a widow who wished to claim her one-third share of her late husband's estate.

He was expecting the Countess de Bar to suggest a suitable match for the rather homely but now wealthy widow, if only for the wedding imposts due Montlimoux. The wealth of an estate was determined by its profits from tithes and taxes.

The chatelaine startled him. She leaned forward and said, "Madam le Blanc, I would advise you to hie yourself to a convent where you will be free from male domination. With your experience, there is no reason why you could not become an abbess and wield broad authority."

Next a weeping maid was pushed forward by a buxom peasant woman in russet homespun, who wore a straw hat over her wimple. Tight-lipped, arms folded, she charged, "My daughter-in-law has aborted her baby."

The tenants and villagers began murmuring among themselves. Thoughtfully, the countess brushed the quill's feathered tip back and forth across her lips. At last, she said, "And the justice you seek?"

"Death. Nothing less than the death she brought upon my son's unborn child."

The chatelaine laid down her quill and addressed the young woman. "You wish to speak?"

The maid stared down at her mud-caked clogs. "I—my husband, he—forced me." She swallowed hard and said in a lowered voice, "He raped me."

"He is your husband," the mother-in-law broke in.

" 'Tis her body," the chatelaine said.

Wide-eyed, the peasant woman forgot herself momentarily. "The bishop will hear of —"

" 'Tis her body, not the Church's," the chatelaine said firmly. "Where is your husband?" she asked the younger woman.

"In the fields."

One of the countess's straight brows raised. Her lips compressed. "As he did not have the courage to come himself, I charge you, madam, and your son to treat your daughter-in-law here as your equal. Should I be apprised otherwise, you will suffer the consequences. Do you understand, madam?"

The straw hat of the peasant woman bobbed in acknowledgment. Beneath it, the woman's face was choleric.

The rest of the petitioners in the great hall appeared to accept the verdict. The beggar was astonished by this blatant blasphemy. Surely this was a solemn comedy being enacted!

His disgust and agitation must have betrayed him. The chatelaine lifted her chin, as if scenting something unpleasant. Slowly, her head pivoted. Her gaze searched the recesses of the room to settle on his shadowy form.

"You," she said, although the word was almost a whisper he barely heard. Her finger beckoned. "Come here, villein."

His feet shuffled forward to stand with the two peasant women. He tugged back his hood and made a clumsy obeisance. "God speed, my lady Countess."

"Last night, I ordered you to leave Montlimoux once you had been fed and received alms, did I not?"

"I was hungry this morning, my lady," he replied with a whine to his voice.

27

She leaned back, her gray-green eyes measuring him. At last, she answered, but not in response to his poor excuse. "You beg to differ with my pronouncement regarding these two women?"

He had not fooled her after all. His answer was guarded. "The Holy Office does not recognize rape if a woman conceives, as this can only happen if she has been sexually satisfied. So in the view of St. Augustine, the female appears to have sinned."

The indrawn breaths of her vassals were clearly audible. Behind her, the Knight Templar shook his shaggy head disparagingly. Her falcon side-stepped across the back of her chair as if impatient with the farce.

He was not certain what to expect next. The countess might have a reputation as a sorceress, but she also had a reputation of one who governed her territory wisely.

"You speak well," she said, her smile thin. "For a beggar. A boorish beggar, at that. I give you until the bells of sext to quit the village of Montlimoux."

By midday, he was astride his chestnut, with his great war horse hitched behind. Behind him, too, were the rose-faded walls of Montlimoux, rising steeply from a country dusted silver. He traveled toward the border of the Duchy of Aquitaine.

That evening he halted at a timber-trussed

building. Above the doorway projected a pole with a garland wreathed on a hoop suspended from it, the customary sign for a drinking place. The tavern was old, with a low ceiling, smoke-blackened timbers, and wattle and daub walls. Inside, noisy patrons thronged, and Captain John Bedford awaited him.

Paxton of Wychchester took a long swallow of the claret before speaking. "The chateau is undefended and well situated for my purpose."

"And the king's purpose?" his captain asked.

Paxton shrugged, his smile dry. "Edward is under the spell of the Round Table stories. He will approve this legendary court. What did you learn of the county itself?"

The red-bearded man leaned forward. "It has some of the finest hunting to be had, Paxton."

He grinned. "I was referring to its social and political leanings."

"Well, I learned there is plenty of anti-French feeling here. The county has prospects for commercial prosperity. 'Tis on the trade route of the Mediterranean and the wine route to Bordeaux. Its graneries and fruit stores are empty but, with good weather, could be bursting by autumn.

"Alas, from what I have been able to gather, even though nearly a thousand citizens have revolted against an imposed salt tax in nearby

Montpellier, apparently in this county the peasants are loyal and supportive of their countess."

"So there has been no successful usurper of her authority," he mused.

"What about her, Paxton? The Countess de Bar? Rumors say that she is as learned as a man."

The image of her in her library had stayed with him, her beguiling eyes and saucy smile. He tipped the tankard again, then replied, "She answers well, for a woman. But I shall have no problem disposing of her."

CHAPTER II

"You were impetuous to challenge the Church openly as you did." Behind Dominique, old Iolande shuffled back and forth across the windowless cellar room deep within the bowels of the chateau's donjon. Her hands twisted as if in constant washing, a hygiene that was not part of the Christian faith as it was the Muslim and her own. "Your ruling on the peasant girl's abortion will have the Inquisition with its torture rack at our gates."

Dominique continued mixing the maleable mercury, the soul of metals. "The Dominican idiots answer to Francis, and he would never countenance their interloping within his jurisdiction. Besides, our good bishop of Carcassone is pleasuring himself in Avignon, hundreds of miles from here."

The stooped woman halted beneath the wavering light of an oil lamp, suspended from a stone wall. "You are still in love with him, my pet?"

Dominique put aside the mortar and pestle and turned to face her old nursemaid. "Francis de Beauvais is the only man with sufficient intelligence not to bore me. If I were ever to subject myself to the inequities of a marriage contract, he would be the one. The only one."

Secretly, though, she was glad he was a bishop, so she would not have to make that decision. To her way of thinking, the ecclesiastical laws of marriage fettered the soul. Francis, with his admirable fluid doctrine, was of the same mind.

Although there were married priests, she suspected quite a few settled for affairs of the heart with the opposite sex. One of the French princes was said to visit a local monastery every morning at the darkest hour for just such a purpose, but seeking an affair with the same sex.

"Bah, there are other men with intelligent minds, if you would but give them—"

"You confuse intelligence with education, Iolande."

"It is merely because Francis dabbles in alchemy."

"It is because he understands that the reality of life is an illusion. That illusion is the only reali—"

"Your mother is responsible for this nonsense of yours." Iolande's seamed mouth pursed. "The Comtessa Melisande and her laboratory! I warn you, the peasants still gossip about her alchemical experimentations. Nowadays their tongues wag that she produced a transmuta—"

Dominique smiled, showing the slight space between her front teeth that was said to be an omen of good fortune. She knew better. She made her own good fortune. "The peasants gossip about your fairy magic with herbs, Iolande," she said, parroting Iolande. "Nowadays their tongues wag that our vineyards bloom because of your incanta—"

"—transmutation that made the de Bar family phenomenally wealthy. And look what happened. Burned at the stake!"

"What happened to my parents," Dominique said with a sigh of expasperation, "is a result of their harboring Albigensians from the Inquisition." As well the old woman knew, but for all her loyalty to the late comtessa she nevertheless had abhorred the woman's mystical avocation. "And as for the de Bar wealth, that was due to my mother's wise management of the de Bar demesnes, if you will but admit it, Iolande!"

"Bah! I admit you are trespassing on unknown borders!" Fiercely, she cupped

Dominique's face between her withered hands. "To force one's will over other people or nature, like converting iron into gold, can only result in the deepest sorrow. Don't forget that, Dominique!"

The Comtessa Dominique covered Iolande's hands with her work-stained ones. "I won't. I swear by all the Pope's relics."

The old woman's mouth twisted in a scoundrelly smile. "One is sufficient."

"The napkin of St. Veronica then?"

They both laughed, but after Iolande departed, Dominique's smile faded as she went back to work. From a seven-hundred-year-old manuscript, she copied, "Man and woman, the lion and the lily, red and white, sun and moon, sulphur and mercury."

She laid aside her quill and rubbed her eyes with the heels of her palms. So, she thought, it appears that the philosophers spoke the truth.

Although it seemed impossible to simpletons and fools, there appeared to be indeed only one stone. "One medicine," she mused aloud. "One law . . . one work . . . one vessel, all identical with the white-and-red sulphur, and to be made at the same time."

Countless alchemists sought the Philosopher's Stone that would transmute base metal into gold. But she suspected it was something far more potent. She believed the Philosopher's Stone was a panacea that would free mankind of all sufferings. If only she knew more. Alas, she was but a fledgling alchemist.

Tired, she settled back into her chair, and, resting her chin on interlaced fingers, closed her eyes. The image of Francis came to mind. Like herself, he believed that it was possible to transcend limitations.

She was at a point in her life where she had to know whether there was something more to this life beyond the Church's one-dimensional concept of the role of man and woman. The Church's description of metaphysical hierarchy, placing women at the bottom of the list, confounded her.

For a long time, she had wanted to believe that there *was* something more. That between the realms of physical and intellectual passion was layered a third: the pure passion of the soul. It would be like finding one's reflection in a silver-polished mirror, she thought. Or finding one's soul in its complement form in the opposite sex. That belief had become an obsession with her.

Francis's marvelously mobile face faded from the back of her lids, to be replaced by that of a villein: the beggar who had sought succor from Montlimoux the week before.

His presence disrupted Montlimoux's harmony and her own. What others called instinct or intuition told her as much. She had sought out solitude in the oratory, seeking to sit undisturbed and enter a state of relaxed receptivity. It had not come; instead, the beggar had. And as quickly left.

Certain details about him had given lie to

his beggar's guise. His aura, for one. She saw it as a luminous vapor around him. It had been a pulsating red and orange, whether from dormant anger or his male aggressive energy, she could not decipher. She only knew the aura was its own truth; it never lied. It told the story of who the person was.

The beggar's educated speech, too, was suspicious. Perhaps he was an itinerant scribe or a mendicant friar who had renounced the order. But most of that tonsured society thrived on the blessings of heaven and the fat of the land. They were a happy and obese community in the midst of the famished.

Though the profession of either scribe or priest could explain his education, there was still his curious accent. He had to be a foreigner. Not one of the French, for his caressing French lacked the coarse dialect of that *langue d'oil*.

Then there was his stance, nothing like that of a villein. Not with his thumbs hooked arrogantly in his loose rope belt as they had been. She summoned the image of his face, that firm mouth with its crisply indented upper lip curling disdainfully in a broad face nicked with scars.

She turned inward to find an answer and, after some moments, reached the conclusion that he was a former soldier. Beneath the short-cropped brown hair, his dark brown eyes betrayed the violence he lived by.

With a sniff of disdain, she dismissed him

from her mind. Undoubtedly, his level of wisdom was far below hers.

"Should the king learn of the rumors and legends regarding the chatelaine of Montlimoux," John Bedford teased, "he'll most likely rescind his order of creating ye its seneschal and establish himself at its court instead."

"Edward would be wasting his time. You know yourself that he would rather devote himself to the tourney and other chivalrous pursuits." Paxton could not understand the king's esoteric cult of chivalry. For himself, there was only the issue of winning.

He glanced back at his baggage train. It snaked over the nearest hill, still coated with winter grass. The trains' tail end of pack animals was out of sight. A reconnaissance partly assured the safety of the caravan, as did his pikemen and Cornish knifemen who guarded its flanks.

He imagined Montlimoux's chatelaine would not be pleased with the cost of lodging such a retinue: personal retainers, armed guards, chamberlain and marshals, mounted archers from Cheshire, men-at-arms, and English knights.

John reined in his mount. The red-bearded man was born to the life of a professsional soldier, although he had come from a family of humble Norfolk squires. "Come now, Paxton. Confess. Ye are like the rest of us. Ye entertain a fascination for the Round Table romances. Ye know—Merlin, Tristan and Iseult, Courts of Love."

Montlimoux a Court of Love?

Paxton recalled the supper he had partaken there and the strutting troubador who had inportuned his mistress's attention with verbose, but conventional, poems of courtly love. Amidst the applause of the knights and their ladies, she had absently rewarded him with a kiss on the cheek and a peacock's feather— and shifted her piercing gaze back to him. The woman was impudent. She would soon know her place as mere chattel, categorized along with his ownership of his prized war horse and other accoutrements. This long awaited confrontation had been more than two fortnights in the planning.

The reed roofs of a Montlimoux hamlet came into view, and soon honking geese fluttered from under the hooves of the horses. Recalling his own humble status at Montlimoux and anticipating his confrontation with its haughty chatelaine, his next remark appeared precipitious and nonsequential. "Let's stop at the public bath, John, and scrub off the dust of the road."

John grinned knowingly, his teeth white against the auburn of his beard. "Aye, my Lord Lieutenant."

"My Lord Lietutenant?"

"To be more accurate, my new title is a seneschal of sorts to Montlimoux."

He had sent ahead green-and-white-capped heralds on horseback to announce his arrival that morning to the Countess Dominique de Bar. In her own Justice Room he would bring to heel that imperious female. For the occasion, he had chosen not the garb of a courtier, but that of a common soldier. Not a jewel, not a ribbon anywhere. Only a shirt of chain mail over a short padded tunic and mail stockings. And, of course, the sword on his left side; on his right the dagger, the *misericord* for the mercy it dispatched to the mortally wounded.

At his mild pronouncement, her eyes glowed like the *feu follet*, those unholy green lights of marsh gas that flitted through England's peat bogs. Her hands clenched the arms of her justice chair. "A seneschal of sorts? By whose creation?"

"By the creation of the King of England, one of the twelve peers of France, Count of Ponthieu, and . . ." He paused to emphasize the last. "Duke of Aquitaine, which my Duke-King Edward III holds as feudatory of the King of France."

She waved a hand of dismissal. "That is common knowledge."

"Perhaps your knowledge doesn't encompass the fact that within the Duchy of Aquitaine's boundaries lies the County of Montlimoux."

Slowly she stood to face him. Her normally tanned face was as white as a winter moon. The barest tremble of her hands betrayed her, as did the rise and fall of her breasts, indecently exposed by a low decolletage embroidered in old lace. Only the virgin white veil mantling her shoulders offered any modesty. "Those boundaries have never been officially established."

She was grasping at straws. He lifted one brow, and his smile was as hard as steel. "Exactly."

He watched her face, the fleeting, warring thoughts that passed over it. The people of Languedoc detested the English only a little worse than they did the French, whose armies had ravaged the countryside a century earlier in a holy crusade against the heretical Albigensians. There was no higher power to which she could appeal. Least of all the pope, since Languedoc's princes and counts had been both tortured and excommunicated countless times over the last century for harboring Albigensians and Jews alike. As she herself had been doing, and her mother before her, and her mother before her.

She drew herself up, reassuming her mantle of dignity and nobility. "Nevertheless, I *am* Montlimoux's comtessa."

"You never were," he said calmly, relishing the moment. "Officially, your fiefdom has been without a suzeraine for twenty years, since France adopted the Salic Law, prohibiting females from either inheriting or passing their inheritance on to their descend—"

"I know the Salic Law!" She moved forward

until she stood a cloth bolt's ell from him. Gardenia, lavendar, rose, and other delicate scents he was not familiar with invaded him, making him feel strangely off balance. Behind him, he could sense John and the bodyguards tense. Behind her, the towering and aging Knight Templar, along with her lackies, stiffened their stance.

"Let me understand you," she said in a low voice, her words clipped, her eyes narrowed. "Montlimoux is to be passed to King Edward of England, who claims this land as an extension of his Duchy of Aquitaine?"

"You do show promise of grappling with the intricacies of politics and diplomacy."

His sarcasm went ignored. She lifted a brow. "Do you not find it curious that the English king claims the duchy nominally his through his French forebear, the *female*, Eleanor of Aquitaine?"

He shrugged. "Your barbarous French passed the Salic Law, not the English." Which had been the source of Edward's vexation to begin with. By doing so, the French prevented Eleanor's Plantagenet descendant from inheriting the French crown, now worn by a Valois, Philip VI.

"They are not *my* barbarous—"

"You are most fortunate," he said in a quiet, but threatening, tone, "that you do not reside in England, where secular law states that the deaf, the dumb, the insane—and the female —cannot even draw up a contract."

41

"That is in England!"

"Well, then," he said with imperturbability, "I shall precede on ecclesiastical law, which bases its curtailment of the rights of a woman on her secondary place in creation and on her primary part in original sin."

A muscle flickered in her clenched jaw. "You are the barbarian!"

"As you are now my vassal, mademoiselle, I could have you whipped in public for such an utterance of disrespect. Let it be your last."

"Your vassal?"

The moment had arrived. His smile was tolerant. "Now that King Edward has at last put forth his claim as Duke of Aquitaine and now that I, Paxton of Wychchester, have been appointed Grand Seneschal of its County of Montlimoux, you are by law in my custody. You may still assume the title of Countess but you hold neither the authority which comes with that title nor the authority which comes with the one of chatelaine."

She stared at him. Comprehension of the enormity of what had just transpired was evident in the sequence of her facial expressions: doubt, followed by horror, then rage, and, finally, the realization of her helplessness. He half expected her face to turn into a domino of tears.

Defiant in defeat, she turned abruptly to leave the room with her chin held high. Her retinue stood frozen, unable to cope with what they had witnessed. He let her get as far as the pointed arch doorway, then called, "Mistress, from this moment on, it would be wise of you to take your leave by my permission."

She whirled around. Her hands were balled, her dusky complexion waxing scarlet, visible even from that distance. "You . . . I can't. . . ."

He crossed to her justice chair and sprawled in it. He was fatigued from the day's journey. "Try," he told her.

She swallowed. The span of a moment passed in which his gaze dueled with hers. "With . . . your . . . permission." Each word was forced, as if she were choking.

"Messire," he prompted.

"Messire!" A cat could not have hissed any better.

His smile was magnanimous. "I grant you permission to take your leave."

For Dominique, Montlimoux held a beauty that was unsurpassed and from her maternal forbears, she had inherited a consuming love for it. As a child, she had reveled in old Iolande's stories of Montlimoux's past grandeur.

In short, the Comté of Montlimoux stood for all that Dominique was, all that went before her, and, in her mind, all that was to come.

Until Paxton of Wychchester had ridden into her mountaintop principality. She should

43

have taken better heed of the beggar's underlying appearance of brute force that first evening.

Her tread measured her chamber's perimeters in one direction, then she would pivot to retrace her steps in the other. Her maids-in-waiting glanced at one another furtively. "This cannot be happening," she muttered. "No warning. No declaration of war. The miscreant just appears with his entourage of soldiers and demands that the chateau and village quarter them."

Marthé, one of her maids-in-waiting, glanced up from the wall hanging she embroidered. "What does he mean to do, my lady?"

"He means to take full control," Iolande said, as she quietly entered the room. She sniffled in indignation. "His aide, Captain Bedford, has instructed me to bring the demesne's ledger to his Lord Lieutenant. The man wants a full account of names and manors within your comital domain."

So, even Montlimoux's revenues, such as they were, he meant to sequester! Palms rubbing together, Dominique resumed pacing, circumventing the stool on which another maid-in-waiting sat.

The curly-locked Beatrix dropped her needlepoint in her lap and, pale, looked up at Dominique. "Does my Lord Lieutenant intend to evict us from the chateau?"

Abruptly, Dominique halted. One eyebrow arched. *"My lord?"* Already the man had usurped her authority. But would he go that far? Put her and her household out into the streets? By her troth, how she loathed the oaf with his cursed abundant dignity!

She swung about. "Summon Baldwyn."

Within minutes, the Knight Templar lumbered to her chamber door. She shooed the others away and directed him toward one of the low stools. Sitting, he was still almost as tall as she.

Never had they consulted in her private chamber, but neither her library nor the Justice Room were now to be considered reliable places for her to conduct private business. "What do you know about this man, Baldwyn? Our *Lord Lieutenant?*" The words on her tongue were as tart as vinegar.

He clasped his hands between his spread legs and emitted a heavy sigh. "It's hard to decipher the man. You know he was at your court earlier this month?"

Her lips compressed. "I well remember."

"He came then as a mendicant, now as a soldier. But he led me to believe he also follows the dictum of the Church."

The Templar fairly spit out the last word. The pope, in league with the late Philip IV, had envied the Knights Templars' wealth and had had them suppressed. Many of the Templars had been burned at the stake. Baldwyn's antipathy for the Church was shared by Iolande, who, with the rest of the Jews, had been expelled from France about the same time. They were but two of the thousands who had learned it did not serve to thwart the power of the pope.

These two outcasts, the Jewess and the Templar, had raised Dominique as their own from the time she was a toddler. Until she had reached her majority, the two had served as co-regents for the county. Despite their loving efforts, she could not shake the feeling of being abandoned, unwanted, so very alone. Perhaps it was because her parents, by electing to harbor the Jewess and the Templar, had chosen principle and death over her. So, there was a vacuum inside her despite Iolande's and Baldwyn's abiding love for her.

Often, she had wished them married, imagined them as her parents, of whom she had but little recollection. But her nursemaid and the Templar were recalcitrantly independent and had no wish for such bondage. In fact, they seemed merely to tolerate each other. She sometimes imagined herself as they were now, old and lonely. It saddened her. Was there not more to this solitary journey through life?

"Your true opinion, Baldwyn. What help can I expect from my vassals?"

"In truth," he mumbled at last, "little."

She stared at the Goliath's visage. This warrior/monk, soldier/mystic had tutored her in geometry and astronomy as well as astrology, knowledge he had acquired while serving as a young knight in the Holy Land. There he had, also, acquired leprosy. "Surely, I have feudal service owed me."

"You know yourself that the last few years, in the absence of wars, your tenants have paid scutage in place of military service."

"Yes, but those shield taxes have gone to building a hospital and other improvements. On how many of our local knights can we depend?"

"Well," he said, ticking off on his thick fingertips, "Richard, son of Jacques holds fifteen knights' fees. Andre of Gaston, six knights'. Robert holds half a knight's fee. All in all, mayhaps thirty-five knights' fees and a half."

"I see," she murmured. She wondered what Francis would advise.

The Templar looked up from his interlocked fingers. His eyes held the regret of a man reduced by the years. "Dominique, I have battled the fiercest warriors of the lot, the Muslims. I know whereof I speak. A thousand knights' fees would not save Montlimoux. Should we battle and defeat Paxton of Wychchester, we would still have his English king to deal with. At Edward III's hands . . . Well, I can only dissuade you from the follies of such a rebellion."

She saw that he suffered as much as she at their predicament. She placed her hand on his stooped shoulder. "I know, I know, Baldwyn."

"No, you cannot. For an old soldier, it's

much worse. Being helpless, being weak. It's like being castrated. Like being an eunuch!"

She almost smiled. She wanted to gainsay him, to tell the old soldier that it was far the worse for a woman. She attempted jocularity. "It was you who instructed me in Latin, impressing upon me that its word for 'woman' suggested her weakness, this one in faith—*feminus*."

"Well, as the peasant says, 'Life and death are in the power of the tongue.'"

She smiled wanly. "I need time alone to think, Baldwyn. Send me Marthé, then see I am not disturbed, will you?"

In silence, a bewildered Marthé helped her change from her tight, tailored gown into a simple undergown of russet linsey-woolsey, then add the peasant's loose surcoat. The maid-in-waiting knew better than to break into Dominique's agitated ruminations.

Sending Marthé away, Dominique made her way down a back turret staircase. At its base, an English sentry stopped her, demanding her identity.

"I am the Comtessa de Bar," she said, barely controlling her temper at this latest impertinence. "Go tell *that* to your Lord Lieutenant."

Abashed, he let her pass with a muttered, "My apologies, Comtessa."

Miffed, she swept by him, heading toward her herbal garden, her greatest source of inner peace. She had acquired her knowledge of plants from Iolande, who, like herself, was a member of a matrilineal society.

Over the years the old Jewess had instructed her in how to cup a plant in her palm and determine its nature and distinctions. By observing the leaves, stems, and roots, she knew whether the plant could be used for healing or food; whether it needed a flood of sunlight; whether it grew harmoniously with other plants.

The fame of Montlimoux's vineyards was a tribute to both Iolande's skill with plant life and her reverence toward all living things. Having absorbed these lessons at her nursemaid's knee, Dominique was loathe to kill even a spider, much less a garden snake.

For over an hour she worked furiously. The warming sunlight of March never reached the chill of her heart. She felt none of the inner attunement that usually came with gardening. Her hands caressed the rich soil, but she received no corresponding comfort.

At the quivering of the lichen, she paused. Someone was coming. The alteration in the lichen affected even her body's vibrating emotions, reducing them to a slower tempo which indicated either fear or anger.

She knew when the man clad in chain mail stepped into the sunlight that it could only be anger that affected her so. She detested the attitude of superiority reflected in his face, nicked here and there with the scars his violence had wrought.

Schooling her expression to impassivity, she rose and faced the Englishman who had appeared in her Justice Room as a beggar. Then she had judged Paxton of Wychchester of being her age. Almost as tall as Baldwyn and nearly as brawny, he had presented an imposing figure, much as he did now. "I was expecting you. What plans have you made for me and my household?"

His experienced eye examined her dirt-crusted hands, her dusty work dress, and her unbound hair. The dark sweep of his brows met over the high bridge of his nose. "Expecting me?"

"Are all the king's lieutenants so slow of thought?" she mimicked. The words had rolled off her tongue before she could halt their flow. Her natural instinct for command, whether by intimidation or by commendation, was a difficult one to subdue.

He hooked his thumbs in the leather belt of his scabbard, a stance that was now becoming familiar to her. He looked disturbingly patient. "Are you planning to make trouble?"

"I am surprised you did not summon me to you like a tenant."

He waved his hand indifferently, its sunburnt skin also notched with scars. "Your feminine games are inconsequential to me."

That pricked her pride. "Do you expect me to placidly accept my subjugation?"

"I will expect you pay homage to me as my vassal a fortnight hence in the great hall."

She gasped.

He continued calmly. "Heralds will be sent throughout the county of Montlimoux, summoning its inhabitants. A tourney, I think, will serve nicely as enticement. Aye, a tourney, guaranteeing safe conduct to knights and esquires alike. That should well set the stage for a ceremonial transition of authority."

So that was what lay behind this visitation. As a woman she might be of inconsequence to him, but not the power she wielded. "I cannot renounce my heritage!"

"Cannot or will not?"

"Either. Both!"

"Mistress, heed me. You cannot even care for your own people. I found here no protection for them, no mercenaries, no army to guard the gates."

"And you found here no violence! Nonaction means simply refraining from activity contrary to nature."

He looked at her strangely. As if she were some unidentifiable species of plant life he had never encountered. "Mistress, do you not perceive—"

"Chatelaine," she corrected. Her gaze swept over the soldier-warrior with unmistakable disdain.

"Mistress," he asserted with the patience of one speaking to the slow of wit. "Do you not perceive that your foolish pride and stubbornness will only beget sorrow for you and those for whom you care?"

"I see that I am as I am. I cannot change." It was a cry from her heart, though her words were stony enough.

"You will learn change if you wish to remain here." He paused, then added, "Of course, you could always become the wife of a yeoman. The marriage imposts I receive as Montlimoux's Grand Seneschal would add something to its coffers. But I do not think you would adapt well to shouldering firewood like a pack mule, while your husband trods on ahead."

He paused, and a glint appeared in his eyes. "Then there is always the convent, is there not? I recall you advising a widow she would find the opportunity to wield broad authority within it walls, aye?"

"I would take the veil before I would submit my free will to a man."

"Free will?" His smile was close to a smirk. "A woman's subjugation to man is the fruit of her sin."

"Sin?"

"Are all Languedoc maidens slow of thought?"

She had never felt more like committing violence.

"Aye, sin," he continued. "Did not woman succeed in seducing man where Satan had proved powerless in the Garden of Eden?"

"I might remind you that while woman was supposedly created from Adam's rib, man was created from mere dust!"

His grin was condescending, infuriating her even more. "And I shall remind you that woman is not the image of God, since she was created in the image of Adam, whereas man alone is the image of God!"

Her lips formed a caustic smile. "Your knowledge of the missals is enlightening."

"I was tutored by an abbot."

"A misogynistic monk, to be sure."

"A monk who knows the truth in Scripture, mistress." He turned on his heel and left her standing, astonished and outraged.

Chengke, an old Chinese sage who had once graced Montlimoux, would have said that her yin power was being challenged. But then Chengke, who had come to her parents' court by way of Arabia, believed in a lot of things that the Catholic Church found heretical. In her experience, her yin power, that feminine and principal force of nature in Chinese cosmology, was not always something she could draw upon at will.

She thought of Chengke's teaching of finding the middle way between extremes.

But how would she achieve that when Paxton's way was that of the warrior?

She had no answer. All she had to guide her was Chengke's counsel and was that enough to withstand the brute force of the sinister Englishman?

CHAPTER III

She knew that a warrior was inclined to force and violence, and because of this violent nature, the violence had a chance to dominate and possess the soul.

But whose? His own or hers?

Chengke, who had claimed to have lived during the late Chou period, four hundred years before Christ, had neglected to tell Dominique that important piece of information. She only knew she felt out of balance, her mind disturbed, a tunnel's vortex of slow darkness. Fear had numbed her.

She glanced up at the high table, where Paxton of Wychchester sat in *her* chair, displaying male avarice and its egotistical concept of ownership!

Beside his officers sat one of the village's burghers, the portly Guillaume de Sigors, who had made his wealth in cloth—and whom she had only recently knighted. How galling! The opportunistic Guillaume and his wife were the first vassals of the comté to curry favor with the foreigner in the six days since his arrival. How many more of her people would go over to the Englishman?

Where was Denys? Buying marble in Carrera? Contracting with a master glazier for the hospital's stained glass? Had her missive yet reached him that within a fortnight's time she would publicly be forced to cede both her county and her chateau?

She and her household were virtual prisoners in the chateau. Her every thought was predicated on how to rid the county of the savage foreigners. Alas, she could only hope that Denys returned in time. A man of the people, he might be able to arouse Montlimoux's inhabitants to action. Mayhaps, some of the county's foremost knights would attempt to raise an army in Montlimoux's defense.

She suspected the English lieutenant was prepared to counter any such rebellion. Late into the nights, he worked alongside his red-bearded captain in her Justice Room. Baldwyn had revealed to her that upon occasion the lieutenant had summoned him to consult about land routes, bridge crossings, and the nearer seaports.

Once, even she had been summoned from her bedchamber to identify the keeps of petty castellans on a local map he had procured from her document cupboard. When she had entered the Justice Room, the Englishman's back had been to her as he poured over the map, spread out on the escritoire. A ring-tailed cat rubbed itself against his hose-encased calves.

Barely acknowledging her, the man had snapped questions, saying, "Here? And here?"

Distastefully, she had watched his large hands, shadowed with hair and scarred, splay across the map's scrolled edges. Inadvertently, she had blurted, "Your given name Paxton, it little befits your calling."

He had glanced up from the map to her. At that moment, she had realized her dishevelment—her wrinkled tunic, her hair *en neglige*, her lids heavy from a restless sleep.

He had straightened to stare down at her. She loathed him so. She found it difficult to sustain his sardonic gaze. "No, I am not a man of peace but one of the sword. And your name Dominique, it little befits your station now, does it?"

If only he did not speak the language in such a caressing voice. "For the present."

She could not bear to be in his presence and had turned to leave the room. "Not so quickly," he had ordered.

She had half-turned, and he warned, "By

your leave. Say it. 'By your leave, my Lord Lieutenant.'"

Her teeth had gritted against each other. "By your leave, my Lord Lieutenant." The profound dislike in her voice had been unmistakable.

But it had mattered not one whit to him. He had already turned back to study the spread map.

Disgusted with her preoccupation with the man, she banished her recollections and returned her attention to the stewed mutton spread like paste on the thick trencher of bread. Aware of the sidewise glances spared her from the others at the low table, her fingers could only pluck at a soggy morsel. Jeanne had obviously gone lax in her culinary efforts.

This was the first appearance Dominique had made in the great hall at mealtimes since the arrival of the foreigners. Her presence had been ordered by the Englishman's wish or, at least, that was how the phrasing was delivered by a surprisingly respectful Captain Bedford.

While she had not actually been ordered to sit at the low table, she had so chosen. To break bread with Montlimoux's enemy would have been to surrender, if only a part of herself.

Was this how one lost one's soul?

A traveling jester in checkered yellow-and-orange silks, soiled and frayed by the years, danced for the guests. The bells of his long-pointed shoes tinkled with his foolish capers. A silent groan welled inside her. Paxton of Wychchester! The English dolt's company lacked the animated conversation, a spirited mixture of wit and wisdom, that was to be found at Francis's board: poets, theologians, physicians all sharing their intriguing knowledge.

Now that Francis had taken up residence in Avignon, she sorely missed his rapier-swift sallies and intriguing stories. But then all the intellects and diplomats of the civilized world were making pilgrimages there now that it was the new seat of the papacy instead of profligate Rome.

As a child she had looked forward to Francis's visits to the chateau. A full ten years older, he had never bored her and never looked upon her as merely an engaging child, but as a child wise for her years and gender.

Out of sorts, she rose abruptly from the lower table. To do so before the lord of the chateau rose, signifying the end of the repast, was a slight to formality and could bring unpleasant consequences. But then he had made it plain she was of no consequence, and she seriously doubted her presence would be missed.

Paxton of Wychchester's officers were growing steadily drunker on Iolande's vintage red wine, and the burgher and his wife fared little better. The lieutenant—Grand Seneschal, she mentally corrected—paid not the slightest heed to the jester's antics nor the scantily clad professional dancing girls who next performed. She recognized that the rage in his energies burned even fiercer, though he appeared to content himself in conversing with his captain. Their wine flagons were virtually untouched.

Within her privy chamber, a fire burned warmly against the chill spring night. Like fireflies, sparks took flight from the cedar logs. Her falcon, perched on its tasseled pommel, flared its wings in recognition of her entry. "It's high time you were exercised, Reinette."

Reinette pleased her greatly. Not only was the female falcon the fastest animal alive, but she was larger and more aggressive than the male tiercel.

Beatrix rapped on the antechamber door, seeking to help her mistress disrobe, but Dominique wished only to be left alone and dismissed her maid-in-waiting. Doubtlessly, the young woman was headed for a rendezvous with the English captain, John Bedford, in some darkened alcove of the chateau. Their dalliance had been remarked upon by Iolande, who let nothing escape her attention. For her part, Dominique cared not as long as the captain did not saddle Beatrix with child when the English soldiers finally left.

And if they did not?

Pensive, she stared into the fire's hypnotic blaze. Her emotional antennae vibrated in disorder. Her jaws hurt from the anger and frustration stored there. Her intuitiveness aided her not at all these days. Like the blaze's fireflies, it flickered in and out of her awareness so that she only knew of its presence after the fact.

The menacing Englishman had disrupted her whole way of life. Her county, her chateau, and now even her mind.

She heard her antechamber door open again, then the massive door to her privy chamber groaned with the thudding of a fist. She shrank from the violence of the sound, the trumpeter of its master of violence, surely. She went to the door and sheathed its iron bolt. As she had expected, Paxton of Wychchester loomed in the anteroom's shadows. At his feet, purred the ring-tailed cat.

"You forget your place," he told her. His face was as dark as his doublet.

His ire at so small a disregard for ritual amazed her. She held her ground, keeping the door's aperture no more than a forearm's width. "The antechamber is an excellent place for cooling one's heels."

The cat streaked past her to crouch beneath Reinette's perch and hiss. The feline's tail licked and curled in anticipation.

"Ca–ca–ca–ca–ca!" The high-strung falcon emitted a rapid staccato screech of perturbation. Its talons curved around its railed perch, as if already clutching its victim. Its wings beat the air wildly, then it flew off the perch as far as its tether permitted.

Paxton pushed the door open and crossed the room to peruse her agitated falcon. "I have always found the weaker female sex tends to be more rapacious," he mused in his heavy-timbered voice. Bending, he collected his hissing cat with a broad sweep of his arm. "Arthur here seems to be of the same opinion. You realize, do you not, that your falcon and my cat cannot live in close quarters. Your falcon will have to be set free."

"Free?" she demanded of his broad back. "What do you know of freedom? I am the prisoner here, sire, not you!"

He turned on her. "I can take care of that, mistress. Off Marseilles' coast are moored Saracen galleys eager to take on white slaves as cargo, especially fair maidens." His fingers boldly reached down to touch her cheek, and she forced herself not to flinch. "Though thy cheeks are not so fair, maiden."

The confines of the room, and the fire's heat, stifled her. "No man has ever touched me without my permission," she said with a quiet anger that left her trembling inside.

"I do not find that surprising." His laugh was short and derisive.

"Do not touch my lady again," a voice rumbled behind them. Baldwyn filled the open doorway. With the Englishman occupying a privy chamber at the other end of the solar, the aging giant was never far away these days. Strangely, his face, mottled by the disease, appeared almost timeless. His peaceful expression was unaltered. "I renounced the use of violence years ago, my Lord Lieutenant, but I would lay down my life in defense of my Lady Dominique."

"I would dislike that, Templar. Your life is too valuable for such a foolish gesture."

"Baldwyn, please," she said. "'Tis all right."

"No, it is not," Paxton countered. He released the cat to withdraw a folded sheet of parchment from his doublet and passed it to her. "Yours, mistress?"

She did not need to peruse its contents. The severed rose-colored ribbon and broken seal of her signet ring proclaimed the missive hers. How it had been intercepted, she did not know. Defiantly, she stared up into the Englishman's flawed face.

"Such encouragement of rebellion is an act of treason against His Majesty King Edward III of England and Duke of Aquitaine." She watched the indentation of his upper lip flatten into a harsh smile. "I do not imagine I need remind you of the penalty for treason, mistress."

She couldn't repress a shudder at the merciless glint in his eyes.

"Perhaps I can enliven your imagination," he said. "Our Duke of Aquitaine's grandfather, King Edward I, shut a Scots countess in an open cage which he suspended from the city walls. Her humiliation was likely as horrible as her death, weeks later, when birds of prey began picking at the rotting flesh of the weakened woman."

"You are a cold-blooded bastard!"

His face darkened, and his hand raised, as if to strike her, and it was perhaps only her missive he held that saved her that debasement. He cast the missive into the fire. "Who is this Denys Bontemps?" he demanded.

"Denys is innocent of any plot."

"Who is he, I asked."

"A friend from childhood. The son of a stonecutter."

He leaned down to pick up Arthur again, twining in and out between his leather boots. Stroking its fur with gentle hands, he said, "I do not slay damosels, mistress, but be forewarned of the consequences. I shall take my reprisal on a male of your household one at a time for any further rebellious act of yours."

Baldwyn waited until the soldier had taken his leave, then warned, "As the peasant says, my lady, 'Let not the hen crow before the rooster.' I shall sleep outside your doorway from this time on."

When he, too, had departed, she crossed to the polished silver mirror. She half expected to find a welt where the Englishman's fingers had touched her cheek, as though the heat of his fury had branded her. She rubbed the back of her fingers across the spot, reflectively.

For the first time in years she thought of one of the manuscripts stored in her library. The precisely illuminated work was one of several that Baldwyn had fled with from the Templar Preceptory before King Philip the Fair had raided their commandery. Many of the works there were said to have been brought from the far lands of the East to the Kingdom of Jerusalem by the Arabs and from Jerusalem the Templars had then brought them to Paris.

This particular one spoke of a particular practice of Hinduism, called Tantrism, where enlightment was sought through profound experience of sensual love "in which each was both."

Even more than the concept, she had been intrigued by the Hindu goddess depicted not as a holy virgin but in a sensual embrace of stunning beauty. A remarkable contrast to the cult of the Virgin Mary, which the famed Abelard had claimed despised that part of a woman from which sons of men were born.

With a harshly indrawn breath, she admitted to her reflected image her deepest fear that she possessed a perilous connection with this English soldier who venerated such a cult. It was no accident that he, out of the dozens of the English king's military leaders, was ordered to take Montlimoux.

A large hand clamped on Iolande's stooped shoulder, and she cried out.

"'Tis only I, old woman," Baldwyn said.

"Don't sneak upon me like that, leper!" The contemptuous form of address was her long-standing way of keeping the Knight Templar at a distance.

Ah, but he had been such a handsome gallant when first he had ridden into Montlimoux's courtyard. And she had never been a beauty. Her hooded eyes appraised his ravaged face, mercifully shadowed because of the high, narrow windows in this part of the chateau. Here, outside the buttery, he was once again young and magnificent and handsome.

But daydreams had never been her weakness. Had she even been a beauty, Baldwyn de Rainbaut, best lance of the Templars, had foresworn marriage, at least, if not *par armours*. And had he even been interested in only an affair of the heart, she would never had been considered, as he was a gentile and she a Jewess.

Despite his disfigurement, he was still supremely male. Not for him the sexless leper's castanets, gloves, and breadbasket. She turned her attention back to her ring of keys, discarding the pantry key for the right one. "What mischief do you seek now?" she asked rudely of him.

"I fear for my Lady Dominique."

She straightened, her keys clinking back together on their ring, and frowned. "I know. I fret, also."

"'Tis not just her way of life that's in danger. 'Tis her very life, I fear."

"Has the English lieutenant said as such?"

The Templar shook his shaggy gray head. "No, but her missive to Denys was intercepted. I listen and watch. The Englishman, I am told, is ruthless, thorough, and unforgiving. I fear his reprisal is yet to come after she has formally yielded her title and county to him."

"What can he do to her?" Unconsciously, she rubbed her age-knotted fingers that ached with the cold. "And on what pretext?"

"The missive to Denys was pretext enough, but the Englishman burnt it. Nevertheless, he could find a reason of one kind or another."

"You come to me now because you finally need my help, do you not, leper?"

"You know what it is I seek." It wasn't a question but a statement.

She lowered her head. Even now this stag of a man had the power to make her foolishly yearn for all that could never be. "I have thought of it, also. But I cannot."

"This is different, old woman. 'Tis our Dominique, she needs our help."

Miserable, she shook her head. "I cannot, I tell you. My knowledge of herbs . . . I can only use it for good. To poison him . . . No, we must trust. We must trust."

He stretched out his hands and flexed his sausage-sized fingers. "I have thought of strangling him at an unguarded moment. I would not mind forfeiting the few years left me to keep our Lady Dominique safe. But if it were not Paxton of Wychchester seeking to claim her county and her life, it would be another like him."

Her words were anguished with the future she feared. "There is no other like him."

CHAPTER IV

Paxton felt as irritable as a dog chained for too long. Outside, a spring rain performed a mad dance, and the wind howled like demons.

From Dominique de Bar's library came the brass rattle of the abacus. He found her at her escritoire, calculating numbers from a ledger. At the same time she dictated to a secretary, a pipestem of a man in his forties.

Paxton's mailed step must have given him away because at once she glanced up from the Chinese counting instrument. Her gaze turned cold and empty, like that of a marble statue. "You desired me, my Lord Lieutenant?"

Desired her? Did he?

He really looked at her. An intriguing damosel, her features arresting. But her intelligence, her willfulness, her remoteness—they put off a man. No wonder the virago had not been taken to wife, despite the county's potential wealth. A man wanted in a woman the softness and gentleness that was his complement, a compassion that did not condemn weakness.

Weakness? If any female would suspect it, surely this virago would. All his weaknesses. Remorse, yearnings, cynicism . . . aye, hatred, even, though the Church condemned that as the most foul of sins.

"The tourney draws near," he said brusquely. "You should be apprised of your part in the ceremony."

"Can you not just send one of your lackeys with the instructions?"

So that she would not have to endure his presence. That was what she implied. Her condescending attitude infuriated him. He wanted to throttle her, but such an act would give her an advantage, confirming her opinion of him as a brutish lout.

With an effort, he stifled his peppery temperament, brought on by the confining weather he told himself. Nudging aside a gold-and-rock crystal chess set, he settled one hip on the edge of her escritoire. The affronted look on her face was worth the delay in his schedule.

From her secretary's quivering hands, he plucked the wax tablet that with a second draft would be transferred to parchment. "I and my beloved are one," he read aloud, his tone insulting.

A blush deepened the rose of her cheeks. "Those are not my words."

"Oh, mayhaps they belong to this bird you talk to."

His scathing mockery elicited a flash of fiery sparks from eyes as green as English meadows. She dismissed her secretary with a wave of her hand. "A Sufi mystic who lived long ago made that statement."

He scanned the rest of the script. "It appears to me to be nothing more than a love song."

"Your derision marks you as a man without a heart."

He tossed the tablet on the escritoire. "I am a trenchant realist. This courtly love, 'tis only frank eroticism that encourages courtly dalliance and idealizes extramarital love."

"A realist? You are a savage, sire."

"'Tis woman who is *sauvage*. She is ruthless in asking her lover to risk death."

She spread her hands, capable-looking ones for her fragile build. "She merely requires he prove his love is more than mere passion."

His finger traced the chess set's rock-crystal castle then tipped it over. "'Tis a frustrated love, the pleasure of suffering, that you would glorify."

She reached out and, with a saucy smile, flicked the gold king, toppling it. "The greater the love, the greater the pain. The pain of being truly alive."

"Such love is irreligious." He toppled the rock-crystal bishop.

Her slender, graceful hand fingered the gold queen. Watching those fingers with their cylindrical strokes, he shifted uncomfortably.

At last, she knocked over the gold queen. "'Tis a higher spiritual experience than that of a socially organized marriage by the Church." With that, she raised a challenging brow and thumped her queen of rock crystal squarely in the chess board's center. "Such love is a refining, sublimating force. 'Tis the burning point of life."

"Or death? I do not agree with Sir Tristan's tragic intrigue, 'By my death, do you mean this pain of love?'" He plucked the knight from its square and nudged her queen from the board's center. "Spare me that, mistress, and I shall live a contented man."

She tilted her chin, surveying him from beneath lash-veiled eyes. "Contented? I doubt that you shall ever know the peace that comes with that word."

He came to his feet and stared down at her with a glib curl to his mouth. "No man would in your embrace."

Her indrawn breath was reward enough.

He turned to leave, then added over his shoulder, "Oh, yes, mistress, after the tourney, there will be a gala feast. I advise you to be prepared at that time to make your homage and take your oath of fealty to me."

"I do not trust this back-country countess."
Following Paxton, John Bedford stepped around scaffolding balancing carpenters, who had already erected the tiltyard's palisades. Behind John scampered Hugh, whom Paxton had newly created as page, and ahead the ever-present cat, Arthur, stalked some prey, a field mouse most likely. April's sunlight was brilliant but the breeze unduly chill.

"The young woman is helpless, Paxton."

"Helpless? John, my friend, you are besotted by that curly-haired Provencal wench, Beatrix. Never believe that of any woman, much less this woman, the chatelaine."

"I tell ye there is no ally to whom she can turn, Paxton. The rest of Languedoc's counts and princes do not wish to attract King Edward's attention, and our spies tell us that King Philip certainly is not ready to declare war over the questionable rights of a rather insignificant county. Not yet, at least."

Paxton halted before a pit where two sturdy yeomen wielded a big two-handed saw on a heavy beam that would help timber the temporary galleries, one on either side of the circular tiltyard. The Round Table work of the tourney was coming along rapidly.

The tiltyard was being created on the edge of a wood that approached to within a league of the village. The field was still dormant from the late winter, although sprouts of grain were shooting up where rainwater pooled. The field was bordered on one side by the river and on the other by the forest, which was fringed with enormous oaks that had to be as old as Methuselah himself and yews that would make the finest bows.

John, witnessing his disquiet, said, "If there is any doubt as to ye power and authority here, the Round Table should satisfy that. When the countess foreswears her allegiance to ye before all her formerly loyal—"

Paxton's attention was diverted. His eye was on the falcon that circled overhead, sprinting through flight, her wings taking on a pointed, drawn back appearance. "'Tis neither her allies nor her loyal vassals that disturb me. 'Tis the woman herself."

He glanced at John. The man's short red beard was split by his grin. His friend cuffed his arm with a fist. "So, at last, a woman has attracted your—"

Paxton's gaze moved back to the spiraling falcon. She maneuvered through the air with spectacular, but reckless, abandon. "No, not that way, John. The needs of my loins can be easily slaked."

"Ah, then, Paxton, ye will admit she does stir your desires."

"Nay, not even that." He began walking again, dodging a cart drawn by a yoke of slow-gaited oxen. He strode purposefully into the field. He considered the headstrong woman. Her indomitable pride, her damnable resolution and impetuousness in choosing to sit at the lower table irritated him. But it was something more that irritated him. "I do not trust her because—"

The falcon ceased her soaring, hovered, then begin her dive for her prey. "Because there is something"—he could have said impenetrable or incomprehensible, but he was not even sure himself if that was what he meant—"something strange about her," he finished with dissatisfaction at his inadequate way with words.

John peered at him with dismay. "Paxton, ye have never been one to be obsessed by mythological tales of sorcery and demons and—"

He raised a silencing palm. At the meadow's far edge, Dominique de Bar's page held the reins of three riderless horses. "I gave you orders to see that she was constantly watched, John. Why is she falconing today?"

"Why . . . she asked permission, Paxton. Except for the one night she appeared for dinner, she has been confined to her suite of rooms."

His mouth compressed, expressing his checked displeasure.

"Riding with her is the guard I posted on her," John added. "And, of course, the Templar and her cadger."

"And her domestic steward, the Jewess?

She is still at the chateau then?"

"Iolande? Aye. I doubt me that the countess would make an escape without the old sibyl."

"The countess can run to the ends of the earth for all I care but not before she does homage to me as a vassal, and her authority is properly and legally transferred to me."

He set out for the forest edge with a purposeful stride. Carried on the air, he heard her musical laugh, the sound of witchery, by the body of Christ!

Dominique loved the bird of prey she had trained. Reinette's fierceness, her clean-lined beauty, her dazzling speed, her courage and daring *élan* on the wing, all personified independence.

If Dominique ever achieved that ability to escape her body at will, as Chengke had promised was possible, and take flight, it would have to be as a falcon. In fact, it had been Chengke who had instilled in her the love of falconry, a sport he claimed had been practiced in China two thousand years before Christ.

She watched as Reinette took sight of a prey somewhere in the forest below. The falcon passed high overhead at full speed, and it was like the noise of parchment tearing. Dominique could even hear the sound of her dive as she pulled out of descent, wings neatly folded. Towering sheer cliff walls of the nearby mountains echoed the impact of her hit-ting her quarry at full speed, a sharp cracking sound.

The falcon, Dominique knew, would stoop, or dive, toward the quarry, her spurs laying open for the prey. Then her talons would squeeze the weakened prey until it ceased to struggle.

Baldwyn's leonine head canted. "Do you hear her bell, my lady?"

Dominique stilled, listening for the sound of the bell attached to Reinette's tail. The bell monitored both the falcon's activity and location and could be heard more than half a league away, depending on the weather. She heard not the bell's tinkle but the faintest crushing of leaves underfoot.

At the rustling of underbrush directly behind them, both she and her retinue whirled. Paxton of Wychchester stepped into the leaf-shadowed glade. The guard John Bedford had saddled her with sheepishly sighed his relief. Baldwyn relaxed his vigilance. Her young cadger released his death grip on the cadge, her falcon's rectangular perch for field use.

She did not move. She knew neither she nor Paxton had forgotten the meeting of their wills and philosophies during the challenging conversation in her library days before. His education was extensive for that of a mere soldier.

His predatory gaze locked on her. She felt as though the two of them stood in empty space, beyond middle ground and solid objects. She could see he was experiencing something unusual, also. His expression was that of a warrior who expected an attack—extreme alertness, registering everything that goes on around him without being distracted by it for an instant.

"You wished something, my Lord Lieutenant?" she got out at last, her tone like lye.

"Merely to witness your expertise at falconry."

Her lids narrowed. She was not certain if he ridiculed her. What was his purpose here? Her eye took note that the hunter's green of his tunic suited well his monotone coloring. All brown. The brown of his sun-and-wind weathered skin; his straight, short hair; his darker eyes. Brown, like winter grass. Brown, the absence of life. No, only the dormancy of life. Black was the absence of life. Black was the center of his eyes, and at that moment she was caught in his stare like a bird in hunter's lime.

Pushing aside the brush, he entered the glade, and she noticed only then that his captain and Hugh followed upon his heels. "I have had little opportunity to learn the sport, mistress."

Still, he addressed her by that common term! "Naturally, for I am told the knaves of England are permitted only the useless kestrel with which to hunt."

Baldwyn flashed her a warning glance. The usually smiling John Bedford shifted nervously. Her gaze darted back to the lieutenant. His face had darkened, and the aura of his wrath was almost tangible. The forest sounds were muted by the moment.

"As you have quite clearly received an education, I would have imagined you have been taught Latin, mistress," he said, his voice almost conversationally pleasant. "As such, you must be aware that in the Scriptures the word 'witch' is of the feminine gender, is it not?"

No idle observation but a warning, she knew.

The cacophony of the forest erupted again, with the falcon's bell tinkling wildly overall. She whirled and hurried in that direction— without asking permission to take her leave.

Twigs scratched her face, as she pushed deeper into the forest. The tinkling led her to a patch of dense scrub oak. Softly, she called, "Reinette," and the bird of prey fluttered from the underbrush to regain her outstretched fist. Her critical eye examined Reinette's plumage, damaged by the thickets.

"My Lady Countess?" At her side, her cadger proffered from the falconry bag the jesses that secured the creature's yellow-scaled gaiters.

Coming upon her, the others rejoined her as she deftly slipped the hood over Reinette. "What have you bagged, my lady?" asked Baldwyn.

"I'm not certain." She passed Reinette over

to her cadger. "You saw how she had raked away."

"Uh—huh, she lost all interest in the pigeon and begun to wander after activity below her. Dinner tonight may not be all that I had anticipated."

Dominique was oblivious to the others until Paxton of Wychchester spoke in a drawl that was as smooth as spiced wine and carried as much potency. "Perhaps you will crawl into the underbrush, mistress, and display for us today's catch."

"My Lord Lieutenant," John offered, "I'll retreive the prey for—"

"No."

Baldwyn spread his spade-sized palms. "But 'tis not seemly that—"

"No!" Paxton folded his arms. "The hunter —huntress—will retrieve her own prey, as the common folk do."

Everyone stood paralyzed. She glanced at the copse and swallowed hard. She had done it again, aroused his antipathy by forgetting her place as his vassal and he was quite clearly reminding her. She had not crawled on her knees since childhood, but she could not give him reason to oust her from Montlimoux, not yet.

Resolutely, she trussed her cotton smock at her waist, exposing the course, gray under-skirt she used for hunting. There was a collective and not quite smothered gasp from her retinue as she went onto her knees and pushed forward into the brambles with the utmost caution. Falcons loved to prey upon snakes.

Her eyes had to adjust to the diminished sunlight. The pungent odor of alluvial soil and decayed leaves, crushing under hand, rose to fill her nostrils. Just beyond, a salamander disturbed the leaves as it took flight from her. Further into the brush a thorn gouged her ungloved palm, and she yelped. She paused to extract the thorn and that was when she spotted the bloodied quarry. A ferret, a raccoon, she couldn't tell which until she turned it over.

Her outcry echoed in the forest.

CHAPTER V

"Please, leave me enter."

" 'Tis unwise, my lady," John Bedford said low, closing the privy chamber door behind him. "I have never seen Paxton in such a mood. I only wish he would vent his wrath at me. I could handle it."

She smiled wanly. "You would have him kill you instead of me?"

His mouth crimped in an attempt to return her smile. "Kill me, no. But vent his anger through fighting. We used to wrestle, and once I held my own with him."

She placed her hand on his doublet sleeve. "What happened today—I am responsible. I had no idea the cat was anywh—"

"Ye don't understand, my lady. The cat was . . . well, Paxton was fond of Arthur."

"Obviously," she said dryly.

"It was more than that." He half chuckled. "Paxton even carried that cat with him when he went to call upon a highborn lady with whom he was, shall I say, enamoured. 'For courage,' he told me."

"Courage? Your lieutenant lacking courage? Compassion he may lack but not courage. Now leave me enter."

She maneuvered around him and opened and closed the door before he could gainsay her. Only one candle lit the chamber, a room much like her own but smaller and used to quarter quests. Paxton sat before the fire. At his feet lay the dying cat. Blood pooled around the animal. It was obvious that death crouched only hours away at most.

At her entrance, the man glanced at her, then back to the fire. "I am sorry," she began.

"My Lord Lieutenant," he corrected in a low voice.

She sighed. "I am sorry, my Lord Lieutenant. Truly sorry."

He raised a hand, and the firelight glinted on what he held. A knife. He twisted the blade this way and that, reflecting the fire's sheen eerily across his face. Her heart stopped.

He must have noted her stricken expression. He laughed nastily. "No, not for you. My revenge will be much more subtle, mistress. The knife blade is for my cat. You see, I am trying to summon courage to end its suffering. As I heard John tell you, courage does not come easily for me."

She crimsoned. There was no retort she could make. She moved past his chair to kneel opposite him, the cat between them. She noted in the man's presence she always felt a peculiar knotting in her stomach, as if an irksome cord united her with him by their navels. "Leave me with your cat for a few moments," she said.

He laughed shortly. "Nay, mistress. I would as soon leave my soul with the devil." He paused and stared emptily at her. "And mayhaps I have."

She lost patience. Time and space were flowing swiftly. "Do not be a buffoon. There is a chance I can heal your cat—if 'tis not too late."

He focused his gaze on her, reminding her sharply of *yarak*, the Turkish word for the firey-eyed stance a falcon assumed when scanning or staring at potential prey. Perhaps it was his brows, sharply peaked at the outer corners, that reminded her of a falcon. "How? Mutter some demonical incantation? Use your powers of sorcery?"

She shivered, more from foreboding than from his contempt. Intuitively she knew that to proceed would be courting a dimension over which she had no power. Nevertheless she was powerless to resist the force at work between her and this Englishman.

The last pulsations of color—gray—emanated from the animal. The cat's eyes were open, but glazed. No breath, no movement issued from its inert body. Its spirit was already straining away. "Stay then. It matters little to me."

For the moment, she ignored the deep slashes that ribboned the cat's back. Iolande's poultices would heal those. Instead, her fingers found the cat's stomach, searched behind, gently pressing with precise touches until she located the sensations stored there. Then she began massaging the cat's body, hoping to bring a balance to it. She picked up various vibrations, confusing to her and debilitating.

She once tried to describe to Iolande what she was doing, that it was like knitting or crocheting, her fingers stitching a web of the life energy, that this creative strength she used slumbered inside her. Inside everyone.

"Do not speak of these things, not even to me," Iolande had warned. "The walls have ears, and others do not understand."

Dominique concentrated on summoning a yellow glow behind her lids, the powerful sensory color she first perceived while playing as a child in a sunflower field. She had told neither Iolande nor Baldwyn of this experience, but she was rather certain they suspected.

Nauseated, she opened her eyes to look at the Englishman. "Please, your hostility . . . '

tis interfering, blocking me." A nerve in his unshaven cheek twitched, and she said, "Please, all I ask is that you allow me a few moments alone."

His eyes probed her face. At last, he said, "Aye, for a few moments."

After the door closed behind him, she returned her full attention to the animal. Her eyes closed again, and she sought that crystal bridge to her source, her soul. Once more she orchestrated her physical energies with her emotional, her spiritual with her mental, and felt as if she were spinning. Perspiration drenched the hair at her temples. How much time flowed by she knew not.

Then the cat's scratchy tongue stroked her palm. She heard its faint mewl. She opened her eyes and sat back on her heels as the animal stirred feebly in an attempt to resettle its blood-matted body in a more comfortable position.

"Whelp of a she-wolf!" Paxton stared at her as if she were vaporizing before his eyes. She had not heard him re-enter the chamber. His jaws clenched and unclenched. He passed his hands over his face, as though to wash it.

"Your cat will survive. At least, it will survive this round with the forces of nature. Now, it has only eight lives left."

Her attempt at a neutralizing smile was met with a frown that made his rather plain face formidable. He crossed the room and dropped to his knees, opposite her, so that his cat lay between them. It twitched its ears at its master's presence.

His stare went from his pet to her. "What did you do?" he demanded.

She drew a fortifying breath. "'Tis a spiritual sleight of hand, one might say. I simply used my hands to work energy."

"What?"

She may as well have been speaking a foreign tongue. She tried again. "When one changes energy, one changes reality. I merely lay my hands on the ill—"

"I watched you," he gritted, his eyes narrowed. "You did something more with your hands."

"No, not to its physical body. Listen, 'tis like . . . I feel my fingertips tingling, as though fire is warming them, streaming out, making contact with . . ."

Her words trailed away as, without taking his gaze off her, he rose to tower over her. "Leave!"

His expression unnerved her. His eyes had the power to do such. Slowly, she came to her feet and backed away. She reached the door, and he warned, "Stay out of my sight if you wish to remain at the chateau."

Pennants waving from the chateau's ramparts proclaimed that the festivities of the Round Table were in progress. The village of Montlimoux was thronged with people, peasants and princes who had flocked to attend one of the first tournaments to be held in a long time, since the Church had prohibited that armed contest of courtesy on horseback.

That was because these combats to the death, though subject to the intervention of the host at any stage by the casting of his baton, had offended the Church's sensibilities. But Dominique found it difficult to understand how the Church's sensibilities were not offended when one of its Inquisitors extracted a woman's teeth or roasted a living man upon a kitchen spit.

These days the combatants would be using blunted lances and following rules that established where on the body the sword and battle axe could strike. Only a few of these combatants—knights, with their pages and squires—had found quarters with the villagers, for Paxton's soldiers were lodged in every holstery, as well as the chateau itself. Beyond the river other knights erected tents of canvas painted with their personal colors and flying their heraldic devices. Declassée knights, those of inferior rank, slept in the open with only a blanket to protect them from the chilly April mornings.

Games, combat practice, dinners, dances, wagering, and quarrels in every language occupied the better part of that first day. For the past week, Dominique had for the most part kept to her room, emerging only when she knew Paxton was away. She dared not even visit her laboratory. Baldwyn told her that

Captain Bedford turned away her vassals from the Justice Room each morning with instructions to come back after the tourney.

Time was as heavy to her as if she were with child, waiting . . . waiting. Both she and Reinette fretted from the lack of exercise and fresh air. Her maids-in-waiting, especially Beatrix, with her mind-numbing chatter, kept her company. More for the opportunity of encountering Captain Bedford, Dominique suspected, than out of duty.

Dominique awaited that last day of the jousting itself, when she would have to renounce her title. She knew there was no quarter from whence she could expect aid, yet she was determined not only to survive but to regain all that had once been hers. How she did not know. Now more than ever she desperately needed Chengke's wise advice.

From her casement window, she spied the banners of the Bishop of Carcassonne. He sat astride a white caparisoned courser. Francis! So, he was also coming for the tourney. It would be another half-hour before he and his retainers could wend their way through the crowded village. A long half-hour until she saw him again.

"Iolande, how many months since Francis de Beauvais paid us a visit?" she asked without taking her eyes off the magnificent man.

The curly-headed minx, Manon, glanced up from her needlepoint. "Monseigneur Bishop? He is here?" The young woman's blush rendered her quite winsome, and Dominique realized she was not the only female who appreciated Francis de Beauvais for more than his religious administrations.

Iolande never took her eye, nor her purple-veined fingers, from her distaff and spindle. "Eleven months by my count."

A respite from her boredom! Memories of the fascinating conversations and heated debates she had enjoyed with Francis quickened her blood. "Marthé, make haste and help me change."

Marthé, with her fine eye toward fashion, chose for Dominique a ribbed indigo-violet satin undergown and over that a long, silver-belted houppelande of red silk lined with linen. The horned headdresses that were becoming the style took far too long for Manon to accomplish so Dominique settled for having her hair plaited and coiled in templets over her ears.

As a final touch, Manon insisted on powdering Dominique's face with fine white flour and scented her throat and ear lobes with musk of jasmine and orange blossom that Baldwyn had purchased at the annual trade fair at Montlimoux and which he had sworn had been brought from the Orient.

When at last she descended the solar staircase into the great hall, there was only one thought and that was relief that Paxton was away, finalizing the last details of the tourney. Then even her preoccupation with Paxton subsided at the vision of Francis in conversation with Baldwyn.

Francis's profile was strong, with clean lines and noble features, and his presence was commanding. He wore the long black robe of the clergy that decreed respect and authority. However, his was hardly austere, with gold cord trimming even his priest's brocaded stole. He did not even bother with the tonsure. Over his thick black hair a sable cap angled rakishly.

It had been her mother who had knighted his father, a distinguished lawyer and loyal advisor, for outstanding service in negotiating a treaty with the Infante of Majorica, at that time a threat to the comté. Initially, Francis had been, like his father, a canon lawyer, able and energetic. And then, after his parents died, tortured on the rack during one of those fanatical periods of the Inquisition, he had turned to the solace of the Church.

"Francis," Dominique said, joy lightening her voice as she hurried to him.

He half-turned toward her and smiled. One beringed hand stretched forth, beckoning her. "Dominique, your loveliness and intelligence are wasted here. I have come to lure you away to Avignon."

"If I but could." Placing her hand in his, she had to smile at the way he believed he could command everything, including the seasons.

"Then 'tis true? There is a claimant to your

county? The man responsible for staging this tourney?"

She grimaced. "An Englishman, no less. Paxton of Wychchester."

The aura of Francis's male force was heavy, dark, confusing her. Her pleasure at seeing him was instantly diminished by the sight of the young woman who entered the room at the head of his entourage. His sister, Lady Esclarmonde. That explained the dark undertone Dominique had sensed around Francis.

His sister, a tall blond beauty with a retrousse nose, possessed little of his brilliant learning and penetrating insight. But then Esclarmonde had not had the opportunity for education as Francis had had. Still, the young woman was intelligent, and Dominique would have liked to have had her as a friend.

It appeared that Esclarmonde had never shared the yearning. As a child, isolated by her rank and privileges, Dominique had joyously turned for companionship to the daughter of her mother's advisor. Gradually, though, Esclarmonde had revealed herself guileful and petty. Having no parents, Esclarmonde's domineering spirit had warred on equal footing with that of Dominique's for Francis's attention, and Dominique had always been left feeling embattled.

Esclarmonde halted beside him and, lightly placing a gloved hand on his arm, said, "Dominique, we have come to pay you our condolences." Her tone was light and airy, for all the darkness surrounding her.

"Your condolences?"

"The rumors circulating at the papal palace say that you no longer administer in the Justice Room." Her meaningful glance took in the soldiers posted at the great door. "How disastrous for you, alone here with no family!"

Dominique focused on a deep breath to gain inner control. "The rumors report a situation that is only temporary." The negative aura emanating from Esclarmonde bleached her energies. "After your long journey, you must be tired, both of you. Unfortunately, the English soldiers have requisitioned almost all the rooms, but—"

"But Captain Bedford will see to it that suites are relinquished for our illustrious guests," Paxton interjected evenly, coming up behind her. Arthur padded along just as silently in his trail. How much had the man overheard?

She was struck by the similarity between him and Francis. While both wore nondescript colors, their presence nonetheless demanded the eye. The two were tall, with Paxton brawnier while Francis was more sinewy. Both exuded restrained power. But that of Francis's had a refined quality, like his profile and Paxton's was . . . what? Blunt. They were like the sword, she decided. Francis its blade and Paxton its haft, both parts used equally well upon a field of combat.

Paxton turned his attention upon her, and she fortified herself against his wrath. Francis's observant eye measured the situation. With his ecclesiastical diplomacy, he smoothly diverted the Englishman. "Lord Paxton, my sister, the Lady Esclarmonde."

Esclarmonde dipped her head respectfully, then tilted it just enough that she was able to deliver a smile that revealed perfect teeth. Dominique had to content herself with the good fortune promised by her pair of slightly spaced front teeth. As it was, her good fortune did not appear imminently on the horizon.

As she should have expected, Paxton had not forgotten her. "Your presence at the high table is desired this evening, mistress."

Simply that. The framing of his order left no room for declining. She raged against the position into which he was maneuvering her. Raged, knowing all the while that such destructive thoughts would only be her own undoing.

By the time the cathedral bells sounded the vesper hour and dinner, she had had time to establish an element of inner peace, infinitesimal though it was.

The dinner was not exactly an ordeal. Minstrels played lulling music from the gallery above. Recently arrived guests overflowed the high table. Francis was an entrancing conversationalist and eased the strain between Dominique and Paxton. Eloquent, Francis was fluent in several languages. He directed his glib wit toward Paxton now, much of which she was sure would go over the soldier's head. "The forests of Montlimoux are renowned for their boar hunting—and more."

"Oh?" Paxton drawled.

Dominique held her breath for the repartee that was surely forthcoming.

"Is not your king a devotee of the Arthurian tradition? Then surely you should inform him of a forest north of here. It lies at the heart of Celtic legend." Francis leaned forward, his blue eyes deep with dark fires. "'Tis said to be the original home of Merlin the Enchanter."

Paxton lifted a sceptical brow, and Francis laughed. "A rational man I behold. Excellent. As for myself, I suppose I am a man of differing sentiments—a renegade monk, a notorious libertine, and a troubadour at heart."

Which was precisely why Dominique loved him. He was his own man and not the Church's.

"'A singer of songs whose sound is damnation?'" Paxton asked.

His pronouncement startled everyone at the table. He shrugged and said, "A quote, I forget from whence."

Francis smiled easily. "From St. Augustine perhaps? I believed the good man also said, 'God, give me chastity, but not yet.'"

Everyone chuckled at his scholastic subtlety, and the rest of the dinner returned to its former geniality. Francis was disarmingly charming, never glorifying his specialness nor repudiating his multidimensional capabilities with false modesty.

The Englishman lieutenant remained quiet, attentive, occasionally asking negligible questions about court life at Avignon. Absently, his fingers traced the blade of his dinner knife. She noted that the fair-haired Esclarmonde also watched that sun-browned hand, contrasting with her pale one, so close to his own.

Tactfully, Francis did not broach the subject of Dominique's position there. He waited, taking his cue from her. Her wits were scattered but she had the presence of mind to discuss the crops, the weather, the castellans, and their state of affairs.

Esclarmonde pressed Paxton for details of English court fashion styles, and he replied cordially, "I profess my ignorance, my lady, as I have been absent, involved in campaigns in the wilds of Wales and Scotland."

Her lips formed a moue of disappointment that was no doubt meant to enchant the foreigner. Dominique would have dearly enjoyed confronting the soldier about the rumors reaching Languedoc of the English *chevauchée*—those vicious tactics of laying waste the Scottish countryside, so that crop, animal, and peasant alike were destroyed. Good sense and apprehension of what wounds he might inflict upon her pride in the presence of Francis and Esclarmonde held her tongue.

After dinner, he was the proper host, escorting his guests to their rooms and escorting her to her own rooms to follow her inside when Manon would have closed the antechamber door. Only a single candle burned in its gilded sconce. The flickering light deepened his facial scars. The one that grooved his upper lip was a wicked path.

"Leave us," he told her maid-in-waiting.

Manon flashed her an alarmed glance. Dominique nodded, and the maid bobbed her head and left. When the door had closed, he asked, "Why is Francis de Beauvais here?"

The question took her unprepared. "Why, 'tis Francis's diocese and we are old friends."

"Bishops are known to be implacable enemies of communal self-government. Known to use their spiritual arsenal to defend their ecclesiastical law courts against a chatelaine's encroachment on potential revenue. What authority does he exert over your vassals?"

She shrugged. "What you would expect. When he is here, he oversees their spiritual lives."

"He is here often?"

"Not that much anymore. Pope Benedict uses him occasionally as an emmissary."

His eyes narrowed. "In England, the clergy has a panoply of powers. The bishops have taken over administrative duties and accompanying income, so that they are indistinguishable from the barons."

"Well, here in Montlimoux I rule—"

"No," he said, "I do, mistress. Tomorrow King Edward will make an appearance at the tourney." The information startled her, but he continued on, "As Duke of Aquitaine, he will officiate at the oath of fealty ceremony. I recommend you comport yourself respectfully."

"And if I do not?"

A frown creased a line between his brows. "To even think otherwise is folly. I had not imagined you a simpleton, mistress."

His attitude of male superiority galled her. "Baldwyn has an old saw perhaps you have not heard. 'Better to have a corpse in your house than an Englishman at your door.'"

His mouth tightened. "But I am here, am I not?" Before she could react, he wrapped an arm around her waist and pulled her to him. His hand anchored in her hair and tugged her head far back. His kiss was swift, harsh, and as much as a surprise to him, she suspected, as it was to her. He started to say something, apparently changed his mind, and, turning abruptly, left.

Her chambers seemed empty without his large presence.

CHAPTER VI

The morning was barely past the tenth hour, but spring sunlight shone brightly on the tourney, too brightly for Dominique. For on the day when she must yield all that was dear to her, a time when she must denounce her heritage, she would have preferred gloomy overcast weather.

A narrow lane between the galleries and field of combat permitted a few peasants a view of the tourney, while most of them gathered on the hills outside the newly erected palisades or climbed atop those village houses that had slate roofs. Several spectators had even occupied the cathedral's bell tower.

If she had hoped no one would turn out for

the jousting, she had erred. Richly arrayed burgers, guildsmen, scribes, castellans, priests, and noblemen of all rank, some of even dubious title, graced the canopied galleries at either side of the tiltyard. Their tumultuous activities and din of voices were quieted by the arrival of men-at-arms and the Field Marshall, an older, seasoned knight, who announced the rules, inspected the ranks of each group, and proclaimed the tourney under way.

Pennants represented knights and esquires from far away locales: Scots, Portuguese, Lombards, Flemings, Swiss, and, of course, the detestable French. Riding two abreast, they entered the gate at one end and cantered to the middle of the round field to face the galleries on one side that were adorned with scarlet-and-gold banners and bunting. In the galleries' center was a canopied dais with arras spread on its three steps.

Trumpets announced the entrance of the English king as he ascended the throne. Dominique had heard that two nights before he had crossed the English channel and slipped into the Aquitaine port of Bordeaux disguised as a common wool merchant.

He looked very impressive today in a crimson knee-length houppelande, its sable collar trimmed with jewels and in crimson boots pulled above his calves. A chaplet of pearls graced his head. His drooping mustache and pointed yellow beard were in keeping with his cult of King Arthur. A train of pages and advisors waited attendance on him.

Her eye failed to single out Paxton of Wychchester but easily located Francis in the midst of the nobles. If only she could have a few hours alone with him, but not to discourse and debate as they had in years before.

She wanted badly to ask his help, but his influence with the pope was of little aid to her since her family had harbored heretics, and she herself had appointed a Jewess as one of her stewards.

With Jacotte and Beatrix carrying her lengthy train, Dominique mounted the steps of the gallery opposite the one occupied by the English king. She was dressed in a splendid white gown heavily embroidered at the hem and girdled below the waist with a chain of old gold. The gown had been her mother's, as was the jewelry. A broad gold necklace overlay the fitted bodice, and a gold crown anchored a gauzy white veil that draped over her maiden's unbound hair.

Her chair was on a dais but pointedly lower than that of the king's, opposite hers. As she took her place, surreptitious glances were cast in her direction. Lady de Sigors, wife of the burgher Guillaume, whispered behind her hand to the woman next to her. Dominique knew the spectators were wondering just what exactly was her status at Montlimoux. First foreign troops occupied the village, and now their king had arrived. Was she princess or prisoner?

No one was quite sure of the proper response in a situation like this and looked to her for an indication. She sat with her head high, her posture regal. She would not cower or be intimidated. Until Paxton indicated otherwise, she was still suzeraine of Montlimoux.

Among the women in her gallery was Esclarmonde. Her tilted eyes glittered with excitement, and, with her hand pressed to her bosom, she leaned slightly forward toward the railing as the knights passed in procession, with their squires in attendance.

Because the knights' visors concealed their visages, their shields' emblems proclaimed their identity. Plate armor protected the vital parts of the knights' bodies. Their war horses were likewise armored, and their trappings were as elaborately decorated as the knights' escutcheons.

Occasionally a knight would halt before Dominique's gallery and tilt his blunted lance toward one of her ladies, signifying the wish for some sort of token from his lady-love to display on his helmet, lance or shield—a glove, her veil, a necklace. One eager lady ripped away her lightly stitched sleeve and passed it down to her knight, a not uncommon act.

Dominique bolted upright in her chair at the recognition of one shield among the calvacade. It bore an equilateral triangle intersected by a square—the emblem of the guild of masons, the *Compagnonages*.

"Denys," she breathed aloud. No one heard her for the shouting and acclamations, and she could only hope her riveted attention went equally unobserved.

Such a hope was denied, for Denys reined in his charger directly in front of the dais. Gasps erupted as he lowered his lance before her. All sound faded. All eyes watched. She could never be his lady-love, and he understood this, but neither could she humiliate him before everyone. Woodenly, she removed her veil from her crown. Leaning forward, her hair falling over one shoulder, she draped the veil over his blunted lance point.

Denys had been trained as a squire but had had little experience in actual combat. Yet there could be only one reason for his entry in the tourney: to do battle in her honor. What he hoped to gain, though, she could not imagine. Paxton was implacable, ruthless, effective, and thorough. Everything the rumors had proclaimed he would be. Everything his kiss had demonstrated.

The procession moved on, and she sat back in her chair, tense, her gaze fastened on Denys's back, until a commotion made it known that she was once more the focus of attention. Another knight had halted before her. Again all conversation among the spectators ceased.

This one's blade-notched shield, she noted,

bore no coat of arms. "I have already bestowed a token on another knight," she told him in a firm voice, clear enough for the ladies in her gallery to hear.

"Then I shall take my own."

The arrogant way he sat in the saddle, revealed to her that it was Paxton without even hearing his mellifluous voice, muffled though it was by his helmet. She should have expected he would participate in the tourney. Every inhabitant in Montlimoux must be made aware that he was the ultimate master of man and beast alike.

And woman.

His horse danced closer to the railing, and Paxton leaned over it, knife unsheathed. Sunlight glittered off its blade. She pressed against the back of her chair. "Come here," he commanded.

"You will do your will without my cooperation." If only this once, she would thwart his intentions. She did not believe he would actually hurt her. If anything, he needed her at least for the ceremony that would cement his authority as Grand Seneschal of Montlimoux. She surmised he would most likely cut away her sleeve.

She should have known better than to anticipate a man such as he. He leaned closer to her, and his gauntleted hand grasped her hair away from her shoulder. Before she could react, his knife began to chop at her hair, more than a forearm's length. With a startled outcry, she tried to pull away.

"Be still," he warned, "or you will look worse than a shorn sheep."

Not everyone, especially those in the opposite arena, could see what he was about. So when he lifted aloft his lance, with her streaming hair secured at its tip by one of his hauberk lacings, a collective gasp went up.

She sat stunned. Willing back tears of humiliation, she closed her eyes. When she opened them again, his courser had trotted on by. She would not, could not, look at the loathsome man. Instead, she sat without moving, her unseeing eyes fixed ahead on the tiltyard. She deafened her ears to the mutterings around her but had no doubt as to their subject: speculations regarding the precariousness of her political position.

At last, the bars of the barricades were lifted and the first course of ten knights, chosen by lots, advanced into the arena. From there, they separated and rode to the opposite and open sides of the circle's rim, and tapped with the reverse end of their lances the shield of the opponent with whom they wished to wage battle. After that, they retreated to the far rim.

Dominique scrutinized each shield and was relieved that Denys was not among the combatants.

At the flourish of trumpets, the two contingents of knights sallied forth at full gallop. The horses were weighted down by chain armor and unable to jump aside. There was no recourse but head-on confrontation.

Dust clouded the field. The thunder of lance impacting with shield echoed across the tilt-yard. The violence of the mêlée imparted itself to the crowd. When the dust cleared, two horsemen had been unseated. Another had had his lance splintered. One had swerved from his charge, the sign of an inexperienced knight.

Prepared to forfeit their wagered horses and armor, the dejected losers abandoned the field and withdrew from the lists. Amidst applause and cheering, the victors returned to their pavillions to await the final round when broadsword and battle axe could also be used if so desired.

Another party of knights engaged in battle, then a third. The afternoon wore on. Dust stung Dominique's eyes, and fear parched her throat, but she was too tense to signal for a refreshment. The sun was hot, and perspiration streamed down her bodice. She unfastened its three top buttons. A page waved a feathered fan, but the stale dusty air didn't alleviate her misery. She felt strangely lightheaded as her hair now fell only just below her shoulder blades.

What she had been fearing occurred next. With nine other challengers, Denys rode out into the tiltyard. His horse cantered directly toward the great black war horse that was Paxton's. When he was directly before Paxton, Denys flouted tradition and struck the sharp end of his lance against Paxton's shield in a breach of feudal code.

The challenger's courage elicited a thrill of anticipated exhilaration that hummed through both galleries. Scarves were waved in approbation, and shouts of support rang out. Wagers were increased.

The ten challengers retreated to draw up in a line at the other end. From Deny's lance tip floated her veil. From Paxton's lance her shorn hair. Sunlight set fire to its incendiary shade.

Trumpets were blown. Horses were spurred. Her heart thudded in tempo with the galloping hooves. Dust flurried. In and out of it, battled the ghostly figures of various knights. The shouting from the spectators was tumultuous. One by one, the knights were vanquished from the tiltyard, until six remained. The field marshall disqualified two combatants—one for striking the opponent's saddle, the other for striking a knight whose back was turned.

Of the four, two she recognized as Paxton and Denys. Their mounts wheeled around each other, each cavalier seeking the best opening to garner points. Breaking a lance fairly on the body of the adversary below the helmet, one point; above the breast, two points; unhorsing, three.

Denys landed a thunderous blow that splintered his lance, and Paxton's charger recoiled on its mighty haunches. Paxton reeled in the saddle but maintained his seat. His heels dug into his mount's flanks, and the war horse sprang forward. Dust swirled, momentarily obscuring the combatants.

Expecting to have unhorsed Paxton, Denys was unprepared, with his broken lance lowered, when the Englishman charged out of the haze. There was no possibility that Denys could sustain the mighty blow that Paxton directed at him and remain seated.

At the last second, Paxton's horse swerved. In the confusion that followed, no one was certain what had happened until the remnants of dust cleared.

Paxton was seen, then, stalking across the field. He thrust his lance at one of his squires who had hurried to him and went to kneel beside a fallen man-at-arms, one of his own soldiers who had managed to remain on the field of honor with him. Immediately the king of England lowered his baton to signal a respite in the battle. Gingerly, Paxton removed the man's helmet. Blood spilled over to tint the dirt.

Like a bird of prey, a deep silence hovered over the galleries. Even from that distance she could feel the impact of Paxton's gaze as it sought her out.

CHAPTER VII

"What happened to the knight?" Dominique paused and remembered to add, "my Lord Lieutenant."

They were alone in Paxton's pavillion with the injured man. Spars of sunlight shafted from the open tent flaps to fall where Paxton sat, next to the soldier stretched out on a straw-filled pallet.

Paxton glanced up from the man to her. "Patric was struck on the upper part of his breastplate by his opponent's lance. It glanced off the breastplate and entered his neck."

"The physician?"

The visor of Paxton's helmet was pushed

back to expose his dirty and sweat-sheened face. "I sent him away. He said nothing could be done."

She crossed the pavillion to stand near the end of the pallet and stared at the Englishman who had highhandedly summoned her from her gallery. Like Baldwyn, even sitting as he was on the temporary, wooden-framed bed, he was nigh as tall as she. Why did his presence impose on her, as Baldwyn's giant form never had? Because the Englishman's beliefs threatened her feminine power as no other male ever had?

"You want me to save him?"

"Aye. As you did Arthur."

"And, should I succeed, you will banish me from your sight, as you did when I saved your cat?"

His frown stretched the scar at his lip even deeper. "Save Patric, mistress."

She moved to the other side of the pallet. Her fingers pushed back the man's chain mail collar. No bubbles of blood foamed from the deep slit of his neck. "I fear his life force is absent."

Paxton closed his eyes and rubbed the bridge of his nose. "Then what I need is a resurrection," he mumbled.

"'Tis happened before." He glanced up at her, his dark brown eyes penetrating, and she reminded, "The blessed Jesus Christ, among others."

For a long moment, he said nothing, only

112

stared hard at her. She sustained his raking gaze. "Do what you have to," he said abruptly, rising. He left, closing the tent flaps behind him.

In the darkened room, she sought to shift her awareness from her rational to her intuitive powers. She blocked out the roar of cheers and shouts periodically erupting from the galleries. Motionless as a rock, she sat, insensible to her surroundings.

Concentrating only on her own breathing, she achieved that measure of serenity she sought at last. Vainly, her hands began to seek the man's aura.

She experienced that subtle change which made her eyes see in almost another dimension, a phenomenon she would have been hard put to explain. She searched for that vital breath that Chengke had claimed was the basis of Chinese medicine and the flowing movements of the dance of the Chinese warrior.

Sunlight retreated from the tent. Silence seeped in. The evening grew cooler. Mildew from damp canvas clogged the stale air. Still, she worked. When, at last, she stood, she was so shaky she did not think she could cross to the tent opening.

Outside, starlight gilded the heavens. A handful of people remained from the hundreds who had filled the galleries that afternoon. She saw anxiety in their faces— Beatrix, John Bedford, Jacotte, Marthé and

Manon, and, especially that of Baldwyn's and Iolande's.

Paxton stepped forward. "Patric is alive?"

She hung her head and bit her bottom lip. "No. His spirit has left the body."

"Why could she not save my man?"

Hugh had led Paxton to the Templar, who had been pacing the eastern ramparts. The night wind tugged at the old man's gray hair. He shrugged his Samson-like shoulders. "I do not know how to describe what she does. 'Tis like a high-pitched, almost inaudible sound, she has told me. Sometimes, no matter how hard she attempts to heal a person, the sound cannot complete its circle from the patient back to her because—"

"Because why?"

He shrugged his shoulders again. "Because of a lack of faith. All I can tell you is that the patient must also subscribe to a belief in this healing gift. Your man obviously did not. My Lady Dominique claims we have enormous self-healing capacities."

The peculiarities of this southern society, and this southern county and it aristocracy in particular, intrigued Paxton. For the moment, he ignored his weariness. The tourney's battles had left him fatigued. He motioned toward the Templar's face. He had forgotten to be disgusted by the reddish knobs that blotched its flesh. "You subscribe to such a method of curing?"

114

Baldwyn raised his hairless brows waggishly. "I subscribe by faith—should our illustrious Bishop ever inquire."

The bishop's *savoir-faire* nettled Paxton. "What is he to Dominique de Bar?"

"Her confessor."

"I have the distinct impression she eschews Church doctrine."

Paxton's expression must have betrayed his impatience, because the Templar said, "They have been friends since childhood."

Paxton turned his gaze up to the scythe of a moon that stared down upon them. "Does he know of this . . . gift of hers?"

"He encourages her esoteric interests, especially the alchemical ones. She has her own laboratory in the dungeon below, you know."

"No, I did not know. I find that interesting." He also found Dominique de Bar cryptic, sharp-tongued, and frank—for a woman. They walked a little farther along the rampants, Baldwyn moving at a ponderous pace. Paxton asked, "Are you doing a spell as sentry up here?"

The old leper glanced askew at him. "No. I was trying to decide whether I should kill you or not."

Paxton laughed aloud. He had also forgotten humor. "Why so?"

"I think you an agreeable man, Paxton of Wychchester. You are a soldier, like myself. So you will understand when I tell you that I shall lay down my life in taking yours before I shall allow you to harm my Lady Dominique."

Paxton peered over the edge of the parapet to espy far below the mill, its paddles glistening with river water. His smile was grim. "I shall keep that in mind, Baldwyn." Then he asked what had been on his mind since the jousting earlier that afternoon. "This Denys Bontemps, who is he?"

"Another childhood friend. He is constructing a hospital for my Lady Dominique."

"Constructing a hospital? He is a mason?"

"He is an architect-engineer, a graduate of the University of Montpellier."

Paxton braced his hands on the parapet's stones. "And he believes himself in love with the countess?"

The Templar's reply was guarded. "He owes her his loyalty. You see, the mother of my Lady Dominique had granted manumission to his father, a stonecutter. Denys displayed such a flair for his father's work that the Countess Melisande had me tutor him alongside her daughter, my Lady Dominique, so that Denys learned mathematics and geometry, in addition to other masonic knowledge that is a professional secret. I also taught him a little of sword play. Without fear of boasting, I might add that the infidels had reason to fear my prowess with the blade."

"He wishes to take Dominique de Bar to wife?"

The Templar peered at him innocently. "He would honor her so. Nevertheless, he is but a peasant and she a countess."

"For the present," he answered, repeating her own words to the wordly bishop the day before. Did Francis de Beauvais act as the pope's emmissary, as she had stated, or as the pope's *agent provocateur?*

"You must realize my Lady Dominique has been raised in a society dominated by women," Baldwyn entreated. "As a ruler in her own right and a free thinker, it is difficult for her to behave as do ordinary women."

Reflecting with irritation on her indomitable pride and resolution, he answered, "She will, my good Templar. She will."

"Well, as the peasant says, 'When donkeys fly, we shall see that happen.'"

A sullen pall overcast the day. Trumpets signaled the start of the second round of the tourney, the battle between the knights earning the most points the prior day. Two ranks of knights spurred their steeds to collision in mid-field. The shock of their encounter reverberated throughout the galleries. After that, the clang of the swords and the groans of the combatants drowned out everything else.

Dust erupted, fairly choking Paxton. Through its haze, he was able to spot at least a good half of the knights, unhorsed by either the skill of an opponent's lance or by sheer weight and strength. Still mounted but with his lance broken, he withdrew his sword and swung it in an arc at his nearest foe. He was allowed to strike but not jab.

A corpulent knight wielded a battle axe that would have surely hit mid-plate on his armor. At the last moment, Paxton dodged the stupendous blow. His mastery at horsemanship had saved him, and the momentum behind the knight's lunging swing pulled the man off balance so that in the next moment he was unseated.

Sweat rolled into Paxton's eyes, yet he fought on, as if his honor depended on it. And in a curious way, it did. Here and there he dealt sweeping blows. Then he sighted Denys Bontemps, afoot. Mounted as he was, Paxton could not engage the man by tourney regulations. With a movement that was most agile for a man of his brawn, he dismounted amidst the mayhem to confront the momentarily startled architect.

"I win this encounter, Sir Denys," he shouted against the din of battle, "and you render me your services for seven years."

Unexpectedly, Denys sliced horizontally with his sword, and reflexively he jumped back. The sword missed by a hair's breadth.

"And if I win?" Denys asked, already short of breath. "The Lady Dominique is released from your custody to me?"

For answer, he thrust his notched sword at the young man's chest and scored a point. Denys struck back, catching him on the shoulder. Two points.

For an interminable time they struck and

118

parried with a *tour de force* that elicited furious applause from the galleries. By now, he realized that if Denys could kill him, he would without any qualms.

Gradually, the field thinned until there was only the two of them. Paxton realized Denys was a man of considerable skill with the blade and a strength in shoulder and arm that must have come from years of stone cutting. The whacking of their blades vibrated all the way to the bone. Denys Bontemps fought recklessly.

So did Paxton, but with a purpose. He felt drained of every last ounce of energy. His broadsword weighed like a boulder. Denys was using both hands to wield his blade. The man swayed. Paxton chose that moment to swing his weapon with a force that sent the man reeling. He stumbled to his knees. The crowd went wild, yelling and cheering and clapping.

Paxton ignored them. Placing his blade tip on the man's shoulder, he asked with shortened breath, "Your services are mine, Sir Denys?"

Denys stared up at him with dull eyes. "Yes," he got out in a wheeze. "But not my loyalty."

"The devil take your loyalty." He wheeled away and crossed to retrieve his splintered lance, with its shorn tresses attached. The French called that reddish cast *la cendre*. Hell fire, he called it. His gaze sought out Dominique de Bar. Her features were expressionless. Well, he was not yet finished for the day.

Nearby, waiting nobly for its master, was his steed, which he had trained to bite, kick, and trample in warfare. Especially trample. After mounting, Paxton trotted the war horse across the expanse of tiltyard toward the gallery where the royal standard of a lion against bright red silk proclaimed the king's presence.

Cheering spectators and waving handkerchiefs greeted Paxton. Several women flirtatiously tossed brooches and rings toward him, and his mouth curled in a sardonic smile. Halting before the throne, he raised his lance in a salute to his king.

Edward III, regal in purple satin, rose and announced, "You acquitted yourself superbly and did well by England, Paxton of Wychchester. The honor, valor, and chivalry that was King Arthur's lives again. As a Round Table knight, you have taken the tourney and its grand prize."

With that, he extended a gold garland adorned with rubies and dropped it over Paxton's lance tip. There would be other prizes awarded the knights who had proven themselves—a suit of armor, a war horse, golden spurs fashioned in Toledo, a fine saddle. But, traditionally, this prize was given by the victor to the fairest maiden of the land. More often than not it was bestowed upon a damsel for political purposes.

He cantered across the field to the opposite gallery. All eyes were upon him. Naturally, it was presumed he would offer the garland to the Countess of Montlimoux.

Instead, he stopped in front of the Lady Esclarmonde, a winsome damsel with fair skin as white as snow on ice. Better yet, she possessed wonderful malleability and, best of all, was Francis de Beauvais's sister.

Astonishment rippled along the benches. The young woman hesitated demurely but in the end could not contain her pleasure and plucked the garland from his lance.

Dominique de Bar stared straight ahead, but a noticeable flush flowed up her neck and into her cheeks, crimsoning even those small, shell-like ears.

Regret at having to break her thus took him by surprise. He had supposed he was empty of all compassion for womankind, and women who spoke the *langue d'Oc* tongue at that. He shrugged away the feeling. Tonight, perforce, he would deliver the *coup de grace*.

CHAPTER VIII

The gala feast held at the great hall that evening rivaled any dinner Dominique had ever given. The adherents of *The Laws of Saint Robert* would have unanimously approved of the proper seating order for the guests.

She supposed the evening's fête was attributable to Paxton's largess and not Montlimoux's revenues. It was, in her opinion, ostentatious, but then this was in honor of the Duke of Aquitaine *and* King of England, titles in that order of importance, which Edward himself preferred.

Essentially, he was French by his mother, his language, and part of his possessions. It was said that he was driven by an antipathy for his father, who had been a reputed homosexual. But then it was also said that Edward was King Arthur reincarnated with his noble words and deeds and fair ladies who graced his court.

The knights had scarcely had time to remove their armor and ladies to freshen their toilets before the dinner commenced. Banners of various colored silks draped the tables. On each one was placed a bowl containing lavender. A considerable staff of retainers and varlets served the nobility.

The dishes were brought in by servants in full armor, mounted on caparisoned horses. Their dung in the hall infuriated Dominique, and she found her hands gripping her table knife. She should have expected as much from a mere serf who aspired to rise above his station!

Incredibly, a hunting horn announced the main course that would be flambéd at the table. A roasted peacock in full plumage, stuffed with spices, rested on a mass of brown pastry, dyed green to simulate a grassy meadow.

As a lesser knight, Denys did not sit at the main table. Although she did, she was placed at its far end, with the King and Paxton installed in the positions of importance at the center. Esclarmonde, Queen of the Tourney, sat at Paxton's right. Her shimmering blond hair was drawn up through and overflowed the garland of gold and rubies he had bestowed upon her.

"Your Englishman has done well by the feast," Francis said, finishing the last of his wine.

"You know he is not my Englishman." The vermillion sugar plums were ashes in her mouth. "By tonight's end, he will be officially my lord."

"Look at me, Dominique." His seriousness drew her regard. Around him was a mystic aura that she could not ignore, had never been able to. Beneath his striking mane of ebony hair, his eyes held hers. "You well know that if conditions were different I would take you as my wife." A wry smile pleated the corners of his supple mouth. "But the Church has a problem with married priests."

"Francis . . ." She paused, then verbalized her curiosity, "Do you . . . uh . . . ever have a problem with celibacy?"

To her, Francis had always seemed steeped in a luxury and sensuality that did not dull but rather embellished his graceful masculinity. The Church had long been having difficulty with homosexual priests as well as the married clergy. Could she have misjudged Francis's sexual preference?

His outburst of sincere laughter reassured her. "Come with me to Avignon and discover the answer yourself, *m'amie*." Then he turned serious. "I do want you to come to Avignon. I assure you, you would be quite safe there under my tutelage."

Her eyes laughed. "What kind of tutelage is that, Francis?"

His smile was one of mock innocence. "Why, t'would be like the days of old, when together we explored the works of Abramelin the Mage and Albertus Magnus in your mother's laboratory."

"No, t'would not. Nothing remains the same but is forever changing in the instant. I thank you for your offer of a haven, Francis, but I cannot forsake Montlimoux."

Her gaze sought out the English lieutenant again. He was conversing with his king, but at that instant Esclarmonde said something to distract him and he laughed. His grin took away Dominique's breath. That smile transformed his ordinary features into an arresting face. The bold dark eyes flashed with a humor that made any woman watching declare him unequivocally handsome.

Every woman, that was, but Dominique. She would grant him no boon.

She turned back to Francis. "Paxton of Wychchester may deprive me of my title. He may drive me from my chateau, but he cannot hound me out of my county. I know every valley, every cave, every pond, every plant. If need be, I could live off the land as he never could."

Too soon for her, the dinner was over, and the ballet was set to begin. At some time during the dancing, she would be forced to make public her renunciation of title. The tables were removed, and the gallery's musicians started to play.

At first, the dances were lighthearted, like the roundeau or chain dance, and the torch dance, in which each dancer held a long, lighted taper and endeavored to prevent the other dancers from blowing it out.

As the evening passed, the dances waxed more romantic. The code of the courts of love, entitled *Arresta Amorum*, the decrees of love, specified that each gentleman was to bend his knee before his lady at the end of the dance.

Throughout Dominique had watched with her maids-in-waiting, particularly Beatrix who glowed like a wax taper when John Bedford presented himself before her.

On her part, Dominique declined to participate. Certainly, her heart was not of the merry vein. She would have even refused Denys when he bent a knee before her, but she did owe him a great debt of gratitude for fighting in her honor today. Her hand in his, they joined the circle of dancers, taking three steps to the left, marking time, then taking three steps to the right.

His expression was brooding, and he moved stiffly. When next they marked time, she teased, "Are you bruised and sore from tilting today, my good friend?"

He made a face and lifted her hand aloft, as the dance steps prescribed. "More than I would have thought." He squeezed her hand, almost hurting it. "Dominique, I would tell you before someone else does. Paxton of Wychchester and I wagered for you today."

"What?"

"If I won this afternoon's jousting, you were to be released into my custody."

She halted in her steps. Her eyes expressed their disbelief until she saw the determined intent in his. "And if Paxton won?"

His determination gave way to an anguished whisper. "I have given him my services for seven years."

"Seven years!" she gasped. "Whatever for?" Other couples were circumventing them, but she scarcely took heed.

"His captain, John Bedford, tells me that my skill will be needed in constructing bridges, forts, things of war instead of things of beauty."

Her hand clasped his arm. "Oh, Denys, you should not have risked your future for me!"

"My future is you. I could not be happy knowing that you are here, endangered by this English churl." He was speaking rapidly now, as if there might not be another chance. "There is yet another reason why I would stay, Dominique. The people who are not locals, they are talking about your efforts in the pavillion yesterday, about your attempt to save the wounded knight."

"I can well imagine what they say, that I am a sor—" She broke off at the tugging on her sleeve and glanced down. It was Hugh. He pointed from her to his new master, Paxton, whose broad back was to her at that moment. The towheaded boy did not need the gift of speech to make her understand she was being summoned.

A flourish of trumpets interrupted the dancing. As the duke-king approached the canopied dais that had been transported from the tourney gallery to the great hall, the vociferous revelers cleared the center of the room. Paxton and Edward's advisors took chairs arranged on either side of him.

For this occasion Edward had donned a sleeveless scarlet robe over his short, tightly fitting cotehardie. If she separated his position from his person, he appeared not much older than herself. Young. Determined to rule. Headstrong. His advisors, it was said, counseled restraint. Among those who did so was Paxton.

The advisors were richly bedecked in plumed caps and mantles trimmed with embroidered velvet. Beside them, Paxton's dress was sober, yet his physique was so commanding that all eyes were drawn to him as well.

When a crier called out, "Oyez, oyez," her heart began to beat in her throat.

Edward III began speaking in a calm, almost concilatory manner. His tone was warm, his voice firm, as he told the assembly that the tourney and gala feast following it were being held in the honor of Montlimoux's new Lord and Grand Seneschal, Paxton of Wychchester. He was treating her ousting as nothing more than a change of administration.

He fixed his imperial eye on her. "Countess Dominique de Bar, I bid you present yourself."

She drew a steadying breath and walked toward the dais, where she knelt, then rose to stand proudly. The duke-king nodded toward a paunchy man on his right, the sergeant-at-law. He completely lacked calves, and the points of his shoes were so long they were attached to his knees.

In a stentorian voice, the man began reading from a scroll: "I, Dominique de Bar, Countess of Montlimoux, make known to those present and to come that I have become liege lady of the King of England, Duke of Aquitaine, who from this day holds the County of Montlimoux in feud. Whereupon, I commend myself to his representative for guardianship, Paxton of Wychchester. I have made faith and pledge homage to His Highness and his heirs. In return, I seek the security and protection of the Duke of Aquitaine, through his representative, Paxton of Wychchester. By the Lord before Whom all is holy, I submit myself to Paxton of Wychchester and choose his will as mine."

Her gaze locked with the dispassionate one of Paxton's. It could have been worse, she told herself. Nominally, at least, she still held the title of countess.

He rose and came to stand before her. His eyes were dark, deep, and demanding. He held out his hand. She placed her cold one in it, signifying she was his vassal. His palm was warm and large enough to hold both of her hands.

"I do so swear as a vassal of my Lord Lieutenant, Paxton of Wychchester," the sergeant-at-law prompted.

She could not help herself. She, who never cried, could not contain the tears that welled in her eyes. She had failed her feminine forebears. Thankfully, only this man who now owned her services could see those tears of shame. "I do so swear as—"

Her throat was choked with her tears. Her hand trembled, and Paxton squeezed it, whether as reassurance or as prompting, she could not tell. She could not bring herself to meet his gaze. Triumphant as always was he.

She started over, ". . . swear as a vassal . . . of my Lord Lieutenant, Paxton of Wychchester."

He raised a brow, waiting. Everyone waited for her to perform the last traditional step in the ceremony. She swallowed hard, forcing herself into action. Closing her eyes, she stood on tiptoe to place a kiss on his cheek. He had to lower his head for her lips to reach him, and even then she just barely grazed his jaw.

His skin was smoothly shaved, and a pleasant male smell reached her.

Quickly, she stepped away and blindly signed the document that the sergeant-at-law held out. Another flourish of trumpets and clarions signified the end to the humiliating ceremony.

She would have gratefully withdrawn from the floor, but Denys picked that moment to come forward. He took her hand, the one she had just removed from Paxton's. Her childhood friend's face was taut, his color high. "Your Majesty and my Lord Lieutenant, I come to seek a boon. The hand of my Lady Dominique in marriage."

Silence claimed the great hall. All eyes watched in expectancy, all ears strained to hear any words of exchange. Edward's amused gaze deserted her and Denys and moved to Paxton. "Me thinks this is your domain."

Paxton took the cue. He rubbed his chin while everyone waited with pent-up breath. At last, he said, "By *droit de seigneur et régale*, Denys Bontemps, I refuse your offer of marriage with my vassal."

Denys's hand tightened around hers. "I pray ask on what grounds, my Lord Lieutenant."

Paxton's smile was veiled. His hand seemed to rest negligently on his sword's hilt. "Since as my vassal she cannot provide required military service, her husband must do so. I can marry off the maiden for far more than your military service would bring me."

Piled atop her humiliation now was her degradation of being bartered like salt. "I will not be—"

He cut her short. "You will be what I want."

His words were loud enough only for those nearest to them to hear. He would not let her challenge his authority. The most she might do was throw a tantrum, for which she quite probably would never be seen at court again but instead spend the remainder of her days chained in the chateau's cellar. Which at that moment seemed a safe and desirable prospect.

He turned to Denys. "I suggest you do as the biblical Jacob did for the hand of Rachel and indenture yourself to me for another seven years." He shrugged and added indifferently, "Perhaps after that period of time I shall reconsider, providing I haven't in the meanwhile found an advantageous union for her with some nobleman."

Denys started forward, but her hand waylaid him. He was courting death. "If I may retire, your Majesty?" she asked, purposefully avoiding addressing the oaf who now officially presided over Montlimoux.

"After the gala is over," Paxton said. He signaled the musicians and held out his hand. She had no recourse but to take it and let him lead her out into the center of the room. The *danse au chapelet* was being played. Other couples formed a large ring, and she followed

133

the steps mechanically, for, to tell the truth, had she been required to think clearly she would have been unable.

When she missed a pass, he caught her by the waist and redirected her. A soldier born, yet an adept courtier who has the education of a priest. She could not make out this foreigner. "For all your coarseness, you ape well your betters," she said.

"For all your high birth, your manners are little better than a *fille de joie*." His smile was as forced as hers, his eyes promising further retribution.

Suddenly, she realized that the end of the dance was nearing—and what it required. Was he aware of this Provencal tradition?

The last note of a flute died away and she glanced up at him beneath her lashes. His head was lowering over hers. She stiffened. Wildly, she wondered how this foreigner could have known that at the end of the dance a kiss was required of the damsel.

Then the thought died away at the touch of his mouth on hers. He moved his lips over her own, lingering at the corner of her mouth, then returning to claim hers in a full and quite possessive kiss.

She felt charged, as if she were soaring, and weak, too. Her fingers clung to his shoulders. His large hands squeezed her upper arms, supporting her. She wondered what was happening to her. How could he make her feel thus?

When he lifted his head, she opened her eyes and saw that the two of them were the center of attention. Once more he had imposed his claim on her, as he would, she suspected, in all ways.

She awoke early, with the memory of last night far in the back of her head. Dawn's golden light shimmered between the heavy draperies. She stretched, feeling good about everything in general.

Then, as she pulled the cord to summon Beatrix, the memory returned. It had been all she could do to retire from the great hall the night before with her dignity in tact. By midday, gossip would doubtlessly have shredded it.

The Englishman's mistress!

She tossed back the covers and dressed herself in a simple tunic that required little lacing. A cloak secured by a gold chain at her left shoulder would protect her against the early-morning chill. Avoiding the just awakening maids, she slipped out of the chateau with only the usher and the barbican guards to challenge her. Most of last night's revelers had drunk themselves into a stupor.

Besides, why should Paxton be concerned if she left now that she had finally signed over her domain?

The village was already astir with activity. Blacksmiths and butchers were among the first opening their shops. Shutters rattled and rusted door hinges squeaked. She met sleepy maidservants going to the wells with buckets and basins.

Once clear of the village, she walked, a long, rapid walk to discharge her energy. But waves of magnetic impulses kept swirling through her with incredible intensity. She returned to the chateau, still charged and restless.

For the first time in weeks, she sought out her laboratory, hoping her work would divert her tumultuous thoughts. Torches of resinous wood cast their light down the tightly descending staircase and onto the rusty bars of the dungeon grate. At its bottom, she stopped short.

Spread out over the cold stone floor like a small Arab carpet was her falcon, still hooded. A scarlet line demarcated its split throat, split by one of the broken vials that littered the floor. The bird of prey's blood pooled on the stones to mix with the mercury, sulpher, and other elixirs that had been spilled.

CHAPTER IX

By degrees the tourney's spectators and competitors departed from the county the following week, and life in Montlimoux returned to normal—if the presence of Paxton's soldiers was discounted. Apparently, only Dominique resented the English troops, for as a result of their deployment within the county, Montlimoux's merchants were waxing wealthy from the increased revenues.

Even Denys was gone, dispatched by Paxton to inspect river crossings for possible bridge sights. Denys's leave-taking had been brief but consummate. He had found her in her library and rashly taken her in his arms in front of Jacotte and some of her maids-in-waiting. "I *shall* return for you, Dominique. I swear by all that is holy. I shall never relinquish you! You know that, do you not?"

Staring up into those impassioned eyes, she could only nod. She had known as much since childhood.

Then, he had kissed her. The first kiss ever from him. She had felt . . . pleasure. But not that sense of losing herself that frightened her when Paxton's mouth closed over hers. Afterwards, she had felt regret because of the pain she witnessed in Jacotte's anguished gaze, as she watched Denys's ardent display.

Why could love not be perfectly matched with the lovers? She could only surmise that there were lessons to be learned, but, oh, at what cost to the soul? Pray, she would not lose herself in such a way!

Not all the tourney's guests took their leave, among them being Lady Esclarmonde, who, upon deciding to stay, had bade a temporary and touching *adieu* to her brother. How long Esclarmonde planned to stay was a question ever in Dominique's mind.

Francis's sister found the serenity of Montlimoux a respite from the whirlwind court life at Avignon, or so she said. Dominique had her doubts. She believed Esclarmonde found Paxton of Wychchester a delicious challenge compared to the pandering courtiers at the papal palace.

At any rate, Dominique chafed under the imposition of this unwanted houseguest, but she no longer had the authority to order the woman out. Was it Esclarmonde who had cast this bleak aura over the chateau? No one else seemed to sense the heaviness. Mayhaps, Dominique thought, it was the loss of Reinette that had left her feeling unsettled. The bird's death had been a cruel, violent act.

Who was responsible? Certainly not Esclarmonde. The young woman did not have the strength required to subdue a bird of prey, much less kill it. Of course, there was the distinct possibility she could have hired some man to do it for her.

Of even more dire consequences was Esclarmonde's possible design on Paxton. She was using all her coquettish wiles upon the bachelor. Today, she had cajoled him into allowing her to ride with him. Mounted, not on his chestnut but his war horse, he had ridden out of the chateau with her at his side, astride a docile palfrey. Too bad it was not a cob.

Paxton could very well end up marrying the woman. The very thought made Dominique shudder. Esclarmonde was one of those petty, domineering spirits bent on exerting every scrap of authority that is theirs. Dominique could not imagine her life being spent in such spirit-quenching humility. Worse, she knew that Esclarmonde, should she succeed in bringing Paxton to the altar, would send Iolande, Baldwyn, and herself packing.

Dominique rubbed her temples with her fingertips, willing away her emotional turmoil. It was Paxton of Wychchester's fault that she could no longer center herself. His condescending gaze, his aggressive male essence, threatened to dominate her receptive feminine side, which had always been a paradoxically powerful force.

Outside, spring was adorning herself with a riot of gaudy, gorgeous flowers. She had missed tending her plants, but even more than the earth, she needed water now. Not simply the bath water from a copper tub. She needed full immersion in that element to experience the wholeness of nature and to live with it in harmony.

When she ordered an equerry saddle her horse, Baldwyn insisted on riding with her. He caught up with her as she strode across the bailey. "Not all of the English soldiers may be so well ordered as those posted within the town, my lady."

"No, Baldwyn, I always rode alone before," she said, entering the stables. She delighted in its earthy odors of manure, leather, and straw. Particles of dust floated on sunlight beams shafting between timbers. "To do otherwise now would only—"

"I shall accompany the Lady Dominique," Captain Bedford interposed.

She whirled around to find him leading her dappled gray to her, along with his own mount. "I thank you, Captain, but I wish to ride alone."

"My Lord Lieutenant's orders, my lady."

He appeared to genuinely regret counter-manding her wishes. She could not find it in herself to be harsh with the roguishly hand-some knave. "I assure you, I shall be all right, Captain."

"I shall stay a reasonable distance, my lady. No closer than last time."

"Last time?"

"Aye. When ye went walking the morning after the gala feast."

"You followed me?"

"Aye, at my Lord Lieutenant's command."

So she was Paxton's prisoner, regardless of the length of rope he allowed her. She told John Bedford as much after they left the noisy town behind and cantered out through the river valley. "My captor is generous in permit-ting me to ride so far afield." She slanted a look at the redheaded soldier. "Or mayhaps he plans an accident for me."

John laughed, a full laugh that came from his deep barreled chest. "Thine imagination is lively, my Lady Dominique."

His humor irked her. "With my death, my fief would then be forfeited to him, isn't that so? Why covet a title like Grand Seneschal when one could be Count?"

"What need has Paxton of the title Count of Montlimoux, when he can be the Earl of Pernbroke?"

She sniffed. "An earldom is no better, especially in your heathen land. Even your king prefers the title of Duke of Aquitaine to King of England."

"Aye, but Paxton prefers Pernbroke, I swear by my troth, lady. Once he completes his mission here—"

"And the reason for that is?"

"Why, supervising Montlimoux."

The afternoon sun was hot, and she wiped the perspiration from her brow. "No, I mean why does he prefer this Pernbroke?"

John's expression clouded over. Even his merry blue eyes seem to dull. "'Tis Paxton's form of retribution for past injustices done him by its former earl."

This bit of knowledge revealed to her that the lieutenant could be a dangerous enemy to those who opposed him. Was *he* responsible for Reinette's death?

And what would happen once he had completed his work here? Whom might King Edward send to take his place? Paxton had yet to beat her or force himself upon her. Overall, she had been treated better than suzerains of other occupied principalities. Better Paxton as her leige lord than some ignorant, porcine soldier.

Paxton's rational intellect, his aggressive force, certainly made him a formidable competitor, as he so aptly demonstrated in the tourney games. Perhaps that was why she was attracted to him. Had not Chengke proclaimed that polar opposites were a unity?

142

Abruptly, she sawed in on her reins, realizing what she had unconsciously admitted to herself: She *was* attracted to Paxton of Wychchester!

"What is, my lady?"

"Nothing." She shook her head, as if thereby she could shake off the provoking thoughts of Paxton. "Only that the mountain stream I seek lies nearby. Wait here until I return."

Leaving her gray in John's care, she followed a hen run that twisted up a hillside forested with magnificent old beech trees and fragrant cedar. Legend clung to the area, supposedly the site of pagan celebrations.

Soon, she heard the sound of tumbling water. She picked her way to the spot where the stream fed a horse-high waterfall. Water frothed like sparkling wine, and rainbows arced through its mist. Golden sunlight sifted through the canopy of leaves. The place was intoxicating.

Chengke had instructed her about such areas. Forests, mountains, and the sea, the mother of all creativity, where the waters in the body moved with her tides, were power generators for the spirit. Water was the most profound conductor. Chengke had compared it to lightning, although she was not sure she really understood.

She did know that by simply submerging her body in water, she could effect a tremendous release of the heaviness surrounding her.

The water whispered, its formless spiritual energy beckoning. She stripped off her linen underclothes and outer robes with what Iolande would surely term undue haste. Once her ties were loosed and her hose were peeled away, she wriggled her toes in the cool, green grass and practically sighed aloud.

Gingerly, she waded into the gurgling stream. Chengke had claimed that moving water released the static energy which occasionally disturbed her nervous system and confused her perceptual abilities. The cold water rushed around her knees, up her thighs, and caressed her belly. When it lapped her full breasts, she laughed out of sheer pleasure.

"Ah," she sighed, turning over on her back to float. "How can nakedness be considered sinful?"

The water streamed through her hair, combing it into a shimmering, silken fan around her head. She luxuriated in its essence, feeling her senses wonderfully enhanced. When her limbs moved freely and gracefully, finally relaxed and supple, she waded from the water reluctantly.

As she reached for her silk chemise, she thought of Chengke. She could imagine him as he was in her court, his hands tucked up in the wide sleeves of his mandarin orange robe in the attitude of a monk. She knew he would have told her, "The negative particles of the turbulent water have not sufficiently purified your emotional system, woman."

'Tis that Englishman, she told herself crossly. *He disorients me.*

Her studies with Chengke had taught her that one will always be attracted to that which will create change within a person.

But who said she was attracted to Paxton of Wychester?

She recalled one of her conversations with Chengke. "The *yin* is the female creative source that allows for the blueprint," he had said. "Like Denys's sketches, it is to be taken out and constructed into reality by the aggressive *yang* male energy."

She began to tug on one hose. She did not need to recall Chengke's lecture on mysticism, she mused, with definite perturbation. She needed practical guidance. She needed to find a way to keep Montlimoux.

At that instant, before she could even cry out, Paxton, mounted on his great war horse, crashed through the underbrush. Whirling, she grabbed up her clothing to hold like a screen before her.

His horse pranced nervously, and he sawed in on the reins. His angry gaze raked over her near nakedness. "We need to talk."

She almost laughed. His eyes indicated something else other than mere conversation. The lust she saw there reassured her. She could deal with mere coarse sensuality. It was the solution to her worries. She must fight, using her feminine wiles to maintain her fiefdom. "Talk about what, my Lord Lieutenant?"

"What is on everyone's lips since the tourney. Your sorcery."

"Then it was you who killed my falcon?"

"What?" His impatient tone warred with the desire that darkened his eyes.

"Someone slit her throat and left her carcass in my laboratory, along with broken elixir vials."

The way he frowned, his winged brows sloping at the outer corners in an expression of confusion, made her doubt her initial suspicion. As if making up his mind then, he said, "That only supports the rumors that began when you attempted to bring Patric back to life."

"What? That I am a sorceress?"

He swung down from his saddle and looped the reins around a stunted oak. Her gaze bypassed the short, hazlenut doublet to fix upon his muscled legs. There was a world of difference between his hose-sheathed calves and the lance-thin ones of King Edward's sergeant-of-law.

"Do you deny it?" he asked. "You work with alchemy. You perform spells over cats and humans. You conspire with spirits."

"What do you mean by that?"

"I spied on you in the oratory deep in a trance."

"Oh." She needed to divert him and remembered her purpose. "Since you are so

well versed on sorcery, my Lord
Lieutenant . . ." She held her clothing loosely
now, so that one hose slithered down to plop
atop her bare feet. ". . . surely, you must
know then that a sorceress—or a witch—
cannot be a virgin because . . ." It seemed to
her she was chattering nervously.

Watching her steadily from beneath those
strong, falcon brows, he listened with a deadly
calm.

". . . because a pact with Satan requires a
woman giving herself to him sexually."

His brows lowered, and a nerve flickered
faintly in the rigid jaw. "So 'tis said."

She summoned courage to let her shield of
clothing slide slightly, revealing a daring expanse of rounded breasts. "Then if I am a
virgin, I cannot be a sorceress, is that not so?"

Passion dilated his pupils. His finger loos-
ened the neckband of his shirt. "Exactly what
are you aiming at, mistress?"

"Of course," she continued with false bravado, "only the man who took me to his bed
would know if I am virgin and, therefore, not
a sorceress."

He reached out and took her upper arm.
Her clothes tumbled to the ground. "Me
thinks you a succubus, mistress, but I care not
that you come to seduce me in my sleep. I
want you in my waking hours as well."

His expression was tortured. His jaw
clenched, the veins in his temples pulsed.
Sweat sheened his upper lip, already shad-

owed with a beard at this hour. His training and beliefs and very philosophy of life warred with this elemental passion. A passion so great that she trembled with fear for what was to come. She knew she would be irrevocably changed before the afternoon was out.

"What of Captain Bedford?" she asked softly.

"I have sent John to escort the Lady Escalamonde back to the chateau."

Then he had intended for this to happen as well as she, whether he knew it consciously or not. This moment was no accident.

Her hands at her sides, she suffered him to touch her face in an almost wonderingly exploratory gesture. For all the roughness of his skin, his touch was light. A curious tingling began where his fingers had been and followed them as they curved around her neck, then traced the curvature of her collar bone. Now she knew that delicious sensation his cat felt whenever he stroked it.

She kept her eyes fixed on his. Fluttering light shone in their depths. She could feel her own body lighting up in response to the translucent subtlety in his. Her eyes closed. The feeling of his touch was wonderfully terrifying. He had an extraordinary power to excite her.

She felt his lips kiss the hollow created by her collar bone, as if he were tasting her skin. Her lids sprang open. "I must warn you," she murmured, her breathing shallow, light.

"There is a legend about this place."

He eased her to her knees and sank to the soft grassy bed opposite her. "That it is enchanted?"

She reached over and began to loose his doublet, saying, "That if you meet a fairy by the waterfall—"

"Are you truly a fairy, what the French call *fée?*" His voice was deep, stressed with the passion he constrained.

"—and drink its water, you will fall in love with her."

His dark eyes never left her face as she divested him of his clothing. "I do not believe in superstitions, mistress."

At that she smiled. "And 'tis no superstition that, according to Saint Thomas Aquinas that the gaze of a woman during her menstrual times can dim and crack a mirror?" she teased. "Or that her blood is injurious to any plant she touches, or this?"

Her fingers stroked the length of that totally masculine part of him, and he shuddered like one of those mythological dragons in fever. His lids closed. In her work of healing, she had seen men unclothed but never a man so perfect of body. She found she wanted to continue to touch him.

"Here in Languedoc," she said softly, "we tell the story of a man known as Fauvel. Actually, he is half man half horse. The peasants vie for the privilege of caressing him. He is the embodiment of sensuality."

With a groan, he grasped her palm and held it immobile. His eyes burned like the bonfires of Midsummer Midnight. "I am no imaginary creature."

She was amused by his seriousness. "I did not think so, my Lord Lieutenant."

"Paxton," he corrected. He pressed her back and stretched out alongside her to rest on one elbow. He stared down at her with an expression that reflected racing thoughts. His breathing became shallow and rapid to match hers. She perceived the latent violence that threatened to take shape as the coming sexual act.

She raised her hand and let it conform to the strong, square line of his jaw. "Sex is not a weakness, Paxton. 'Tis the life force. 'Tis divine." Her hand dropped to touch him between his legs again, and she delighted in the lightning that sparked his eyes and in his smell, heightened by his heat. "'Tis not only here but in your hands when you touch me and in your throat when you speak. To take me with any other thought is the misuse of your sexual power and will only leave you splintered, Paxton of Wychchester."

She did not know whether he understood what she was trying to teach him, but when he pulled her under him it was with a ginger movement that might have been the forerunner of gentleness.

Her mind, eager for knowledge through experience, took note of all.

Breath was the spiritual energy that animated everything, and the sharing of his breath with her in the form of his kiss was the key act to experiencing her, whether he knew it or not. The delicious moment continued when his tongue stimulated her upper lip, thereby stimulating the moist spot between her legs.

She took the lead, her tongue making contact with his, that first act of penetration. He seemed not threatened, only more thoroughly aroused. His tongue joined with hers so that they went beyond individual boundaries into that mating act of passion. In that deep kiss, she drank of his essence and life force, beginning the union of their polarities.

After that, all her analysis ceased as they began the dance of creation and destruction. Wherever he touched her—her ear lobes, her breasts, her waist, her thighs—came alive so that her entire body was aquiver.

Wherever she touched him—his thick mahogany hair, his groin, his muscled throat, his hair-garlanded nipples—the heat of passion danced between them.

She was moist and needy. He was hard and wanting. There was no pain of entry, only the dance of union. Then came that moment, just before he emptied his energy into her, that she could feel herself being pulled from her body: a wind, the sense of spinning, faster and faster, an intensity of sound and spiraling, a humming that grew louder and louder, echoing with the crescendo roar of the waterfall.

If she could but stay with it, she knew she would achieve that state of ecstasy that would verily allow her to pass through walls.

Yet there was that fear, too, that if she did not hold tight to her will power she would be peeled away and sucked into the cracks of oblivion, that she would expand to the point of disintegration.

Her body was wreathed in a finite, sweet torture instead.

She came crashing back down through the cracks of the sky to find herself in Paxton's arms, holding her tightly. His breathing was raspy but, to her delight, it was not that exhausted breathing that came with promiscuous sex.

A slight smile curved her lips. She was fertile ground to be revered, and he the rain that nourished her crop. She was the chalice for alchemy, he the magic wand.

He raised on one elbow again and stared at her with perplexity tugging his brows down even further at the outer corners. His gaze wore a slightly dazed expression. "Me thinks you have given me some kind of potion, mistress."

She laughed lightly. Her fingertip traced the line of the scar that indented his upper lip. "Impossible! Have you drunk from the waterfall yet?"

"Nay, but I shall do so now, if only to prove

you are no sorceress and have no hold over me."

She drew her hand between her thighs and held up for him to view her fingers, smeared with his male seed and her virgin's blood. "This should prove it well, messire. I am no sorceress and have made no pact with the devil."

"Paxton is not the sort of man to be obsessed with a woman, is he?" Dominique asked insouciantly. The tapestry she tried to embroider looked like the work of a hand palsied by chilblains. Gone for the moment was her dexterity with the needle.

"That is not for me to say, my Lady Dominique," John Bedford replied cautiously.

She could not understand Paxton, why he behaved as he did. Baldwyn called him a man's man in a comaradely tone, which put her on edge, and confessed to enjoying his rakish company.

Paxton had permitted her to resume her lifestyle, though she was hampered by his soldiers quartered there. Fortunately, he was absent more than present at the chateau. He continued to travel the countryside, inspecting the fiefdom of which he was now in supreme charge. The day following their tryst alongside the waterfall's grassy banks, he had chosen to ride out from the chateau again. Supposedly to meet with one of her estates' castellans about surplus crops. Or so John told her.

Although she had heard reports that he was far from popular among her people, the bourgeoisie and petty noblemen were said to respect him. In the Justice Room, she grudgingly witnessed that he ruled intelligently with a velvet glove rather than an iron gauntlet. Nonetheless, she resented his appropriation of her authority.

"Oh!" she gasped.

"What is it, my lady?"

She held up her forefinger. A tiny spot of blood tipped it, where she had pricked herself with her embroidery needle. Inactivity was causing her to be careless these days. "I would never make a knight, John. My aim with the lance would be as poor as with my needle."

He left his seat in the window embrasure and crossed to her prie-dieu chair. He knelt and took her hand to examine its minor injury. "Me thinks ye possess the courage of the best of knights," he said, smiling.

"Courage, mayhaps. But not accuracy." Now why had that needle prick happened? Symbolic of something else?

His eyes widened. "Why, 'tis already ceased bleeding!" His gaze deserted her fingertip to peer up at her with amazement.

"Then you may cease your tender ministrations, Bedford," Paxton said from the doorway. His face was beard-shadowed. He looked weary but nonetheless formidable. She could feel his force from halfway across the room. It was like the lull in the air before the onset of a sultry spring storm, motionless but threatening with unseen power. And something in her responded to his masculine force, deny it though she may.

Beside her, John rose to his feet in an easy stance. His ruddy complexion was none the redder for his lieutenant's derisive words. Surely, he guessed what Paxton's suspicious mind was wondering.

That two of her maids-in-waiting were also in the room did not alter Paxton's suspicion. His assumption of ownership of her irritated her. Did not the ownership of her mind give her the right to also own her body?

She composed her features into a tabula rasa. "How are the affairs of my estates progressing, my Lord Lieutenant?"

His mild gaze lowered on her. "Your domestic steward has been teaching me about over-ripe grapes and mold." He turned to leave but paused to hurl her a smile that pricked like her needle. "Noble rot I believe it is called."

So, even Iolande was consorting with the enemy. The old woman admitted as much, while Dominique dressed for dinner later that evening. "You should be delighted the Englishman is showing an interest in Montlimoux's vineyards, my child. You are too young to remember, but during the Albigensian crusade, many of the French soldiers ripped up the vines of the various fiefs they occupied. Fortunately, a considerable portion of Montlimoux's escaped the crusade's pillaging."

"Ah, but not its torturing." She pulled her wrist away from Manon's grasp and, sending the startled maid on her way, she fastened the multitude of buttons tightly seaming each sleeve.

She could not help her testy mood. She feared Paxton of Wychchester's methods might not appear as brutal as the crusaders, but they could accomplish the same ends.

"I must make him marry me, Iolande."

"Paxton?" The Jewess stared at her as if she were in the throes of an epileptic seizure. "Have you taken leave of your mind? Bind yourself to the service of a male?"

"The man cannot bind my soul, Iolande."

"Can he not?"

Iolande's nose twitched so that Dominique had to laugh. "Well, at least, he has not seduced you over to his side, as I had feared."

She grabbed up her mantle to leave, and Iolande called after her, "Be careful not to sell your soul for Montlimoux, as *I* do fear."

Jugglers demonstrated their agility before the high table that evening. Bells dangled from their hoods' two elongated points. Some jugglers tossed ahigh knives, baskets, and brass balls, while others walked on their hands or threw wonderful somersaults. One even had a clever monkey that pantomined the guests.

Dominique felt distanced from the frivolities. John Bedford's blue eyes twinkled with tears of laughter. At the table's center Esclarmonde giggled charmingly and turned her lovely face up to Paxton's in a moment of shared amusement. Watching Francis's sister, Dominique sensed an unevenness about the young woman's aura. It was as if Esclarmonde were not in touch with her reality, as if she performed like the monkey, cued by tugs of the juggler's rope.

Of course, it could be that Paxton's tremendous male force blighted the energy from those around him. She knew she alone was a worthy adversary for him. And he knew it, too. His calculating gaze clashed with hers.

The sudden heat that coursed through her took her by surprise, as did the peculiar lurching in her stomach. On reflection, she supposed she should have expected as much. The battle was going to be for the retention of the soul.

CHAPTER X

Was Paxton taking Esclarmonde to his bed?

Dominique was not certain. If not within the chateau, the two certainly had the entire countryside to conduct their trysts.

Her memory recalled with annoying clarity his strong, confident body, that tall, battle-hardened torso. Her hands still held the memory of his long, muscular back. Her dreams, some of them anyway, revealed again and again his proud chin and intelligent dark eyes.

The other dreams . . . Lately they had been unpleasant, though she could not identify exactly why. When she awoke, her memory of them would be blurred with only an impression left of a forewarning. Ever since Paxton's arrival she had felt disoriented.

Apparently not Paxton. Was his energy, the energy of the violent warrior, stronger than her own?

And what what his design on Esclarmonde? A design to infiltrate himself into the French court at Avignon? Was that the amorphous warning in her dreams?

She knew that he was currently instructing Francis's sister in backgammon. For the last three evenings, the couple had adjourned to the Justice Room to play the game. The clatter of the rolling die mingled with their laughter and murmured voices.

Dominique experienced frustration at having failed in her purpose to capture Paxton's unrelenting interest. If only she could convince him to marry her so that when he abandoned Montlimoux for this Pernbroke he coveted, his—and her—heirs would retain Montlimoux.

But how? When already his masculine ego was being stroked by the most fairest of what he contemplated as the weaker sex, albeit one whose chief vice was "carnal lust, insatiable and incalculably stronger than man's."

At least, that was the gist of the conversation between him and a Goliard. At dinner that night the wandering scholar argued brilliantly, for all his youth. "Publicly our clergy decry pleasure experienced purely for the sake of pleasure as a sin but you will notice, messire, that they have no qualms about privately making their housekeepers their mistresses."

Esclarmonde's silence was explained by her disinterested expression. Dominique likewise remained silent, although she had the impression that Paxton wanted to bait her. While she had championed the Goliard's viewpoint, she deplored an argument solely for the shock value of irreverence. These wandering scholars spared no one and no subject. God and the devil, Aristotle and the Pope, canon and feudal law, all were held up to ridicule.

"My Lord Lieutenant, I wish to retire. Tomorrow will be a long day."

Leisurely, he swallowed the sweetmeat and drank from his goblet before he deigned to answer her. "You have my permission."

If Hugh had not been behind her, her chair would have toppled, so abruptly did she rise from the table. His permission! Never had she behaved so overbearingly and unreasonably with her own vassals. Why on earth was she attracted to this lout?

Fuming, she paused at the minstrel gallery's balustrade and glanced into the banqueting hall below. Paxton *did* hold the possibility of revitalizing her county, she reminded herself, as she watched a teasing Esclarmonde slip a sugared almond between Paxton's lips.

Strangely, Dominique felt no jealousy, only a poignant sense of loss, a wistfulness, for what might have been. She had had this feeling that her path and Paxton's had not crossed by mere chance. How else to explain the color and sound that had inundated her when she had merged with him? That exquisitely light, out-of-body sensation afterwards?

But then she had been inexperienced in the patterns of sensuality woven between man and woman.

"I have been waiting for you."

"Waiting for me?" He watched her fingers fly with incredible nimbleness, and from her distaff and thread there slowly formed a delicate piece of lace. She wore an overdress that had a dark red-violet bodice shot through with gold. The bodice left her breasts almost bare.

She put down her lace and fastened on him those odd green eyes. No other maid looked at him so frankly, so openly. "Yes," she said quietly, "forever and a day."

This was not the coquettish reply Esclarmonde might make. With uneasiness, he realized Dominique de Bar was perfectly serious. Delaying, he rubbed his chin. He realized he did not want to know the truth of this woman, this peculiar woman with her extraordinary feminine powers.

Then why was he here?

Irritated with his irrationality, he broke the bond of their gazes and crossed to the traceried window. Below, in the bailey, John drilled the guard. Paxton told himself he should be out there with his men, not here, dallying like some fool page.

Behind him, he thought he heard her sigh.

His hands pressed down hard against the stones of the window embrasure. Their cool, rough feel, so unlike his memory of her body by the waterfall, restored his common sense. She was a mere woman, his chattel. "The villagers are staging a festival for tomorrow."

"Yes, I know. 'Tis for May Day."

Her voice haunted him, chaining him in the most confining of dungeons. Exasperated with his infantile reticence, he turned back to her. "I think it expedient you appear with my retinue tomorrow. Show your vassals that you are not my prisoner after all."

To occupy his hands, he bent to pick up Arthur, who had followed him into the library. Paxton's hands were accustomed to fashioning his elaborately tactical plans into reality. Yet this young woman was elusive, and some chimerical cognition told him that his hands could never really hold this complex woman, as complex as a spider's web, as strong and yet as fragile. As complex as the web of heaven and earth.

Her gaze tugged away from watching his fingers stroke a much-improved Arthur to fasten on his face. "Expedient for whom? Me or you, my Lord Lieutenant?"

"I want no revolt such as occurred in Montpellier, mistress."

"The people there were revolting against imposed salt taxes, not on behalf of a deposed countess."

"I take no chances."

"That is why you sent Denys away, was it not? You feared he would foment opposition to you among my people."

Was she in love with the young man? Yet, the countess had given herself for the first time to him, son of a baseborn serf. For the price of her fiefdom? His teeth ground against each other. "I sent Denys away because he is more useful as my military machinery engineer than your lap dog."

Her eyes darkened to the green of a stormy sea. "This then is an order, my Lord Lieutenant? That I accompany your retinue into the village?"

The way she emphasized his title . . . She really was a vexing wench. Somehow, she had managed to ensnare him neatly in a net of dilemma. Bed her, as he wanted, and she would prove her power over him. Avoid her, and he would prove his fear of her.

Both were equally true, and he churned sleeplessly and sweated through the dark hours of the night with this new knowledge of himself.

He could make love every night to any one of a dozen different maids, and he knew he would still be unfulfilled. It did not matter how beautiful their bodies or how perfected their technique, as aptly demonstrated by the adept Esclarmonde. He sensed he would never achieve that sense of feeling at one with himself unless the fulfillment he sought was reached in unison with someone like this vital woman, Dominique de Bar.

Was there anyone like Dominique de Bar?

God forbid! By the blessed Mother Mary, the very thought of the possibility made his stomach knot.

"Aye, Captain Bedford will escort you to the Mayday festivities," he growled, and abandoned the room abruptly.

The first of May dawned with all the splendor the spring ritual promised—blinding green and fairy blue-and-yellow bright. The cathedral bells pealed at inordinate hours in a sort of gay abandon that characterized the mood of the village people.

Paxton's mood was erratic. He was annoyed that he could not concentrate his thoughts wholly on his work. One part of him wanted to complete his mission at Montlimoux and return to Pernbroke, a project which was still a year or more away.

A separate part of him yearned to establish himself here, to lay down his guard, to explore himself. A daunting prospect. A facet of himself he had not suspected was opening like a spring flower. But flowers were fragile and vulnerable. Easily crushed.

The morning was still early with the scent of fresh dew, but already faint laughter of eager revelers beckoned through the open painted shutters. With a curse, he threw down his quill and crossed to the window casement, where Arthur lazily sunned himself.

Below, John and Dominique, with her maids-in-waiting, were riding beneath the barbican's hoisted iron portcullis. Some of the household servants, released from their duties for the day, made up the entourage.

Abruptly, he turned from the window and called out, "Hugh! Summon the barber for me."

Almost impatiently he sat while Hugh held a basin of beaten silver beneath his chin and the barber wielded a blade that left him clean shaven and with no more nicks to his face then he had begun with. Hugh watched the process with wide-eyed interest. "Begone with you," he told the mute lad. "The day is yours to celebrate."

A wide smile split the boy's face. His sandals slapped against the stone stairs as he scampered off to the festivities.

Within the hour, Paxton also took his leave of the chateau with a certain amount of anticipation lifting his spirits. He supposed the excitement of the spring day was contagious.

The hubbub down in the village was reminiscent of fair days. Peasants and their wives, burghers and their damosels, knights and their ladies crowded the streets. Gaudy spring flowers spilled over window boxes. Taverns were noisily thronged, and jongleurs sang on the cathedral steps. In the square before the cathedral, a Maypole had been erected with colored ribbons streaming from its top. Later in the day a king and queen would be selected to lead in the dance wrapping the ribbons around the Maypole.

Even though the crooked streets were narrow, the crowds parted for Paxton's great war horse. Wherever he went, he was recognized. When first he had come to Montlimoux as a beggar, their behavior had been merely that of indifference. Today their expressions were respectful and deferential, if not friendly.

Respect would be enough.

As the morning wore on, he became disturbed when he could not locate John and Dominique. Her vassals might be loyal to her, but today's celebration would draw the usual travelers, among them flocks of thieves who would think nothing of holding an elegantly bedecked young woman at knife point. Although John was quite capable of defending himself and Dominique in an evenly numbered match, Paxton felt he should have appointed a contingent of guards to accompany them.

At last, he discovered the two before a stall displaying exotic spices—saffron and cinnamon from the Orient, salt from Salins in Franche Comté, and the small black wrinkled berry so costly that the longshoremen who handled the peppercorn were closely watched and frequently searched.

Dominique was holding a single peppercorn in her palm as if it were a solitary diamond. She looked up at Bedford, and her parted lips and sparkling eyes were enough to make a man hurt with wanting.

"To cultivate its shrub for medicinal purposes, John, would be a delight beyond—"

Paxton flipped a gold *écu* from the purse at his belt. "A peppercorn for the lady," he told the startled spice merchant.

Open-mouthed, Dominique stared up at him.

"Bedford," he said, "I shall escort the Lady Dominique from here."

The reins of his horse in one hand, he took her by the elbow with the other and steered her past the passers-by who had recognized their countess. It would be hard not to. There was an air of assurance about her that had nothing to do with her finely made gown of rose muslin with its oversleeves slit to reveal the inner ones and nothing to do with her clear-cut countenance that was all the more beautiful for its subtlety.

"I once told you we needed to talk," he said, keeping his eye on the cobbled path for potholes or pools of human waste. "We never did. I think 'tis time, mistress."

She stared up at him obliquely. "Do you think you could address me by the same title you used with John, 'my Lady Dominique?'"

He glanced down at her and felt himself momentarily smiling, forgetting his qualms about ths strange woman. "Aye, mistress . . . my Lady Dominique."

He was somewhat astounded by the soft feelings the young maiden engendered in him. He had thought he hated all things Provencal, and for him to trust again, well. . . .

With everyone gathering in the square, it was easy enough to find on the nearby riverbank a spot secluded by bullrushes. The merry noise of the revelers was only a faint and distant whisper here. A lazy, meandering stream, the water floated dollops of water lilies that looked for all the world like fallen stars.

The overhanging willows reminded him of the dance of Brandon, that nocturnal festival in which the men and women went out with lighted candles to worship the trees and the sacred rites of spring. The oak had been the most revered of trees, but the closest trees had been willows. With his brothers and sisters, he had danced around just such a willow in a nearby meadow.

Dominique paused by the bank and watched him with her untroubled, clear green eyes. Gray, he had once termed their color, and at another time hazel. Now green. Perhaps it was the reflection of the rushing water. Pale green against her sun-burnished face.

He found himself wanting to touch this

uncommon maiden. Instead, he busied himself with securing his mount to the nearest tree trunk.

"That particular tree you tethered your horse to," she said, "is called a lotus."

"A what?" Had she perceived his thoughts about the Brandon rites? With a show of nonchalance, he dropped down opposite her and braced his arm on one upraised knee. She had chosen a sandy patch just beyond the treeline where the bank sloped toward the slow-flowing water. The air was ladened with the scents of reeds and wild flowers that grew in profusion around the venerable trees.

"You have never heard of Odysseus and the lotus-eaters?" she asked. "Well, of course not. Your abbot would have ignored Greek knowledge as a font of heresy." She paused to emit a sigh of disgust.

"Supposedly," she went on, "Odysseus was the king of Ithaca. He and his men visited a land of lotus-eaters. The lotus was a magic food that made people forget their homeland."

That explained the eerie pull of the Provencal land. Languedoc— Montlimoux— possessed some kind of exotic air that made him feel light of body. Was that why the sunlight filtering through the leaves overhead seemed to rain its golden dust around them? He felt absolutely foolish. He did not believe for one moment in such nonsense. And yet, he had witnessed her work her magic with his cat. Was she a sorceress? A pagan, yes. But a witch?

Before he could halt his tongue, he blurted out what had been plaguing his thoughts. *"Did you give me a love potion?"*

She flashed him that saucy smile, displaying those two front teeth slightly and intriguingly spaced apart. "Are you in love with me, messire?"

His reply came readily. "I think not!"

"There, you have your answer."

"But . . . you are ever in my mind," he said, hearing the acknowledgment with surprise and no small amount of resentment.

Reflectively, she sifted the fine sand at her feet through her fingers. "Perhaps, 'tis the recognition of the soul's twin in the other person."

"You speak beyond my comprehension."

"Baldwyn will tell you that the peasant says, 'When the student is ready, the teacher will appear.'"

Her cleverness made him uneasy. "You would make light of what is serious."

Her tone became mildly impatient. "'Tis easier to accept what you have been told all your life, Paxton, than to imagine other worlds outside your own realm."

Should he humor her? "And how do you find these . . . these worlds?"

She shrugged. "There are way showers to guide us. Dreams, for one. And plants and animals to warn us of natural disasters. Angels even of whom, you will note, the Church bestows only male names, like Gabriel and Michael."

With the last statement, a small frown drew her quiver-straight brows low, but she said no more.

He rubbed his own brows, then his smoothly shorn chin. "Your thoughts . . . You know they are blasphemous and dangerous should others learn of them?"

"I know. But danger is part of living. Life without that edge of danger is not life, is it? You should know that as a fearless and mighty warrior."

He had to grin at the prankish way she stressed the last. "Aye. 'Tis what makes the other moments sweeter."

"The grass greener. The sky more brilliant."

Why, yes, he thought, that was what he had felt when he awoke this morning, what he was feeling now.

She plucked a yellow flower, he knew not its name, and, entwining its stem with that of another scented flower she plucked, said softly without looking at him, "I, too, find my thoughts full of you. When I am around you, I feel . . . I feel more alive."

"Because I am a danger to you?" Surely, she had guessed that.

She canted her head and eyed him from beneath her thick lashes. "No more than I am to you. 'Tis true, is it not? To accept me, you

172

must rearrange your entire way of thinking. And if what you once believed is no longer true, then what is?"

The way her rich auburn hair fell smoothly from her wide brow to cascade over one shoulder stirred him more than the sight of any other maiden completely disrobed. "I do not have to accept you. I could just take you, as I already have before."

With dismay, he heard the low growl in his voice, but she appeared not to notice. She added yet another flower to the chain she was creating. "But your pleasure would die as quickly as these flowers without the sustenance of soil and water and light."

The floral scent was heady, intoxicating. "And if I take the time to explore you, what sustenance does that bring to our . . . our relationship?"

She raised the flower chain aloft and viewed her work with a critical eye. He saw that she had fashioned a wreath. Her gaze fastened on his. "Are you brave enough, my mighty warrior, to find out?"

He tried to answer as objectively as he could. "By my troth, I have my mistrust of you, fairy maiden, but, aye, I trust I am brave enough to test my values of life against yours."

She smiled, and he felt the breath go out of him. Truly, the place was bewitched.

She raised on her knees and placed the garland atop his head. "For today you are my May king."

He could not help himself. He captured her wrists and drew her hands around behind his back. She left them there. Other women would have already had their hands boldly inside his tunic. Merely the light pressure of her hands was enough to generate a wondrous heat.

Her lips were parted, half-smiling in an enchanting way. Her upper lip, he noted with pleasure, was a perfect archer's bow. "I wish to start with your mouth. A most lovely place to explore."

Her mouth was as soft as the petal crown she had fashioned for him and as scented. Just touching her somehow no longer made the urge for immediate completion paramount. Slowly, tantalizingly, she brushed her lips back and forth across his own. He could not resist tasting them with his tongue.

"Like the mead of the gods."

Still clasping the breadth of his back, she moved away slightly to peer up at him. Dimples at either side of her mouth drew it into a delightful curve. "Ah, then your education was not entirely devoted to sermons!"

He chuckled. "I confess that I did not confess, leastways not all my sins. Not those that involved loving village maids in musty haylofts."

Something that was almost akin to pity shadowed her eyes. "Is loving a sin?"

He touched the curve of her cheekbone. "You are a strange one, Dominique. You would give me freely what other maids barter for?"

She hesitated, then asked, "Esclarmonde? She barters her love?"

"Francis's sister covets Montlimoux though she has never admitted as much."

He watched Dominique's expression closely. Her lids lowered, so that the black half moons of her lashes concealed what he suspected he would find in her eyes.

"I know what you think," she whispered. "'Tis true. Montlimoux is part of me, of my lineage, and to lose it is to lose myself. I would fight in whatever way necessary to keep it alive." She lifted her anguished gaze to his. "But this—this thing with you. 'Tis something else apart. Something I do not understand."

"Aye, I know," he muttered. Without realizing it, his hands tightened on her shoulders.

Her eyes stared beyond him, as if she were puzzling over her selection of words. Her gaze found his again. "'Tis not as if I have no will of my own. I do have a choice about this moment, Paxton, but I know if I do not respond to this sacrament of loving then everything afterwards will be dulled by having missed this experience."

Loving, a sacrament? Not a sacrifice?

He did not hold with this philosophizing. Not with her power to confuse his thoughts and feelings so easily. He drew her down with him on the sandy bank. Gone was the leisure of the moment. A seizure of passion convulsed him. His kiss beseiged her. Her lips parted willingly to his invading tongue, but her own met his in a mating that felt like . . . like the way she described her healing hands . . . like lightning coursing through him.

The laces and buttons of her robe, her houppelande's wide sleeves, and her chemise's full neckline made disrobing her a simple act. His clothing was as rapidly strewn across the embankment.

She was as impassioned as he. Entering her jolted him. Beneath him, her hips moved in exquisite timing with his. Her fluid bathed him, nourished him. He felt that moment coming, that whirling point, as if his finite body were poised at the threshold of another of those dimensions of which she spoke. If he could but sustain this feeling!

Her head lolled back against his arm. With a little laugh, she said, "I know what you are feeling, my Lord Lieutenant. That spinning force. The first time we merged it left my hair in corkscrew ringlets for more than a day!"

His laughter was liberating. "You have me trussed fast in your love-lock dungeons, fairy maiden."

Her finger traced the scar that deepened his lip's crisp indenture. "You are experiencing these exquisite sensations because you are coming close to uniting your energy with a greater force. Do you know that? Do you understand what—"

"Hush!" he said, closing his mouth over hers to silence her disturbing words. He reveled in kissing her, but she ended it, by pushing him to one side. "What are you doing?" he rasped.

She rolled atop him. Her hands pressed against his heaving chest, and her hair curtained their faces. "Showing you that a maid can make love in this position as well."

The feeling of her pumping his loins was agonizingly breathtaking. Still, it seemed unnatural. He groaned aloud at the thought.

Her laughter was like quicksilver that slipped through the fingers. "Unnatural? Why? Because the man should have the upper position?" Her eyes twinkled. "Your St. Augustine doubtlessly thinks this supreme way of demonstrating love disgusting. But then me thinks if there was a better way of dealing with procreation, the Creator would surely have invented it."

There was no way he could disagree with her at that moment.

"The next time we do this, my Lord Lieutenant, I shall show you yet another way." Her fingers caressed his nipples, changing them to hard little pebbles. "One that I am sure your abbot-tutor would denounce as imitating animals with the male mounting behind the female but one that the Indian Hindus describe as quite delightful." Her lips sweetly wreathed one aching nipple. "I am curious to see if they are right. What think you? Should we experiment with this Hindu practice?''

He could only groan again as bliss bathed him.

Beneath their entwined bodies lay his wreath, the flower petals crushed.

CHAPTER XI

Through eyes glazed by Paxton's intense and intimate lovemaking, Dominique studied the man asleep next to her: the hard line of his broad cheekbones and angled jaw; the way his brows peaked over the outer corners of his eyes before sloping down sharply; his body powerful even in repose. In the pale, pre-dawn light, his facial scars were not even notice-able.

A handsome face, it was not, but an inordi-nately interesting one.

He was a quick student of the metaphysical arts. He pleasured her in ways even she had never imagined. Goaded by his lovemaking, she came dangerously closer each time to an emotional abyss. After that first time of experiencing his affect on her, she had been most careful to exert her will, even during the throes of their passion.

As if her thoughts had disturbed his slumber, Paxton's eyes opened. As was his habit, he quickly scanned his darkened chamber before moving. Then, rising on one elbow, he planted a kiss just below her ear lobe where it joined her jaw. She tilted her head to one side to allow him access to the fully exposed length of her neck, and he chuckled. "You will weaken my reserves, Dominique. Today I must ride to one of the garrisons being restored to its former strength."

The thought of Denys leaped into her mind. How was he faring with the troops to which Paxton had assigned him? She dared not ask.

Paxton rolled from her and began dressing, shrugging into his tunic and the wide-sleeved, leather surcoat, before even bothering to light a candle. Did he think because she could not see his back that she was unaware of its scars? Her fingers were not sightless. By now they had memorized every sinew, every muscle, yes, even every welt of his body. Honed by a soldier's life, it was a magnificent specimen of male beauty.

She sighed, almost purred. She felt satiated, replenished. Like Paxton's cat, she stretched languorously. *We both bask in his presence*, she thought. That he had yet to mention marriage disturbed her, but she was becoming adept at putting the unsettling thought from her mind.

She watched him stride to the open window. He walked with such confidence and assurance that he could combat anything. He stared out at the dawn, its first pale glow muted by a light rain. She loved its refreshing scent and its lulling patter on the roof slates. She sat up, tossing her heavy hair away from her face. "The rains will be harder come summer," she said, her voice still husky from their lovemaking.

He did not turn from the window. "I plan to show Montlimoux's tenants how to gather the soil that has slid to the bottom of the hills after such a rain, and haul it up to the top." He paused, then added, "I believe the soil's shaly slate is responsible for the region's superb crops, but it will not always be so if precautions are not taken."

For a man trained in warfare, his knowledge of the earth amazed her. There was so much she did not know about her warlord. Wrapping the linen sheet about her, she walked up behind him and put her arms about his waist. "Is it just possible you appreciate and love the land as I do?"

His answer was a harsh, "No."

"But, Paxton, Mother Earth is a living system just like the human body, and like the human body she needs attention and care and love."

"She will also take the sweat of your brow and the blood of your hands and more often than not render you nothing in return."

Dawn's breeze was redolent with rain, chilling her, and she hugged him close. "A farmer would disagree with—"

"Tell me nothing about farmers and their love of the land. I, too, cultivated the land, but t'was not for love. I pulled the plow for my mother. I was the mule, the ox, because as serfs we had no such animals. I was the animal!"

A serf! Impossible. A contradictory image of his haughty assurance, his autocratic mein almost that of royalty, crossed her mind. "But your education?"

He braced his hands on the sill, and the veins stood out on their backs. "Baldwyn would certainly appreciate this one. 'When two nobles quarrel, the poor man's thatch goes up in flames.'"

"I do not understand."

"Our landlord disputed a boundary line with the Earl of Pernbroke."

Her breath caught at the name, but she said nothing as Paxton continued. "The earl's men rode down all the serfs and their children. I was quicker than the rest of my family. My mother, my brothers and sisters were trampled. I watched their skulls smashed open like melons. I kept thinking, 'This cannot be happening!' I was literally blind with fury. For days. The earl's abbot was on the scene. He took me in and nursed me back to a sanity of sorts and eventually tutored me."

"A kind man," she murmured.

"The very same one you claim is misogynous."

"Kind but ignorant."

"Lucky for me," he quipped over his shoulder, "that he taught me more beneficial subjects than woman-hating, subjects like mapmaking and surveying."

That explained so much about him. Laying her cheek against his back, she summoned the courage to ask softly, "And the welts that stripe you here on your back?"

Beneath her palms, his stomach muscles tightened with his sharply indrawn breath. "Those are more recent."

She knew enough to wait. Mayhaps some day he would share that part of his life with her as well as other things she wished to know about him. Had there been a woman he'd loved?

On the heels of that thought came another. Was there a wife back in England? Unexpected pain tugged so harshly at her heart that she gasped.

"What is it?" he asked, turning around to take her in his arms.

"Nothing, only a chill."

His brown eyes lightened with amusement then darkened with passion. "I can remedy that." He caught her behind her knees and swung her up against his chest to stride back across the room to the bed. "You heal your way, Dominique de Bar, I shall heal mine."

* * *

"Now I understand the true fear of a woman for a man. The love for another that ultimately demands the loss of oneself. I would rather feel nothing at all than this . . . this fear."

"You? Afraid?" Iolande was amazed. The child had seemed dauntless, mature with a knowledge far beyond anything Baldwyn or she could impart. But Dominique the adult?

"Pass me that vial of salt."

Iolande searched among the laboratory's rack of vials until she found the one requested and passed it to her mistress. "At my age, I can safely promise that you have many feelings still to suffer, my Lady Dominique."

"The sulphur, please. Do you know that Paxton is avoiding me now during my life-giving flow. He dared to refer to it as that 'secret malady of women!'" She sniffed contemptuously and added, "As if t'were some distasteful feminine weakness."

Iolande shrugged her stooped shoulders. "I have never had that problem, my child, since no man ever desired me to begin with."

Dominique flashed her a penetrating look. "Has there been no man you felt drawn to, as if compelled by something beyond yourself?"

Iolande's jaw ached. She told herself it was her remaining teeth that plagued her so. But the ache, she knew, came from swallowing back those feelings all these years. An image of those ebony eyes half masked by the straight line of his lids came to her when in truth there was but the knight in rusty armor. "There was one for whom I felt the feelings you described."

"And?"

Dominique's perceptive sympathy was the last thing she wanted. Endurance was all she wanted at this point in life. "And nothing came of it."

Dominique flashed her a skeptical glance but only said, "The mercury now, please."

She thrust the vial of mercury at her mistress, who added the third ingredient to the mixture. "Mercury, sulphur, and salt," Dominique murmured to herself. "Spirit, soul, and body."

The elements bubbled and hissed and steamed, prompting Iolande to speak of what was troubling her. "I fear, my Lady Dominique, that your quest for hidden knowledge may lead you into a dark and evil force beyond the veil."

"There is no such thing as evil, Iolande. Only the misdirection of power. Life's powers lived backwards instead of forwards. 'Tis no accident that the word 'live' spelled backwards is evil. No, I believe my quest for hidden knowledge will end with initiation into divine truths."

Iolande shuffled toward the staircase. Yes, there were still many feelings for her mistress to suffer and ambitions to abandon, all feelings that overtook those unlucky enough to survive infancy. Fervently, she wished her Lady Dominique could be spared the consequences of old age.

Another garrison refortified, another bridge built, another arsenal created. Dominique watched Paxton dress in preparation for leaving to reconnoiter a potential fortress site. No half-day trip this time but an absence of almost a week. He no longer avoided baring his back to her, and she could only gaze upon the wine-purple welts with a sort of horror at the violence they represented. The scars she knew, ran all the way to his soul, where she doubted she could ever reach.

Was she falling in love with him? Truly, she did not know. Her fear of what he represented blighted any other emotions. No longer could she even detect the differences between people's malevolent and benevolent energies.

Mayhaps, he was indeed her warlord.

As the last of his dressing ritual, he sheathed his sword and dagger at his sides. In the morning's half light, his dark brown eyes found hers. Feelings of passion and, yes, compassion, inundated her, threatening to weaken her even more, so that she had to turn away. She must remember herself. She could not care for Montlimoux and her people if she did not care for herself first.

"Today promises to be perfect," he said, coming up behind her to take her in his arms.

She closed her eyes, resting her head back

against his chest, and savored the feeling of him: his strength as counterpart to her softness; his rational complimenting her intuitive faculties. Then, too, there was the extraordinary sensuousness she felt when with him.

"Travel with me as far as the next hamlet," he said, his warm breath stirring the tendrils of hair at her temples. "You can ride pillion with me and tether your gray to the camp wagon. John could escort you back to the chateau."

"Mmm, I would like that," she said. She turned her head against his shoulder so that she could see his face, and he winced. "What is it, Paxton?"

He dropped a kiss on her nose. "Probably an old shoulder injury. It aches occasionally."

She said nothing, but she knew that the source of his pain, his left shoulder, was also the source of the heart's conflict. For some reason, there was most likely a congestion of energy there. Prospects of the diversion of a trip lightened her mood, and she hurried to ready herself.

By the tenth hour, Paxton's calvacade had already left the village of Montlimoux far behind. She clung tightly to his waist as his war horse picked its way across a pebbled brook. The courser was so enormous, she felt as if she sat high in a belfry tower.

"The day turned out as beautiful as you foretold," she teased. "Perhaps 'tis you who is the sorceror."

Paxton's laughter was as sparkling and warm as the sunshine. She rested her cheek against his back. A contingent of maybe fifteen knights, thirty or so archers, and a score of foot soldiers accompanied them, but she felt a oneness with him that excluded all peripheral distractions. She doubted he would believe her if she told him her heart was actually singing. Every part of her being, radiated life and light.

Did he feel the same? He was so closed off to his emotions, he was impossible to decipher.

When they reached the hamlet of Brisceu, he relinquished her to John Bedford with what might have been a fleeting look of regret. But not enough regret that he wanted her permanently in his life. Her efforts to extract a contract of marriage from him had failed miserably.

On her return trip to Montlimoux, she tried to pry more information about Paxton from John, but the captain, who acted as an intermediary at the chateau between her and the soldiers garrisoned there, would reveal little.

"What about the Earl of Pernbroke?" she pleaded. "Please, can you not confide in me anything? Paxton told me about the horrible act the earl's men committed, trampling his family to death, but he will not elaborate."

John's usual merry eyes were sober. "All I can tell ye is that at one time the earl thought highly of Paxton and came to love him like the son he never had." Beyond that enigmatic piece of information, he would divulge no more.

Upon her return to the chateau, Esclarmonde was waiting for Dominique in her library. In her lap, lay Arthur, lids closed, throat arched to her stroking hand. At Dominique's entrance, she glanced up. Her smile matched the cat's satisfied expression.

For a long moment Dominique stared at the distant and cool blonde. Where was the childhood playmate? What had happened to the laughter and glee enjoyed in the games of Blind Man's Bluff, Hide and Seek, and the May Day celebrations of Robin Hood and Maid Marian? She recalled the shared secrets of mischievious misdeeds that somehow Francis always managed to worm out of them. Even then he had made a perfect father confessor.

Over the years, childish disagreements had evolved into fissions of discord that not even Dominique could mend. She only knew that Esclarmonde had developed an unreasonable jealousy as Francis's regard for Dominique had deepened.

Esclarmonde ceased stroking the cat and reached for a scrap of parchment on the escritoire. "I believe this was meant for you," she said, waving it as charmingly as she had her handkerchief at the tourney.

Dominique's eyes narrowed. "What is it?"

"A copy of a missive. The messenger mistook me for the chatelaine of Montlimoux. At my importuning, your scribe kindly copied it from the original. I forwarded the original to Paxton, where I thought the missive would catch up with you." Her painted lips made a moue of simulated sympathy. "Obviously, it did not."

Dominique jerked the parchment dangling from the young woman's outstretched fingers. The epistle was penned from Denys himself.

"To My True Lady, the sergeant has allowed a respite in the arsenal construction. My message is thus brief, only to inform you that my love for you is ever strong. Seven years time seven I would wait if I thought to gain your hand. The work I do for your Grand Seneschal requires no aesthetic efforts. My soul languishes for its once consummate creativity, as it languishes for you. Only a month, and I still have more than six years to serve Paxton of Wychchester. When my hands pound the mortar, me thinks of pounding his skull or conspiring against his rule. Seven years! How can I endure it? This loss of my plans, my grandiose dreams of creating the most beautiful of cathedrals. Only you can understand how my soul is dying. Give me solace, my Lady Dominique."

Dominique's eyes lingered over the last words before she looked back to Esclarmonde. "Why? What have I ever done to you that you wish to cause me or Denys harm?"

As if she had not the courage to meet her gaze, Esclarmonde returned to stroking Arthur. Her voice was so low and tense that Dominique was not certain she heard aright. "You have everything I have ever wanted."

"What are you talking about?"

Esclarmonde lifted eyes bright with unshed tears. "Paxton, if I would let you. And Montlimoux. 'Tis a crown that needs the proper jewel."

Dominique flipped the parchment scrap onto the writing desk. "And you are that proper jewel? No, I think 'tis more than that. 'Tis Francis. You resent me because of his affections for me, do you not? All along it has been Francis between us. We could have had a friendship that few men ever dream of, but your perverted jealousy prevented it."

"Perverted?" As she rose to confront Dominique, Arthur sprang from her lap, as if glad to be released. "You call me perverted when you dabble in works for which the world would burn you as a witch!"

"Your brother, I might remind you, holds alchemy in the same high—"

"And speaking of my brother," she spat, "'tis perverted for you to lust after a holy man of God, Dominique de Bar." Holding her skirt away, as though Dominique was the leper and not Baldwyn, she swept past her, adding, "And by all that is holy, I hope you suffer the consequences of God's righteous wrath!"

* * *

As much as Dominique had looked forward to Paxton's returning from his expeditions, she dreaded this particular return. Had he intercepted Denys's missive? And, if so, what would be the consequences to Denys and herself?

From the north tower, the direction in which she and Paxton had set out the week before, a spiraling cloud of dust was reported, signaling the approach of a caravan of some sort. Then came sight of Paxton of Wychchester's blazing banners that announced his imminent arrival.

Hastily, she had her hair washed by Jacotte and then changed into a sheer, summery gown with a decolletage so low she risked coming down with an ague. But then, she would risk just about anything for Montlimoux.

Paxton did not come directly to her but first heard petitions in the Justice Room since it was the third day of the week. On the floor above, she paced her library with a barrage of unsettling emotions bombarding her.

At that moment, anger was foremost among her emotions, anger that he had usurped her authority and dared to preside in her place in the Justice Room. He was insufferably high-handed.

Of course, there was also apprehension of what reprisal he might take because of the missive. Surprisingly, mixed in with the other emotions was joy at his return.

Against the corridor tiles, there came the

tapping jingle of his spurs. She went still. Her heart pounded against her rib cage. The door opened. She saw only his suntanned face, those deep brown eyes that had the power to excite her passions. He seemed to fill the entire room, making it difficult for her to breathe. Why did he not say anything?

At last, he unfastened the silver chain at his shoulder and flung his dusty mantle over the back of her chair. Vainly, she tried to read his expression, but it seemed those days of her gift of discernment were past. She could only anticipate.

Every forethought she had given this reunion now proved erroneous. As usual, he did the unexpected. "I missed your challenging mind, Dominique. Soldiers have little interest in any concept that beggars their minds to ponder anything deeper than the tankard's depth of ale they swill."

Uncertain still of the direction of his intentions, she stayed rooted where she was. "I have missed you, too, my Lord Lieutenant."

"Come," he said, pulling up a chair before her chessboard. "Entertain me with a game. Pit your mind against mine."

She felt it now, not as strongly and clearly as had once been her wont. But now she felt his aura, or rather perceived it dimly. The vibrations of the oranges and reds. Pure male anger. Warily, she took a seat opposite him. "Gold or rock crystal?" she asked in a most casual tone.

"Your pleasure, Dominique."

"The gold."

Deftly, his scarred hands set up the board. In no time she realized that he knew more than the rudiments of chess. His fame as a military tactician had preceded him to Montlimoux, and he demonstrated that skill now superbly on the board. At first, she had been distracted by watching his sun-browned fingers fondle the pieces he eventually selected to move. The large fingers so powerful, the slender crystal so dainty and fragile.

As though his skill were not enough for her to cope with, she had also to deal with his running commentary. It appeared idle enough, but she knew he was leading up to something, only she was not sure just what.

"Our misogynist monk taught me the basics of chess."

"Our?"

"Of course, he instructed me in much more than chess. Latin, literature, mathematical sciences—"

"Your move."

"Check. I learned Scripture, also. Vanity, foul temper, greed, fickleness, and promiscuity are faults and sins of the woman, according to Scripture."

Her mouth dropped open.

"Your move, Dominique. You are in check."

"Sins of the woman?"

"Especially promiscuity. Move."

Before she could draw a calming breath,

her fingers, seemingly of independent will, clutched her castle and hurled it at him.

He dodged but not in time. The edge of the castle's base clipped him on the temple. She gasped at the crimson spot that emerged. At once, her fingers shot out in the instinctive act of healing. His hand grabbed her wrist and forced it flat upon the board. Chess pieces toppled off onto the floor, where the crystal ones shattered.

She stared at him, aghast. That she, Dominique de Bar, was capable of violence, appalled her. What was happening to her? "I am sorry! I have never done anything like that. Please believe me."

"Oh, I do. I have the distinct impression you are usually much more subtly cunning in your attacks."

The angle at which he imprisoned her wrist was beginning to hurt, but she could not budge his hold. "I know why you are angry, Paxton, but I had nothing to do with Denys's epistle."

Across the width of the table, he stared her down. "I do not imagine you did unless encouragement can be attributed as a factor."

"You know that is not true. What occurred between Denys and me is far less than—than that which occurred between you and Esclarmonde."

His smile was harsh. "You speak of the fair maiden as in the past. What occurs between Esclarmonde and myself I shall decide. Just as it is in my power to decide your fate and Denys's."

With his free hand, he wiped away the blood that trickled in a thin line down his jaw. Dazed, she watched as his thumb smeared a dab of blood on the inside of her wrist. "The two of you conspiring against me could—"

"Denys means no ill will, my lord! You must understand. For him to labor in the quarry and on the walls is for him a slow death, a torture worse than anything a Dominican Inquisitor could think up."

"You plead well for your lover."

"He is not my lover."

Abruptly, he released his grip. "Nay, I do not think he is. 'Tis Francis you fancy yourself in love with. 'Tis Francis you think of when you compose your lays and love songs, is it not?"

She could not confess her love for this man who ruled her so thoroughly, too thoroughly, if she were not careful. She affected a shrug of indifference. "Think what you will."

He rose. "I am tired. The day has been long. I bid you *adieu,* mistress."

She waited that night for him to come to her bedroom, and when he did not and when the hours passed all too slow, she surrendered to her instincts and went to him. When opened the door, he raised on one elbow to watch her. Moonlight spilled over him. Above the whiteness of the linen sheet, his bare chest was swarthy. "I have been waiting for you," he said.

She heard the mockery in his voice as he echoed her own words to him once. It mattered not. Her bare feet crossed the cool tiles to his bed and she lay in his sensuous embrace, now a necessity for her physical well being. Yes, and emotional, as well.

CHAPTER XII

It would seem that Paxton had decided to put Denys's missive from his mind as the subject was not broached again. Yet neither did he send Esclarmonde from Montlimoux.

But what of the nights, few though they were, that he did not come to Dominique's bedroom or carry her to his? Piqued by his withdrawal at those times, she would have resisted him when he did come to her in the deep of night, but she suspected if she had he would have turned his sensuous attentions away from her.

What he did with his time during the day she was not wholly certain. She only knew that when he was present at meals,

Esclarmonde appeared to please him. She was gay and attentive, asking questions from him that elicited elaboration. Of Dominique herself, Esclarmonde shunned all conversation. The largest of castles could not contain two embattled women, and Dominique sensed the day of confrontation coming unless the woman left soon.

By day Dominique felt an emotional and mental paralysis that was relieved only when Paxton took her in his arms at night. Even then, she tried to maintain her guard, having relaxed it only that once, that night of their chess match, when she had gone to his room. His energy had overtaken her will and, netted within his lovemaking, she had achieved undeniable bliss.

But she had pulled back. That wildly delirious sensation extracted a price she was not prepared to render.

Her numbness was from fear, she knew, a compact, slow-moving fear that robbed her of her centeredness. Constantly, she was nagged by the worry she might lose Montlimoux to the English, that the people who counted on her might lose the livelihoods that had flourished under Paxton's rule.

Worse, was she losing herself in ways other than the result of her physical unions with Paxton?

Those fears crescendoed in the last lingering days of May, when Dominique discovered she was with child from that one night of relaxcd vigil. Would Paxton's interest wane as she grew large with child, and would he then take, instead, Esclarmonde to his bed? If he was not doing so already.

There were, also, yet other fears to plague Dominique. Would Paxton wed her off to some nobleman as he had once threatened?

To lose not only Montlimoux but her independence, as well, to become by dint of marriage a man's chattel was a heart-stabbing prospect.

No, if she had to marry, better Paxton where she could remain at Montlimoux.

But would he marry her?

Now, more than at any other time, she needed all her wits, her clarity of vision, if she and Montlimoux—and her unborn child and its inheritance—were going to endure.

"Care to ride with me, my Lord Lieutenant?"

Paxton glanced up from the scrolled parchments over which he labored. His eyes narrowed. Dominique stood beneath the pointed arch of the library doorway. Never before had she asked him to accompany her. "John is busy?"

She waved a hand. "He is occupied elsewhere."

With the sunlight gilding her, she appeared nigh transparent, an etheral loveliness that was almost painful to behold. Leaving her would be one of the more difficult things he had ever had to do. "Where do you ride?"

"I go to call on some of Montlimoux's tenants."

He rubbed his bearded chin. Had he overreacted to the intercepted missive from Denys Bontemps? His thinking was not as rational these days. He did not believe this young woman fey, but then there was so much he could not explain about her, about the way she made him feel when they lay together at night. She was a contradiction to everything his five senses perceived, an abomination to all his church education.

Esclarmonde and women like her were safe, and if no more trustworthy, they were at least predictable. Esclarmonde, in particular. Like a she-dog in heat, she fairly gave off the scent of sexual hunger.

As if sensing his indecision, Dominique said, "'Tis not just the petty noblemen, castellans, and bourgeosie whom the lord of a demesne must supervise."

He battled a grin. "Be you telling me how to rule Montlimoux, mistress?"

She stiffened, taking umbrage at his term of address, as he had known she would. Then her smile grooved dimples beneath each cheekbone. "You will admit 'tis your first gambit at ruling a county."

He gave up and, letting a grin come, tossed his quill on the writing desk. "Aye, I shall take a lesson from you, mistress."

Late spring sunlight swept the cobwebs from his brain and body. Riding beside him on her palfrey, Dominique appeared to reflect that sunlight. It purified the air and set heat to her hair, caught in that net of pearls. It glossed her tanned skin and tinctured her cheeks.

Sensing his gaze, she turned her head to flash him a shy smile.

Shy? This maiden who had ruled an entire kingdom and whose maneuvers in chess were worthy of any battlefield tactics?

"There is something wrong with me?"

Aye, she beguiled his senses, confounded his judgment, tempted his spirit. He almost genuflected, a habit the old abbot would have exhorted, especially in this situation. "No, you merely puzzle me."

Her brow arched. "Merely? I had hoped I was not that commonplace. How about 'truly'? Or 'absolutely'? Or 'unequivocally' puzzle you?"

His smile came grudgingly. "I concede you are like no other." The pleasure in her eyes quickly faded when he added, "But then the temptations of this earthly world are never commonplace, are they?"

She returned her attention to the path her mount was taking. Her profile was as stony as a pontiff's. "How do I puzzle you, my Lord Lieutenant?"

He preferred the use of his familiar name, but "Paxton" only passed her lips during the hours she lay in his arms. He missed her slender arms around him, like that afternoon she had ridden pillion with him.

His mouth tightened. *That afternoon he had intercepted Denys's missive to her.* "Aye. Why 'tis you have never taken a husband?"

"Why be the servant girl when I can be mistress?" Her answer was flippant; then she added, as though seriously given thought to his question, "Have you observed, truly observed, your cohorts, once they take a woman to wife? Even those few appreciated women who have been allowed their freedom, soon even they are taken for granted. Each marriage partner ceases to seek that specialness in the other."

He shrugged. "Propinquity results in boredom."

"No." She turned sharply toward him. Her brows knit, as if she were searching for a better answer. "Boredom has nothing to do with constant propinquity of two people. Boredom is the ever distancing of their souls."

Her words took him by surprise. This kind of talk made him uneasy. It made him think, whispered a voice, which surely was only a breeze.

A clearing made for a swine pasture heralded the nearby croft of a tenant. His allodial land might render him a free man, but likewise he was free of the benefits of a liege lord's protection.

The peasant's house with its patch of kitchen garden was little better constructed than that of Paxton's childhood, a windowless, mud hovel containing but one room. This one was a timbered hut walled with cob, its roof thatched with river reeds. An iron plowshare and iron-bladed scythe and sickle that would harvest autumn's crops lay unattended next to the entrance.

"Jean-Luc and his wife are the new cotters," Dominique explained, as he came around to lift her down from her palfrey. Her waist was so slender that he could span it with his hands. The scent of her lavender and gardenia and other unknown fragrances assailed his senses. He found himself wanting her now, although they had lain together little more than ten hours earlier. This power she had woven around him like silver ribbon around the Maypole disturbed him for he acquiesced so easily to its taming strands.

Following her like a lap dog, he entered the windowless cottage. The animals that shared it were not favorite hunting dogs, cats, or falcons but pigs, chickens, and even a prized cow that greeted them with a nasal snort. The floor was bare, trampled earth. Against a wall, a pallet bore a flock mattress. Smoke from a fire burning on the hearth stung the eyes before fleeing through the eaves.

A fetching girl with light brown hair worked at a kneading trough for dough. She glanced up with a welcoming smile that reminded him sharply of his sister, Alienor. Only when she came around from behind the trough and into the light did he realize this barefoot girl was older than Alienor had been when she was murdered—and this lass was heavy with child.

"Comtessa de Bar!" She attempted a curtsy, which was little more than an awkward bob because of her condition. Only then did the girl appear to notice him. Her smile turned cautious. "My Lord Lieutenant." Once more, she bobbed respectfully. So, even the newest of tenants was aware that he now oversaw the affairs of Montlimoux.

Dominique placed her hand on the girl's thin shoulder. "No need for that, Marie. We merely come to inquire of the progress you and your husband are making."

Marie's cheeks reddened with the unaccustomed attention. "Jean-Luc is out tending the family plots, my lady."

"Rye and barley and oats with the second field fallow, is it not?" Dominique inquired as she stroked the milk cow's muzzle.

He was amazed at her memory for the tedious details of agriculture. But then, her own garden proclaimed her devotion to plants, as if they lived and felt and breathed the same as humans.

Her display of interest eased the girl's shyness, and the two females discussed the crops, with Dominique admonishing as she took her leave, "When the birthing time draws nigh, send Jean-Luc to the chateau. Either I or Iolande will come at once."

After he and Dominique began their ride

back to the chateau, he said, "Your allodial peasants live little better than English serfs."

"But they *are* free. With that freedom will eventually come self-sufficiency."

"More aptly freedom to starve." Now why did he feel quarrelsome? Mayhaps it was the way the day had turned overcast, with clouds boiling off to the north.

She sent him a puzzled glance. "They are better off than living in your larger cities, where a weaver's family huddles in a single room with not even a blade of grass to call their own."

"You love the land, is that not so?"

A look of pleasure softened her angular face. More pleasure perhaps than when he and she made that journey together in passion? He did not know, for he had avoided looking at her face at that ecstatic moment for fear he would glimpse his ultimate damnation.

"The land," she replied. "The sky. The water. I would perish were I a weaver holed up in an attic like a rat. The child I carry will know the freedom of her heritage."

For a moment her statement did not register with him. Then he reined in sharply on his steed. When she continued riding, he spurred ahead, catching up with her to grab her palfrey's bridle and yank the animal to a halt. He leaned over her, close enough to see the green flecks in her eyes. "You are with child?"

"Yes."

"With child like Marie back there?"

Her expression made him feel stupid. "Yes."

That was what this outing was all about. Dominique had arranged it, down to the meeting with the young lass, large with her own unborn babe. "You are certain?"

"Why, yes. I am my own body."

"You said 'her.' You know that the child you carry is a girl."

"Of course."

"How?"

"I just know. 'Tis a communication of sorts."

He turned his head to stare off at the constantly shifting clouds. Now they formed castle battlements, enclosing, confining. He shivered. Memories of the taunts of childhood playmates flooded through his mind; the chanted "Bastard! Bastard!"; in the fields, fair days, or Mass at the cathedral, when others accompanied their fathers. And he was alone, a boy taking on the responsibility of himself.

He became aware that she was watching him, waiting. This extraordinary and strange young woman who had captured his fancy. No, more. Captured his imagination. He aligned his hand with her cheek. That singular curve of cheek, of breast, of lashes that set her apart from all other women. She stared up at him, searching his face, for what he knew not. "The child will not be baseborn, Dominique. We shall marry."

Relief softened the tension of her mouth, and her lips regained their enchanting fullness. "You do not ask who is the father. I am grateful for your trust."

His fingers slipped down to the hollow created by her collarbones, such fragile bones to conceal such a formidable will power. He felt her pulse accelerate. "Were I to suspect any other man of fathering your child, my answer would still be the same. It—she needs a father."

He could tell his answer stung her, yet she maintained her composure. "But? I hear further reservation in your voice, Paxton."

His fingers dropped away to seek the familiarity of the hilt of his *misericord*. His lips compressed. "Aye."

She caught his hand between hers. "I speak truly, Paxton. I am not asking for your love, only your name. And the right to remain at Montlimoux."

He wished he could read behind her eyes, peer behind the layer of flesh and skull into her vital and unconventional mind.

"Is it the fear of being tethered like a mill horse to the grinding post, the fear of boredom with me?" she prompted quietly.

He had to smile. "Never that. Not with you. Nay, but it is a fear." He squeezed her hand gently for all that his words were stern. "A fear I am certain the Church will dissipate when your Francis marries us."

* * *

"The banns have been published."

Dominique nodded her head in acknowledgement of Baldwyn's latest news and laid aside her spade, her garden work forgotten. Two more successive Sundays with the banns posted for all to read at the cathedral steps and then . . . then she would be owned by a man. That the man was Paxton of Wychchester weighed heavily in favor of submitting to the marriage.

Still, she had hoped, nay yearned, for that one person who would love her fully, unconditionally, who would be her equal in all ways, who would vanquish not the occasional lonesomeness but the loneliness. That aching feeling of incompletion. Of emptiness. Of being like the unicorn, the only one of your kind on earth. Sometimes, she felt such sorrow for what would never be that tears would come to her eyes.

The thought of Francis's visit anon eased that pain. There was yet another pain, that of rejection, of not being enough of a woman to hold a man.

Hesitantly, she spoke to the Templar of it. "Baldwyn, with the exception of you, I have had little experience with the male sex. I . . . Paxton has not . . . We have not shared each other's bodies since I informed him I was carrying his child. Am I already . . . repulsive to him?"

Baldwyn lowered his bulk to one knee,

careful not to crush the sprigs of thyme. "Verily, I have not had any experience with maidens who were . . . whose child I fathered. But, mayhaps, 'tis like when a knight prepares for a holy crusade. Fasting and abstinence, you know."

She rubbed the moist earth between her fingers. "He is not fasting, Baldwyn."

"So, you fear he is not abstaining either?"

"He rode out again with Esclarmonde yesterday."

"I see. It could be worse. Passion invokes in some men all that is base and vile."

"Unfortunately, this is not the case. His passion is . . ." She searched for the right word and finished by saying, ". . . is both exciting and disturbing."

The giant's black eyes laughed. "Mayhaps you have met your match in this male."

"I should hope not. Paxton's male egotism is so thick it would take a pickaxe to penetrate it!"

He peered at her from beneath his hairless brows. "You are certain, Dominique, you want to go through with this yoking?"

"There is the babe."

"I might remind you that for the major part of your life you were raised without parents. You realize, do you not, that marriage with Paxton of Wychchester may be worse than no marriage?"

Her lips pressed together. "I shall abide."

"He is a pragmatic man trained to violence."

"He is capable of gentleness."

He lumbered to his feet and stared down at her with a wealth of compassion in his rheumy eyes. "Well, as the peasant says, 'Wake not a sleeping wolf.'"

CHAPTER XIII

"Francis!"

Dominique flew down the staircase to greet the bishop. His slender fingers tilted her chin up so that he could look into her joyous face. His black eyes glinted with their familiar appreciation of her. "You grow more beautiful, Dominique."

Laughing, she withdrew her arms from around him, albeit reluctantly. He was her security. "But not enough that you would forsake your calling for marriage?"

His lips were curled in reproof. "You swore long before I to remain unfettered by the chains of marriage. Now you wish to forfeit your freedom?"

"'Tis a choice between the lesser of—" She

broke off at the sight of Paxton and Esclarmonde striding into the room. Their faces were flushed from the summer's heat. Both stopped short, then Esclarmonde broke free from paralysis and rushed to hug her brother. "Francis, Francis!"

Paxton paused to collect Arthur, who had padded across the great hall to greet him. Then, the cat cradled in the hook of one arm, he strolled on toward the guests at a more leisurely pace. His gaze skimmed Dominique with an indifference that made her blind with fury. She carried this man's child! Physically, they had become momentarily as one, if not spiritually and mentally. Surely, he owed her the courtesy of deference, at least.

"We are obliged that you will be performing the marriage ceremony, honorable Father." Paxton's tone was polite enough, but Dominique sensed a derogative undercurrent. For a man who revered the Church, Paxton did not seem to apply the same esteem to this vicar of Christ. From between narrowed lids, he surveyed the man from his embroidered shoes, past his brocaded gown and the gold pectoral cross, up to his bishop's mitre.

Francis appeared not to take umbrage. Though not as tall as Paxton and without his physical presence, Francis possessed an imposing demeanor that came partly from his *savoir faire* and partly from an intense psyche that made her even forget that he was also most handsome among men. "Why, this is an opportunity for the Church. Church tradition sanctifies marriage."

"It sanctifies marriages but not love," she said derisively. Yet, all the same, her eyes were fixed on the powerful hands that stroked Arthur so gently.

"Love—or passion?" Esclarmonde retorted, her lips parted and her heavy-lidded gaze directed meaningfully at Paxton.

Dominique swung away, ostensibly to order refreshments but in actuality to collect herself. Instinctively, she sensed Paxton and Esclarmonde had lain together recently.

Her self-control was practically demolished. Her intuition regarding people and situations was now unreliable. Was this all the result of harboring another life within her?

Later that evening, Francis persuaded Dominique to adjourn with him to their childhood haunt, her mother's laboratory. At the prospect of sharing her passion for alchemy with another who appreciated its powers, old excitement stirred in Dominique.

Francis swept one long finger over the dust that lay upon the counter. "You're interest in alchemy has waned?"

She picked up one of the philtre vials and held its prism to the candlelight. "No, Francis." Her voice sounded weary even in her ears. "'Tis not lack of interest but the inability to concentrate. These days all I do is pace. And fret. It seems I have no control over my destiny."

He took the vial from her, standing so close it was as though his black velvet mantle enveloped her. In contrast to the candlelight glow, his black eyes appeared bottomless. "Your present life is analogous to alchemy, Dominique. Putrefication, the rotting, of one substance merely begets another. You stagnate, here, Dominique."

She sighed. "Mayhaps I do, Francis."

"In Avignon, the most adept at astronomy and alchemy and metallurgy gather to discuss the soul and body of matter. The most intelligent of philosophers come from as far as Arabia, Greece, and the Orient to argue and debate in the papal palace."

An ember of interest flickered in her. "To such as they, I am but a fledgling."

"There is much I could teach you," he said low, his breath barely stirring the hair at her temples.

"My Lady Dominique?" Iolande called.

Both whirled as the Jewess rounded the last steps of the spiral staircase turret. "What is it, Iolande?" Dominique asked.

The old woman glanced at Francis warily, and Dominique said, "'Tis all right to speak before the bishop."

"A soldier arrived with a missive for my Lord Lieutenant."

"Yes?"

"'Tis about Denys Bontemps."

Dominique's floundering insight momentarily regained its former strength. "What about him?"

"He has fled the Lord Lieutenant's regiment quartered at the quarries outside Les Baux. He killed one of the guards in his escape."

Dominique snuffed out the candle and pulled the coverlet over herself. She missed Paxton's large, protective body lying next to hers, his warm skin, and cool breath. Missed the way in sleep his arm draped almost possessively over the indenture of her waist. It was more than missing. It was an ache. Now that she was to be his possession, he no longer was interested in her.

The uninitiated on his pathway always and only wants what he cannot have and is indifferent to what he already possesses. Yet if someone else coveted that possession, then the owner would battle to keep it. That probably explained Paxton's repressed anger that apparently only she perceived that evening. Francis's arrival challenged Paxton's total possession of her.

This internal warring made her sleep restless that night. Even when dreams visited, she knew she would not recall them lucidly the next morning, as had been her ability before Paxton's arrival disrupted her life. Would the hurting inside, this wanting of him, ever go away?

Wisdom told her there was security only in

oneself, that there one finds the source of all happiness that makes it possible to give that happiness away, the source of all love that makes it possible to love others. But her emotional body cried out at Paxton's easy dismissal of her, that she was of no consequence.

Her latent senses stirred within one of those nebulous dreams, warning her that something was amiss. She struggled to regain consciousness, the kind of struggle where one tries to cry out at some impending disaster and cannot. Consciousness surfaced at last, emerging to find a darkness darker than the night hovering over her like the owl of death.

Her scream was smothered by a human hand. Hard, rough, sinewy. She could smell dust, perspiration, and anger within its palm. Her flailing arms and legs were weighted by a body much larger, heavier, and more powerful than hers. She groaned against the silencing hand. Her teeth sank into its flesh, and she was rewarded with a curse and momentary freeing of her mouth.

Her scream was cut short as the darkness coalesced into features that she recognized. "Denys!"

"You would not wait for me!" His growl of rage was laced, too, with anguish.

"I do not underst—"

"The banns, damn your soul. You and Paxton—"

Tears streamed from the corners of her eyes. "I had no choice!"

His hot breath was a hiss. "You always had choices, Dominique. You made the choice of keeping Montlimoux. I loved you. I would have given my very breath of life at the tourney to have you and love you. I would have labored seven years for the privilege merely to gaze upon you each morning for the rest of my days. But you sold your body to Paxton for Montlimoux!"

"No! There are circumstances that you do not understand. That go beyond just myself or Montlimoux or Paxton."

"My God, Dominique. Seven years!" She heard the frustration and hurt rasping his voice. Sweat—or tears—dripped from his face onto hers.

"I did not ask this of you, Denys. Nay, I even tried to tell you that there was no hope for that which you desired."

"Is it Paxton's hands you desire? Touching you like this. And this?"

She wriggled beneath his groping hands, stroking the inside of her thigh, squeezing her breast. "Such a long time," he gasped. "So long without you."

Her fists pounded his shoulders ineffectively. "No, Denys. Do not do this thing. Please, do not—"

Suddenly, his weight was lifted from her. "What—" Denys yelled, then came the sound

219

of scuffling, the thud of her priedieu over-turned. Candles carried by alarmed servants flooded the room with their light. Like two magnificently built wrestlers at a fair, Denys and Paxton thrashed on the floor. Paxton was naked, proclaiming he had just come from bed. But whose?

He slammed a fist into Denys's nose, and blood splattered on the hems of those nearest the two grappling men. Their writhing bodies, their hoarse grunting, the odor of their perspiration mixed with blood, their fury that tasted like sulphur in the air . . . Her dreams had turned into a nightmare.

Screaming. Could that be her high-pitched voice, reverbrating against the walls like that?

She bolted from the bed and threw herself at the two. "No! Stop it!"

An elbow, a fist, something slammed in her temple. Red and green lights shot behind her eyes. Hands tugged her, yanking, dragging. She was being quartered, her limbs to be rendered separately to the four spheres.

Then, the blackness of the void.

"The dungeon is forbidden to ye, my lady."

The excuse of working in her laboratory was not believed by Captain Bedford. "John, Paxton cannot execute Denys for treason. Denys did nothing against Paxton."

Regret at gainsaying her plea softened his reproof. "The man dared to touch Paxton's future bride."

She paced the library anteroom, rubbing her palms together. "This is foolish! One man's life in retribution for another's pride?"

"'Tis something a woman would not be understanding."

She whirled on him and, her hands on her hips, snapped, "No, a woman does not understand violence and brutality and murder. We understand living and nurturing and loving and giving!"

He almost winced from her counterstroke. He folded his arms. "Ye cannot visit the dungeon."

She returned to her bedchamber. Her chattering maids-in-waiting could discern from her tight lips and flashing eyes that silence was imperative, and they industriously applied their needles to their linens.

Only Iolande dared approach her. Her face was a mask of tortured wrinkles. "Denys must not die."

Dominique roused herself from her preoccupation. "I know that! But what can I do? I have been a virtual prisoner here myself for months."

The old woman rubbed at her gnarled hands, aching and disfigured by chilblains. "Paxton would give heed to the Church. Ask Francis to intercede for Denys."

"Paxton might listen to the Church, mayhaps, but not to Francis. He mistrusts Francis."

"You, then, are Denys's only salvation. You

must appeal to Paxton of Wychchester as a last resort."

Dominique's footsteps slowed. She sighed. "I know. I know."

The old Jewess shuffled to block Dominique's tred. She caught the younger woman's forearms and fixed her with a fierce gaze. "You will do what is necessary?"

In the darkness, his hand shot out and captured her wrist, twisting it sharply so that she fell across him on the bed. At the cascade of her hair across his face, he gasped. "Dominique?"

"Yes," she whispered. She trembled, whether from fear or desire, she was not certain. Mayhaps a powerful combination of both. She had no idea what she was going to say.

He took the burden from her. Releasing his hold, he asked, "Why have you waited to come to me until now?"

"I did not think you desired me, my Lord Lieutenant."

"But you think I do so now?"

His sardonic tone was a slap, and instinctively she reacted by smacking him back—with her hand. The thud of the impact resounded in the room. Then he grabbed her and rolled atop her, and her breath went out of her with a whoosh. "You came to plea for Denys's life, is that not so?"

She could feel his heat, his anger, and, yes, his desire. She wanted to lie, but a higher truth responded. "Yes. He is my friend."

"Your friend?" His growl was almost a purr. "Then show me what your friend is worth."

She hesitated, unsure what to do, and his hand tangled in her hair, turning her head so that her lips were crushed beneath his. This invasion of his mouth, an act of passion with no tenderness, no care, no giving, no deep intimacy infuriated her and incited her. She bit his lip, and he nipped hers back.

"That is the best you can do?" he taunted.

Somehow, without understanding how or why passion took fire inside her, consumed her. Her entire body throbbed. Her emotional and physical body screamed for more of this addictive passion. And yet, after he took her and momentarily slaked the frenzied desire in her, she lay within his arms, feeling drained, tired, empty.

As if he could feel her slipping away from him, he said, "I am pleased that you hold by your pledge to King Edward to choose my will as yours."

"My will is my will," she murmured, and turned her back to him.

Later in the night, she turned to find him gone. She sat upright, sensing something was amiss. Then, there came a terrible blood-curdling howl that was more animal than human. Paxton never returned to his bed.

The next morning she learned the horrible truth. At first, she attributed the heavy air to her own gloomy agitation. But Jacotte, helping dress her, was all thumbs. Dominique peered at the maid's face. Her eyes were red from obvious weeping. "What ails you, Jacotte?"

She sniffled but did not meet Dominique's searching gaze. "My Lady Dominique, there is something you should know. There is talk."

Dominique half-turned to stare at her maid. "Yes?"

"The soldiers are saying that the Lord Lieutenant relented during the early-morning hours and spared Denys Bontemp's life."

A relieved sigh eased from Dominique's fear-blocked throat. "Then I can go to him."

"No." The single word was drawn out reluctantly. "He was removed from the dungeon and taken to the barbican."

Her hand going to her throat, Dominique stiffened. She sensed there was more. "And?"

The maid-in-waiting's face was sallow as candlewax. Her voice trembled with pent-up horror. "They say that the Lord Lieutenant ordered Denys Bontemp's hand, the one that dared touch the mistress, be chopped off!"

CHAPTER XIV

"Denys Bontemps would have raped you, Dominique! Can you not see that? He is fortunate Paxton was charitable enough to spare his life."

Dominique glowered at her reflection in the silver-polished mirror. "His life! His sculpting was his life! Without his work, without his right hand, he has been reduced to a common beast of the field."

With gnarled and trembling fingers, Iolande readjusted Dominique's bridal mantle, edged with gold lace. "Which was what he behaved as when he tried to rape you. My point exactly."

Dominique closed her eyes. She felt weak,

nauseated, depleted of her powers. Was it the child, Paxton's child, she carried who could do this to her? Or the horror of the past week? If there was only some way she could get to Denys, some way to console him.

She stood like a statue, lifeless and as cold, while Iolande arranged her clothing for the forthcoming wedding. She wore her best: her finest linen chemise; her best silk tunic, trimmed with fur and a velvet surcoat over it, embroidered with gold thread; her shoes of the most expensive morocco leather were worked with gold; and on her head, the small veil was held by a narrow gold band.

She stared dully at her mirrored image. How could she go through with this wedding? A sham. The joining of two physical bodies only. Not their souls. How sad. How painfully sad!

When, at last, she and Paxton met in the courtyard for that momentuous trip to the cathedral, his expression appeared as apathetic as hers. Whatever emotions the warrior possessed, they passed behind the impenetrable curtain of his brown eyes. They reflected nothing at the sight of her in her bridal finery. He, also, was dressed in his best: a short, girdled coat of mahogany satin, tightly fit over his muscular torso; a long, wide cape; and a stiff, broad-brimmed hat.

Side by side in the merciless morning sunlight, they rode down the spiral road to the village. Tapestries decorated the streets, and spices burned in all the squares, where torches and tambourines welcomed them. A little troop of *jongleurs* preceded them, playing on flute, viol, and harp. Behind rode the wedding guests, a cortege several leagues long. All along the way people crowded the sides of the street to watch.

In the square in front of the cathedral, Paxton dismounted and came around to her side. His large hands encircled her waist. She stared down into that broad, impassive face. The hands she placed on his shoulders as he lifted her down trembled.

This was to be the man with whom she would share a bed—and her body—for the remainder of her days. This was the man who would own her. This was the man who would dictate her life. Panic fluttered in her heart.

She and Paxton were opponents. Each abhorred what the other stood for. He, her paganism, as he called her spiritual mind set. She, his violence. Only one of them could emerge the victor. But which one?

The sight of Francis, waiting under the portico, restored a small measure of inner strength to her. In his hands, he held an open book and the wedding ring. His face was dark with a nameless passion she was unable even to begin to identify, such was her own turmoil.

He began the traditional interrogation of the bridal couple. "Are you both of age? Do you swear that you are not within the forbidden degree of consanguity? Have the banns been published? Finally, do you both freely consent?"

At that point, Paxton took her right hand in his. She, almost inaudibly, he, tonelessly, repeated the vows. Then Francis blessed the ring, which Paxton took and slipped in turn on each of the three fingers of her left hand, saying, "In the name of the Father, and of the Son, and of the Holy Ghost." Finally, he fitted it onto her third finger, and uttered, "With this ring I thee wed."

She felt as if a part of her disintegrated at that moment, and in a daze she helped Paxton distribute alms to the poor, who had collected outside the portico. Before the two of them entered the church with the rest of the wedding party, he gave her a fleeting, searching glance. She met it with a blank stare.

Inside, the flickering lights of candles did little to dispel the cold gloom of the massive church. Incense smothered the air. She felt chill, feverish, faint.

She caught sight of Esclarmonde. The young woman's expression was one of agony warring with anger. A wedding, Dominique thought, should have been a time for rejoicing with friends. How lamentable that she and Esclarmonde would never be friends. But then there was little to rejoice about this wedding either.

Dominique clung to the sight of the familiar, Francis's face. Here, he ruled supreme, ruled over Paxton even. Francis's dark eyes seemed to reassure her as he read the nuptial Mass. If only the tedious ceremony would end.

Too soon it did—disasterously.

Traditionally, the priest bestowed on the groom the Kiss of Peace. In turn, the groom was to transmit the Kiss of Peace to his bride. But Francis blatantly and blasphemously disregarded tradition by taking her shoulders and kissing her not on the forehead but fully on the lips. The kiss was little more than the duration of a heartbeat, but it was a kiss she had unconsciously been yearning for from Francis almost all of her life.

A collective gasp of disbelief zephyred through the members of the wedding party. Francis's smile taunted Paxton, who moved as if he might grab the priest by the golden silk tippet draped around his neck. But the kiss happened so quickly, and in that sacred place Paxton, out of childhood indoctrination, checked his violent reaction. Relief from the others was almost an audible sigh.

Led by the little troop of minstrels, the bridal procession returned to the chateau, where an elaborate wedding feast awaited them: spiced wine by the barrel; legs of beef, mutton, veal and venison; capons; a boar's head; and a swan in its plumage.

Refusing the meat, Dominique tasted only the wafers, confections, cheeses, and fruit. At her side, Paxton touched only the wine. Both of them devoted only a measure of attention to the acrobats and juggling acts performed in their honor.

The guests danced, and storytellers recounted tales of Hero and Leander, Charlemagne, Paris and Helen of Troy, Samson and Delilah. Wedding gifts were presented, and there was even one from the English king. Edward had ordered made for them an immense round table of English oak.

Throughout the celebration, concern was reflected in the eyes of John Bedford, Iolande, and Baldwyn.

The festivities continued all day and into the night. At last, Francis rose from his place at the banquet table. As bishop and priest, he was signifying that it was time for the bridal couple to adjourn to the nuptial bed.

Led by their priest, the guests accompanied her and Paxton to the bridal chamber where Francis was to give his blessing to the bride and groom. Paxton's chamber was scented with summer's lavender, rose, and jasmine. With feigned reluctance at her part in the ceremony, the cantakerous Iolande inspected the bed to make certain no ill-wisher had secreted anything there to impede conjugal relations, such as two halves of an acorn or granulated beans.

Paxton fixed Francis with a veneer of a smile that was nonetheless lethal. "Do not even think of pilfering more than the kiss you took in the sanctuary of the church. So help me God, I have no qualms against beheading priests who have wandered astray."

Francis's smile was as thin. "You will forgive my proprietary interest that derived from our being childhood playmates."

"The bed is ready for the bridal couple," Iolande's gritty voice interrupted.

Everyone backed out of the chamber. Francis's face was the last Dominique saw before she turned to Paxton. He appeared weary and his expression seemed so closed to her. How could she surrender to a soul that knew nothing about the possibility of dancing through another soul?

A soul that courted only war and destruction? A soul that recognized only and always male dominance?

As always, he took her by surprise. No demands or orders. Simply, "Will you kiss me, Dominique?"

Wary, she gauged his features. His expression was empty of all subterfuge. She tried steeling herself against any tender feelings for this invading warrior. But her attempts to create an emotional barrier as solid as any wall failed abjectly at the vision his eyes held: a need for another human, a need for her.

She heeded her inclination and took the three steps separating her from him. Rising on tiptoe, she brushed her lips across his. The sensation took her breath away. It was like standing at the very edge of a cliff. She could fall—or she could fly.

Her palms splayed against his chest for

balance, and she felt the tremble that rippled through his massive body. That she could be responsible for such a reaction should not have amazed her, but nonetheless it did.

He took her hand in his and tugged her toward the iron chest in the chamber's corner. "I have a wedding gift for you."

Perplexed, she watched as he knelt on one knee to open the metal locks. When he rose to face her, he held cradled in both hands, almost reverently, the length of her hair he had cut away at the tourney. "What I did was a form of striking out. You did not deserve that, Dominique. Between us, there must be no more separation."

She accepted the shorn hair. Next to her own tresses which had grown considerably, the swath appeared dull without the vibrant red cast that life gave it. From beneath her thick fringe of lashes, she peeked up at him. "Because I carry your child?"

He stared down into her eyes. "Because I know that we are opposite beings, but opposite can also be complementary, as are our bodies when they join."

He took the length of hair from her hands, laid it atop the chest, then turned back to her. "Kiss me. Really kiss me, Dominique."

A whisper of energy murmured in her mind, *Surrender does not result in loss but in gain. It is the birth of change.*

She wrapped her arms around his neck and

tilted her head so that she could fit her mouth over his. Their lips joined in perfect complement, as Paxton had told her was possible. His experience caused her a pang of jealousy for the other women who had known his passion. His kiss was soft and giving and hungry, also, like a man who had waited a lifetime. Her heart beat so fast, she was losing all control. She felt lightheaded.

Any thought of why he and she were destined to share a span of life together dissipated under the touch of his hands, smoothing down her spine, clasping her waist, cupping her hips so that she was pressed against him. His heat, his scent, his body, all inflamed her. She was fire and wind and water. And earth's fertility.

At last, he released her. His breathing was rapid, his voice raspy. "I once said I would prove you were no sorceress, that you had no hold over me."

She tilted her head, puzzled by his words. "Yes?" Her own voice sounded ragged in her ears.

"I still hold to that." Wry amusement glinted in his dark brown eyes. "Sorceress, no. But, enchantress, maybe."

The afternoon sunlight was merciless on Iolande's face, a patchwork of wrinkles. She sighed. "Look at them. 'Tis as if the two were meant for each other."

Beside her on the battlements, Baldwyn said in a hushed voice, "Me thinks you are right, old woman."

Together, the two aging people watched the two younger ones cavort on the list below. The older couple's dreams of what might have been, what could have been, but would never be made the afternoon air heavy with remorse and sorrow.

At that distance, the shared laughter between Dominique and Paxton sounded like the pealing of Whitsuntide bells. Paxton's cat scampered and pounced amidst them in pursuit of a butterfly.

The young couple, wed scarcely three weeks, ceased their frolicking to pick flowers, growing wild along the walls. Deftly for such large hands, Paxton wove a chaplet of the blossoms and placed it on Dominique's brow. Unaware they were being observed from above, the two moved into an embrace, their kisses unabashed, wild, and surely as sweet, as the rapidly wilting plucked flowers.

This time Baldwyn sighed, although his gravelly voice came out more as a grunt. "As they say, 'Love and a cough cannot be hidden.'"

"Bah! What know you of love, leper?"

"Love?" He turned his despoiled visage on her. "I would lay down my life this very moment for love of our Lady Dominique."

Iolande's nose twitched with a sniffle. "Yes, I can understand that kind of selfless love."

There was a part, hidden far below Iolande's crusty surface, that yearned painfully to love and to be loved by a man. Nature had created everything, every single thing, to unite with its counterpart. Everything, everyone, but her. Why she had been so destined she had long ago given up trying to divine. "I never would have believed that this savage Englishman could bring our Dominique joy."

"As the peasant says, 'Bitter medicine may have sweet effects.'"

"A plague on your proverbs, Templar! Just watch them. The two fairly radiate with their bliss."

"Do you remember when our lady Dominique was small, no more than knee high—"

"*Your* knee high, mayhaps."

"—and, climbing that elm in the outer bailey, she accidentally knocked down that beehive we kept for candle wax?"

"Came running to me, sobbing, she did, and with a face full of welts."

He chuckled. "She looked like a leper, herself."

"But, as I recall, within the hour she had use of your shoulder as a perch. She was bent on climbing that elm once more, with the bees still swarming."

"I remember, that I do. They clustered all over her. Never stung her. Not once. Stung the fire out of me, though!"

"Remember that time she and Francis and

Esclarmonde and Denys got into the battle with the stable's clods of manure?"

This time Baldwyn's chuckle was almost a wheeze. "Do I! Esclarmonde did not duck quickly enough and—"

Iolande cackled and clapped her twisted hands. "And she looked like one of those black-faced Moorish servants the Saracens keep!"

Their laughter was as one, as their love for Dominique was one. With their fond gazes fixed on the couple, Baldwyn mused, "Denys, the poor young man. I cannot help but wonder what is to become of him, locked in the barbican that way. With but a stump for a hand. I tell you, old woman, no good can come of that episode."

"Our Lady Dominique would disagree with you."

"To be sure. But for the life of me, I cannot see how everything happens for a reason that is to the betterment of our souls. No wrong roads to be taken? Simply lessons to be learned from our choices? Me doubts it hardly!"

"She is an advanced one, our Lady Dominique."

The Templar spared the crone a sidewise glance. "Do you think the English soldier and our Lady Dominique will produce children? Children who we could take as much delight in as we have her?"

Iolande cackled again. "Every chance. I

secreted a small gemstone of jasper between the sheets for childbirthing powers!"

Paxton heard Dominique's laughter, and like a man bewitched, he followed its siren's beckoning call to her chapel. From the door he spied upon her with a lover's delight. She sat on the floor like a man, cross-legged, and faced Hugh, who held a wooden tablet. She was reading from a Latin grammar, and the boy laboriously scratched into the tablet's green wax.

"'A is created by God, therefore A exists,'" she read. "'And similarly this. A does not exist, therefore A is not created by God.' Of course, Hugh, the word God is a neutral term for an all-powerful, all-knowing force. God is not masculine or feminine. Do you understand, what I am trying to explain?"

Hugh nodded vigorously, but Paxton had his qualms. His pleasure in his newly acquired wife squelched these qualms, as it squelched his occasional jealousy when her attention focused on other men. His best friend, in particular. Was not John bedding the brunette maid, Beatrix?

Yet would it be easier for Dominique to love John, the son of a squire than himself, a baseborn serf?

She glanced up and spotted him. Her smile came readily. "I felt someone watching."

His mouth crimped in a wry line. "That does not surprise me."

Her lax attention afforded Hugh the opportunity to avoid any further schooling, and the boy shot past him. She chuckled. "You would think I were a Dominican monk quizzing Hugh on the torture rack."

Paxton grinned but could think of no retort. Why was he here? If nothing else he could be cleaning the rust from his armor with sand, as the other soldiers were busy doing. It was a perfect summer day for shedding the shirt and engaging in combat practice or hunting. The partridges were so thick a blindly shot arrow could not miss bagging one. "I thought I would take you fishing."

Her amazement at his statement only surpassed his by an increment, but after he said it he realized that that was exactly what he wanted to do.

"What a delightful idea," she said, rising gracefully from what would have been an awkward sitting position for him. Her hem caught on her girdle link, baring one shapely leg all the way to her thigh. His appreciation of her womanly contours was nudged aside by his sudden wanting of this woman who was now his. Only an acquired refinement was able to subdue what Brother Thomas had designated as "the dark animal that lurks within every man's depths."

"Change into something more—something simpler," he said, "while I have our mounts saddled."

She did more than change into a simple

linsey-woolsey tunic; she prepared a basket of cheeses and fruits, along with a sheepskin *boleta* of wine. Her joyous smile, her high spirits, were infectious.

They mounted and left the chateau, heading for the far meadows where ponds reflected diamond sunlight and trees flourished like Irish clover.

While she spread their repast beneath a shady oak, he set out to rig two poles. Baldwyn had told him that bream and pike as large as beavers were stocked in the pond.

"'Tis been so long since I last fished," she said, coming up behind him to take one of the poles. "Since I was maybe twelve and hooked more fish than Baldwyn." Deftly, she secured the line and hook. "After that he refused to take me."

A noblewoman fish? Her capabilities were truly astonishing. He eyed her askance as she seated herself in a grassy spot beneath an oak and dangled her line. She saw his bothered expression and smiled. "We women are not the weaker sex, you know, Paxton."

"I did not say you were."

"Ah, but I can tell from your expression and your demeanor that you think so. I know well how the Dominican Inquisitors word it. 'The cunning enemy Satan seduces a member of the weaker sex, who is inconsistent, wavers easily in her faith, is malicious, and has no control over her feelings and instincts.'"

He had to smile at her deep-throated parody of a priest. "Mayhaps, my lady, you are overly defensive. The Dominican friars could have been referring to the male."

"Aha! Then you will freely admit the male is the weaker sex?"

"I admit nothing." He laughed.

His wife was utterly and charmingly unpredictable, and he watched her, fascinated, waiting for what next her ingenious mind would produce.

She fixed him with a saucy look. "Do you likewise disavow the charge that Peter's thrice-repeated denial of Christ was actually that of the voice of a woman?"

He dropped his pole and took hers, laying it aside. "I will admit only that if any woman could perform such a feat, it would be you. You have captivated me from the very beginning, Dominique."

She aligned her hands on either side of his face and stared at him solemnly. "I know. I experienced the same when first I beheld you as a beggar. That tug at my innermost being. Ridiculous but true, Paxton."

He splayed his hand over the small mound of her belly. A gentle warmth spread through him, a feeling of being home, although home, he would have said, was Pernbroke. "This child of ours—"

"This daughter—"

"This daughter of ours, you will raise her to be like yourself?"

"You want that? For her to be like me?"

"Very much." And then he could contain his desire no longer, and his hand deserted her stomach to slip beneath her skirts and find the moistness there. There was home. All the home he would ever need.

"Paxton only married you to better cement his authority of his newly acquired fiefdom," Esclarmonde taunted. "The entire county of Montlimoux knows that."

As much as Dominique regretted seeing Francis return to Avignon, she could only rejoice in his sister's imminent departure with him on the morrow. Dominique had been doing her best to be agreeable with this long-term guest, but annoyance got the best of her. "You are merely disgruntled because Paxton did not want you."

The two women, along with Dominique's maids-in-waiting, were wandering through the stalls set up for the annual trade fair at Montlimoux. The hubbub was diverting. The tables in the cloth hall were a kaleidoscope of colors. From the spice market could be heard the traditional call of "Hare! Hare!" From the pungent district of stalls came the smell of the fish merchants, the butchers, the linen makers, and most noxious of all, the tanners.

Esclarmonde smiled slyly. "Did not marry me, mayhaps. Marriage ties, after all, are based on political calculation. But want? Can you say truly that Paxton does not *want* me?" Her lower lip made a mocking moue. "Tell

me, Dominique, do you truly know what
Paxton does with all his hours?"

Dominique would not let the vindictive
woman spoil the growing pleasure she was
taking in her marriage. Paxton was an attentive lover, with a delightfully lingering hand
and his wry humor was totally unsuspected.
His abbot had done well in instilling a measure of knowledge about a variety of subjects,
so that they often conversed into the wee
hours of the morning. Only the thought of
Denys, imprisoned and mutilated, marred
these first perfect weeks as Paxton's bride. "I
have faith in my husband."

"Tell me, is he as faithful to you as he was to
his first wife?"

Dominique felt as if she had been hit in the
stomach. She stopped, closed her eyes, and
drew a fortifying breath, then waved away her
maids. In a low voice, she asked, "What are
you saying, Esclarmonde?"

"Are you slow of wit? That your beloved
husband has been married before."

"How do you know this?"

The blond young woman shrugged prettily
and turned away to fasten her attention on an
accumulation of costly pearls brought by Arab
dhow and pack train. They were spread on
black velvet like tempting, but untouchable,
stars. "The soldiers. They talk."

The hurt Dominique felt was unbearably
heavy. Despite her love for Paxton, he was so
closed off, so unsharing of his inner self.

Would she always be an outsider with her own husband?

She waited until after Paxton returned from stag hunting and had eaten. They were alone in the bedchamber. She sat on the great bed, staring at him as he removed his doublet and tunic. Clad only in his hose, his battle-honed body had the power to take her breath away. She dragged her gaze from his muscular chest and fixed it on his face. The way he smiled at her now, how had she ever found that face plain?

He knelt before her. "So solemn? I know. I forgot to bring you a chaplet today to crown your *cindre* hair. But I brought you something much better."

The teasing gleam in his eye made resistance impossible. "What did you bring me, Paxton?"

He opened one large hand. A small gray pouch lay in his palm. "Look inside."

Tentatively, she reached out to grasp the velvet bag by its draw cords.

"Pearls," he told her, too impatient to wait for her to unveil his gift. "From the deepest seas."

She spilled the pearls into her palm. "How did you know about—"

"Jacotte. When I asked your maid-in-waiting what caught your interest at the fair today, she told me you and Esclarmonde had stopped at the pearl stall."

Dominique stared at the opalescent orbs so

she would not have to judge the truth in her beloved's countenance. Her words were barely a breath on her trembling lips. "Paxton, I want to know about your previous marriage."

She saw the ridges made by an abruptly clenching fist. "So you know."

"Is your . . . You are not still married, are you?"

He rose and turned from her. "No. I am not still married." He paused, then said, "Elizabeth is dead."

A portion of her turmoil evaporated. "Why have you not told me of this, Paxton?" she asked. And the next in words of pain, "Why did I have to learn this from someone else?"

"'Tis no one's business but mine."

"You are wrong, Paxton!" She sprang from the bed and slung the pearls like chicken feed. "On our wedding night you spoke of no more separation. Well, pray tell, what do you call this?"

He rounded on her. "*This* is my past. It has nothing to do with you and me."

"Do you still love her?"

"No."

"Did you love her?"

His head lowered. "Aye, at one time."

"Tell me about her." Did jealousy prompt her question? "Was she from your village, from Wychchester?"

"No. She was the Earl of Pernbroke's daughter."

"The Earl—he had the people of your village murdered! And you married his daughter?"

He rubbed his fist into his other palm. "I had meant to seduce her—an act of revenge. But, before I knew it, Elizabeth had become an obsession with me. So beautiful. So untouchable. I thought. And so passionate when at last I possessed her."

"How did she die?"

He stared at her stonily. "She was murdered."

"Murdered?" she whispered. "How?"

"It matters not. The fact is *she* is dead and *our* marriage is legal in the eyes of the Church." His words came too rapidly. He caught her by her shoulders. "You are my wife, Dominique."

His kiss hurt her, a possessive kiss that she struggled against. Struggled and lost. His touch bathed her in bliss, however fleeting it was. Perhaps *he* was the sorcerer. She understood the power of sexuality, but this was something more, something that would take more than her will to withstand.

That certain "something" came to her in a dream later that night. She awoke with remnants of the dream meandering like the breeze through her sleep and lingering briefly on her conscious thought. "In chess, the Queen is free to move in any direction."

She understood the import of the dream's

message. She had the power to do anything, if she wanted to badly enough. But was she truly queen?

Beside her, Paxton slept deeply, his arm heavily and reassuringly draped across her ribs. She could feel the crisp hair of his legs on her. Such delight to be taken in one's opposite!

The morning brought the departure of Francis and Esclarmonde. Their pack train was lengthy enough to flow out of the bailey, span the drawbridge, and creep down the village road. With Francis's leavetaking, Dominique felt, as she always had, that she was losing her last touch with civilization. Nevertheless, Paxton's gaze was upon her and made her farewell brief. Esclarmonde would have prolonged hers with Paxton, her hand tarrying overlong on his sleeve, but John Bedford interrupted the *adieu*.

He drew Paxton aside. His voice was low, but his words were obviously urgent. Dominique watched Paxton's countenance darken. The muscles in his jaw tensed. He issued some order to John, who hastened away.

"What is it, Paxton?"

He flicked her an inquiring look. "Your friend, Denys. He has escaped his dungeon cell."

At once, Paxton left with John and a few soldiers to scour the woods and nearby mountains for Denys. Her husband had given her the briefiest of good-byes, and she sensed he suspected her of engineering Denys's escape. She feared for her friend's life. This time Paxton would certainly not spare it.

By evening, Paxton had not returned. Now she feared for *him*. What if Denys managed to ambush Paxton and his men in one of those narrow mountain files? Paxton did not know the lay of the land as Denys did.

Bored, worried, restless, she wandered down to her laboratory, where she had not been since Denys's imprisonment. Whatever relief she expected to find in her alchemical work was immediately quenched by the sight of Arthur. Its feline body lay upon the counter. A swath of dried blood semi-ringed its furry neck.

CHAPTER XV

Observing Dominique as she ministered to Hugh, who lay coughing with the ague, Paxton supposed he should be filled with admiration at the demonstration of her skill and her compassionate touch.

More often than not, though, he found himself dismayed and a trifle uneasy at the continuing revelations of heretofore undiscovered facets to her. It was unsettling enough that she read and wrote as well as any man and that she made him earn his victories at chess. Quite indomitable, willful, incorrigible, she challenged his forebearance.

Clearly, she was a pagan. Her interest in alchemy was a conjuring of nature's dark secrets best left alone. Those trances she went into, calling them "meditation periods," confounded him. Before their marriage she had been intriguing but now he found her a vexation.

Yet the idea of anyone else possessing her was . . . He pushed the thought from his mind.

Overcome by the reek of the mustard poultice she applied to Hugh's chest, he fled the boy's room and headed for the Justice Room.

John's mailed steps caught up with him in the corridor. "Denys is at it again. He and his *routiers* looted a packtrain from the Mediterranean this time."

Paxton rubbed his jaw with the heel of his hand. The knife had shaved dully this morning but then the shaving had been by perforce a hurried act.

"Last week," John continued, "he set fire to the graineries in the hamlet of Briebaux."

Still that urge to turn and see if Arthur followed. Paxton missed that hissing ball of fur. When he apprehended Bontemps, the *routier* would this time pay with his own life for killing Arthur. "Get together a contingent of men," he told John. "I shall set out after sunrise, at the ringing of the prime bells."

The Justice Room was doorway deep with petitioners. He sighed. He had thought he was blessed with patience. Patience to wait stealthly for the stag to drink from the pond. Patience to wait for the enemy to make that one false move. Patience to outwit a chess opponent, to sacrifice small pawns, for the capture of the opponent's queen.

Yet this kind of waiting was a trial of endurance that taxed him to the limit. Listening to the haggling, the mundane and petty complaints for hours on end when he wanted to feel the sunlight on his skin and stretch his kinked muscles in a round of jousting or chopping firewood wore on him. Was he truly qualified to rule a fiefdom justly?

Dominique taxed his patience also. The wench was becoming prone to throwing things more often. He supposed her volatile temperament was due to his child she carried. An image of her, silhouetted against the light of dawn in their bedchamber, taunted him even in that crowded room of peasants and bourgeoisie: her belly softly rounded; her breasts full, straining with her milk. On his tongue, the taste would be tart and tantalizing. So tantalizing he could not forsake those generous breasts this morning in time to sit through a proper shave.

When midday arrived, he abruptly ended the administrative tasks in favor of preparation for the forthcoming expedition. Forsaking the noonday meal, he went to find the blacksmith sweating over his fire.

Bertrand's smile displayed his missing teeth. "You be needing a lantern forged for whiling away your nights with the chatelaine, messire?"

He chuckled. "No, I shall need forged a pair of spurs by the morrow's sunrise, Bertrand. Knitting needles have sharper points than these spurs' rowels."

Dominique appeared in the doorway. Dust particles floating in the sunlight made her seem as if she were a shimmering apparition. "I learned from Baldwyn that in the Justice Room today you confined the miller's wife to the stocks for adultery."

Her terse tone told him she was highly annoyed, which puzzled him. "Aye, that I did. Better a period in the stocks than to cut off her nose or to lash her naked through the streets."

She put her hands on her hips. "Alieson was only getting her revenge on her husband. The miller has been taking his pleasure with every willing woman in the village for months now."

He found his temper growing shorter than a burnt candlewick. "A wife without chasity is a criminal blot on the husband's escutcheon."

Her eyebrows shot up. She put her hands on her hips. "So, you are saying that female virtue is the counterpart to male honor?"

"I shall not have my decisions in the Justice Room questioned, even by you."

"You, sire, are unsufferably highhanded!"

She dared criticize him before a vassal. In England, a man would throttle a woman for such disrespect. He could not understand her, this strange woman. His teeth clenched. The blood in his ears pounded out his anger. He drew a deep breath that helped check his runaway fury. Without a glance at her, he stalked past her and out of the stables.

That night he did not sleep in their bedchamber but stayed below in the Great Hall, drinking with his men and falling asleep on a proffered pallet. His last thought before sleep caught up with him was that his wife was an affront to his masculine ego. She may have been accustomed to ruling her domain, but he was now Grand Seneschal of Montlimoux —and she was his wife.

Clearly, he would have to see that Dominique mended her ways.

Nothing was going right these days.

Dominique's fiefdom was no longer the peaceful countryside it once was. Violent winds and heavy rainstorms harrassed the county, the graineries were being overrun by rats, and, worse, Denys was stirring dissatisfaction among the peasants. This time, Paxton had sworn not to return until he had Denys in chains. She wished Denys would abandon this vow of revenge and take sanctuary in another country.

More importantly, she fretted for Paxton's safety, and chaffed at how they had parted without reconciling their differences.

The problem was, their differences were so great that reconciliation was an improbability. This man to whom she was joined mentally, physically, and emotionally . . . There had to be a bridge of light to reach him spiritually as well. With such a union, she was sure they would experience a rapture greater than any bliss brought them by the joinings of their bodies.

But how did you communicate with a man who was aware only of his physical body? Who did not realize that fighting weakens while harmony strengthens?

And why did she have to love him as she did?

She tried to tell herself that he was a soldier, trained for violence and brutality, but she had to acknowledge that he had brought to fruition many of the plans she had conceived for Montlimoux, that he had a humor that always caught her off guard, that he was sometimes capable of tenderness though he would deny it vehemently.

Well, she had had enough of her misfortunes. She could only be thankful that the Summer Solstice was upon them.

Finished with her herb-gathering, she collected her straw basket. When she went to rise from the garden row, she winced at the sudden stitch in her side. With a gasp, she pressed her hand against the pain. Most likely, she had been kneeling in an ungainly position.

"What is it?" Iolande asked, coming up from behind her.

She sighed. "Either you are becoming lighter on your feet in your old age or I am becoming less in tune with my surroundings."

The old woman's eyes peered at her from beneath their hooded lids. "You are in pain?"

"No longer. Truly." With a tender smile, she placed her hand on her swelling belly. "Just a stitch in my side, that is all. That I would willingly endure a hundredfold for the sake of the babe."

Only then did she notice that Iolande's mouth had taken on a tighter grimace than usual. If eyes could ache, the old woman's eyes looked as if they did. She touched her nursemaid's brittle wrist, its skin veined with purple. "You have always wanted your own child, have you not, Iolande?"

She sniffed like a sweating wrestler on fair day. "A child? Nothing but a whelp with a snotty nose and a dung-smeared bottom."

"If what you proclaim is true, then why did you care for me so lovingly?"

The old woman's mouth crimped downward. "Duty. 'Twas my duty."

"I do not believe you. I believe you wanted a child so much your insides were torn with the wanting."

Silent tears blurred eyes already blurred by age. The old woman stared at nothing but the past. "Yes, my insides were torn. Torn from repeated raping."

Dominique gasped, but Iolande appeared not to hear. Her knotted fingers interwound around each other in a slow dance of emotional pain. "I was young, not yet of twenty years. And pampered. I was descended from a

255

royal family of the kingdom of Jerusalem. Nothing more than a name, really. But our fortress at St. Jean d'Acre rivaled those of Languedoc. Then one afternoon, a party of crusaders stormed our gates. Because we were Jewish, we were agents of Satan. Or so the one said, the one who first raped me."

"Enough!" Dominique cried, blocking her ears with her hands and shutting her eyes.

The old woman continued in a bitter tone. "I was locked in a tower room for almost a year. The crusaders brought me food and watched while I relieved my bodily functions —and availed themselves of me when they pleased. Their brutality ended any hopes of childbearing. The savagery of those Holy Wars, God damn the popes and their self-righteous adherents!"

Dominique was weeping raggedly. She threw her arms around the woman. "I love you, Iolande!"

The old woman shrugged her off. "As I said, babes are a nuisance."

"You have not forgot 'tis Summer Soltice?" Baldwyn asked.

Dominique sighed and laid aside the manuscript of Marie de France's poems. Her romances were full of Celtic atmosphere and made use of Arthurian materials, but Dominique was nowhere nearer understanding her English husband. "No, I have not, Baldwyn. I shall make my appearance in the village for the celebration. I swear."

Summer Solstice was the longest day of the year, and for as long as the Provencal people could remember, the occasion had been celebrated. The longest day of the year was looked forward to as a source of joy and renewal. Come eventide large bonfires would be lit. In the square of Montlimoux the villagers would gather to laugh and dance and wait for the ruling comtessa to pass among them, distributing coins and fruit.

This evening, for the first time in centuries, a man and not a woman should have been presiding over Summer Solstice, but Paxton had not returned. So Dominique donned the best of her looser fitting tunics and, with John at her side, her maids-in-waiting, and retainers riding behind, rode down to the village square.

"The Celtics of our country celebrate this day, also," John told her, as they watched the flames leaping high, the firelight dancing eerily over the faces of the villagers. "But it has a more mystical value." He grinned. "Spirits and that sort of knavery."

"You do not believe in the mystical?"

In his narrow face, his eyes seemed to reflect the dance of the fire, and their blue centers were as heated, for his gaze had often turned back to Beatrix, riding demurely behind them. "I do not accept the rumors that sorcery is the wellspring of thy power, my Lady Dominique, if that is what ye mean."

"'Tis no sorcery, John," she said gently. "'Tis the power that comes from within me . . . from within you. The Divine power. You have merely closed yourself to it."

He genuflected, and his voice was as impassioned as the horror of his expression. "Ye know, my Lady Dominique, I shall guard your very life with my own, but I beg ye not to speak as ye do."

She began to feel that sighing was about the only thing she could freely do these days. She seemed to have not one iota of control of her reactions. How could this have come to pass, how could she have handed over the reins of personal power so easily?

With the merriment of the festivities, the evening went quickly enough, and soon it was time to return to the chateau. Everyone in her party was yawning and yearning for their beds. All but she.

Once she closed her chamber door on John, she summoned Baldwyn to her. The Templar's massive body lent reassurance to her nocturnal objective. "I have fresh mounts ready, my lady."

She nodded. "Midnight is rapidly approaching."

The night was lovely, with stars marking the passage of time across the vast heavens. The heaviness began to slip from her as she and Baldwyn made the trek to the traditional ceremonial site for the de Bar Summer Solstice. A rocky, climbing path and tall firs hinted at the higher elevation that made the stars seem within a distance of a mere fortnight's journey.

She would be there sooner. Tonight, in fact.

The air was fragrant and cool, cool enough to build the bonfires. Together, she and Baldwyn gathered branches and twigs and piled them in small mounds that formed a path across the moonlit clearing. By striking a fire iron against flint, the Templar lit fires. Soon smoke spindled upward from each mound. Crackling and snapping of the wood punctuated the silence of the deep night.

The two sat and watched the play of the flames, watched until the mounds burned low and flickered to embers. The heat they gave off was still enough to warm her face. Soon the embers disintegrated into hot ash, pulsating with energy. That energy was the life force, the bonfire the symbolic energy cleanser.

"Ready?" Baldwyn asked.

She nodded.

He hefted his bulk from the ground and crossed to his mount to remove from his saddle the short rake he had brought along. While he racked the glowing cinders, she removed her leather slippers and hose. Minutes later, he was finished raking. He had leveled the red ash into a glowing, carpeted walkway.

She stood at one end of the walkway and

closed her eyes. A circle of pastel, a lovely, lovely purple, began to expand on the backs of her lids, filling her inner vision. From within the circle, a white light began its own expansion so that she was completely filled with its purity. A serenity spread through her, insulating her and her unborn child from harm. In that blaze of white light, she came in contact with her spirit, surrendered her will.

The transformation was beginning as was her fire walk. Her state of mind transcended her body, transcended pain, refused to register painful signals. How long it took her to transverse the cinder carpet, she had no idea. She simply knew when she reached the far end, a glorious feeling suffused her. Smiling, tears in her eyes, she opened her arms wide and whispered, "I am! I *am!*"

Whether the fire walk put an end to the random misfortunes, as was claimed the ritual could accomplish, she did not know. But she did indeed feel renewed. Overflowing with joy and good will, she turned to look back along the cinder carpet she had walked, to look for Baldwyn.

She found him—and alongside him John. Then her gaze collided with Paxton's.

His anger blazed across the intervening distance. Her serenity destroyed, she avoided the cinders as she walked toward the three men. Paxton was already striding toward her. His every step was like a thudding hammer on her heart. When he was almost upon her, she said, "You do not understand what you witness—"

His hands shot out to grab her shoulders. He shook her so hard her head snapped back and forth. "Have you lost your mind? If you ever had one. The peasants are right. You are not normal. You are not like everyone el—"

She jerked away. Her voice seethed with derision. "Even a common serf should know that what the mind thinks is possible—is!"

"The fact that I had been a serf did not bother you enough to keep you from my bed or to keep me from siring my child in you!"

"You fear woman's life-giving power," she taunted him. "For whoever can give life can take it away!"

Pain and fury contorted his face. His hand lashed out, and she staggered with the impact and fell to her knees. The hot cinders barely had time to sear her palms, before Paxton was scooping her into his arms. "Dominique, *ma mignon,* I am so—"

Whatever he had been about to say was cut short by Baldwyn's massive hand clamping on his shoulder. "I shall take my Lady Dominique."

Hampered by the burden of his wife, Paxton could only shrug off the hand. "She is my wife, Templar. I shall care for her."

John stepped in between the two. "Hold off, both of you!"

Something of the anguish in Paxton's face must have reached through to Baldwyn. "See that you do, Englishman. 'Tis your life in balance."

On the return trip, she rode cradled in Paxton's arms. The hard, steady beat of the horse's hooves commingled with that of his heart to echo through her ear, pressed against his chest. The thudding reverberated through her body to fill her, fill her so completely there was nothing else but him. This warrior was the man she was destined to love.

When they arrived at the chateau, he carried her into their bedchamber and gently lowered her onto their bed. Iolande pushed past him. "You are all right?" the old woman asked and took her hand.

Dominique winced, and Paxton rolled his eyes. "She burnt her hands, Iolande."

The Jewess shot her a puzzled look.

"I lost my balance," Dominique explained.

Gingerly, Iolande turned over Dominique's palms. Blisters bubbled the flesh. "I shall make up a salve."

After Iolande departed, Paxton said, "Dominique, I let my anger get the better of my will. I ask that you—"

She shut off the flow of his words with her finger. "Not now, please. Words . . . They are nothing. You are a soldier, a warrior, a fighter. A man of action. Later . . . show me what it is you want to tell me."

His eyes darkened with the agony her words inflicted. He took her hand and kissed the

burnt fingertip she had held against his lips.
"Later, then."

Later brought tremendous pain ripping
through her. In a feverish haze, she felt
Iolande's cool hand on her forehead, she
sensed Paxton at her side, but the pain in her
stomach overwhelmed all else.

She was losing the babe. Their babe. She
could not even be four months into her term.
She overheard Iolande saying, "The babe did
not take hold. It was not meant to be. . . ."

Then darkness was all around Dominique.
Stifling air. Disagreeable voices. An argument.
Paxton closing the windows for her health,
Iolande battling to keep them open. An ex-
change of words about leeches and bloodlet-
ting. Iolande's adamant refusal.

From afar, she heard Paxton's voice now.
The one word: "Witch."

She tried to deny it, but no words would
come. She tried to fix her will, to affirm her
perfect health, but the blood ebbing out of her
drained her of all strength. Then at last, at last,
blessed oblivion.

Sweat dripped from John's face onto Beatrix's
ecstatic one. The rhythm of their pumping
bodies was fast and furious. Mayhaps, he
could persuade the countess to let the country
lass return with him to England for a spell.

"For all your rutting, John, your arse resembles more a boar's than a stallion's."

Taken by surprise, John shot back onto his knees. "Paxton! What the hell—"

Paxton's laugh was grim. "You have better things to do than seduce country wenches, Captain Bedford. Meet me in the Justice Room."

John scrambled into his clothing and, bestowing a peck on Beatrix's bewildered face, hurried off to the Justice Room to meet with his commander. The big man was pacing like a unsettled mastiff. "Trouble, Paxton?"

"Aye, trouble. Denys Bontemps is slitting the throats of Montlimoux cattle and peasants alike. He is as illusive as a field mouse and as dangerous as a Pyrennes bear. I leave again to go after him."

John decided to risk the truth. "To go after him—or to escape yeself."

"Myself?"

"Aye, yeself."

Paxton planted his hands on the desk. "Now listen to me. We are here for one purpose only. Not to fertilize the Languedoc maidens with English brats. Not to come to terms with my past. Only to prepare for Edward's invasion."

John recognized the clenched jaw and flaring nostrils as a sign for him to retreat from the subject he had introduced. "Do you really think the French will accept a foreign ruler, Paxton?"

He shrugged his massive shoulders. "We

English have always had foreign kings. Normans, Germans, Scotch, Welsh, Angevines. And we are none the worse for it. At the most, a few French barons might have to yield to English ones."

"Me thinks that not everyone will yield to us. Not Denys Bontemps—or the Comtessa de Bar."

Paxton's mouth flattened into that adamant line that John recognized as intolerant of interference. "I will prevail, Captain Bedford. Believe this if nothing else."

"Paxton has gone out riding, my Lady Dominique."

She turned her gaze from John's soulful eyes and stared up at the ceiling. "My Lord Lieutenant is restless these days."

He shifted from one foot to the other. "There are many administrative matters to attend to around the county, my lady."

She pushed herself up in the bed and closed her eyes at the dizziness that overtook her. Three days abed was too much.

"Please, sit down, John." When he remained standing, staring at the tiled pattern of the floor, she said, "Please? I need so to understand your lieutenant. My husband. John, I know you care for him greatly. I love him, too. Please help me to understand him!"

Reluctantly, John went to fetch a stool from a corner of the room. He sat beside her, clasped his hands dangling between his spread legs, his gaze fixed on her embroidered coverlet. "What is it ye wish to know, my lady?"

She wrapped her arms around her knees. "What drives Paxton now? What drives him at all? His anger, it frightens me."

John's mouth tightened. "That night you fire-walked. You must understand that he was secretly afraid of what it could mean."

"I know he does not understand me. But does he even understand himself? Oh, John, I know he must be suffering at the loss of our child, but so am I!" The pain of that loss was like an open wound. It was as if she could actually feel the blood seeping, seeping, from it. It hurt!

"Aye, he is suffering." John raised an abashed gaze to hers. "But 'tis more to it than the loss of the wee one, my lady."

"I know. You do not have to say it. I should never have taunted him about woman's life-giving power. 'Tis just that since men cannot experience birthing directly they fear us, they fear that separation they remember from birth."

John's smile was wan. "I do not understand ye either, my lady."

Her short laugh was mildly self-derisive. "I expect not. But I know that I am meant to learn something from this relationship I have entered into with Paxton of Wychchester. And I sorely need your enlightment, John."

He seemed to be concentrating on the way

his thumbs interplayed with each other. His words were almost mumbled as he broke his silence about his commander. "Well, ye see, my lady, Paxton's wife—"

"Elizabeth of Pernbroke?"

"Aye. She was highborn, French on her mother's side. Provencal French. As I understand it, Elizabeth was enchanting and fun-loving but, also frivolous and self-centered."

He stopped, but she knew there was more he could say. "Go on," she prompted.

"A story is told about her as a girl, about a trick she played upon her dowager aunt. The old lady had a lap dog that she adored like her own child. Anyway, one day when the aunt was watching from a balcony overlooking the nearby river, Elizabeth picked up the dog and pretended to play with it. She wandered closer to the river, calling the dog. Then, when near the bank's shrubbery, she screamed that the dog had jumped from her arms into the river. The aunt saw the animal being carried away by the swift current, and fainted."

"'Twas no accident?"

"Actually, the animal floating down the river was not a dog but a piglet Elizabeth had pilfered from a family of the demesne's serfs and substituted for the lap dog behind the concealment of the shrubbery. The old dowager was delighted to discover her lap dog safe, but the family of serfs lost a piglet that would have provided for many meals. To them, it was a great loss."

"She was still as fun-loving as Paxton's wife?"

He rubbed the back of his neck. "I suppose ye could call it that. Up to the time she found she was with child." He made a grimace. "Ye see, she went to a midwife to rid herself of Paxton's unborn babe."

Dominique's held breath rushed from her. "Oh, no." She could better understand Paxton's attitude. He had learned not to let others see his vulnerability, especially those who could wound him most, those in a position to become dear to him. Nevertheless, she was still hurt by his inability to trust her.

A full four weeks passed, four weeks of grieving and recovery, four weeks of rejection, of barely speaking should she and Paxton pass in the corridors of the immense chateau. Her soul was hurting, desolate and crying out for communication with him.

One night, she lay alone, awake when all the countryside slept. Tears that had quietly and willfully spilled over her lids had left dried tracks on her cheeks. Suddenly, candlelight stole across the room to blind her. She put up a shielding hand.

Paxton stood at the foot of her bed. The light of the candle he held shimmered over the muscles and tendons of his naked body. "I tried to stay away, Dominique. But the traditional six weeks, 'tis too long." The slightest smile tugged at his mouth. "You have been like a plague in my thoughts, giving me no rest."

She would have wished that he would have said that he loved her and needed her. But those few words would have to do. She sat up, the sheets falling away to reveal her breasts, bare and still overly full from the pregnancy. She held up her arms. He blew out the candle and, setting it on the chest, knelt over her welcoming body.

He buried his face between her breasts, taking great gasps, as if her smell alleviated his own pain. Together, the two of them sought assuagement in one another. He loved her far into the dawn, until their bodies were surfeited with pleasure.

But the pleasure ebbed each time as quickly as it had come. Because Paxton could never understand the joys of intimacy and warmth, she could never allow him the opportunity of breaking through her emotional barrier.

As it was, his virile sexuality weakened her physical resistence. She could not help but resent the way he had invaded her senses, moving without restriction into her thoughts. When he took his leave, she felt curiously disoriented and drained, yet filled with a burgeoning need of him again and again.

She tried to minimize this need by reminding herself that she was the triumphant one during those moments of merging, because she could achieve the greater pleasure without giving any of herself away.

The tall man with blond hair and beard did not mix well in the crowd of boisterous men who drank at the noisy wharfside tavern of Bordeaux. His regal mein was suspiciously eyed by tavernier, maidservant, and sailors alike.

His companion who tipped the tankard with him was much taller and heavier muscled, though not as handsome, but his arrogant posture would have proclaimed him the equal of King Edward. And of those in the tavern, only Edward knew that the man had in fact been baseborn.

Edward took a draught of the ale, inferior in his estimation to English ale that was blended from the same Bordeaux grapes. What he would have preferred would have been brandy. The marvelous golden fluid, that *eau d'or,* would have restored some of his flagging energy. "The time we have been awaiting has come. Philip has demanded that I go to Avignon and pay homage to my right dear cousin, swearing in the cathedral to become the King of France's man for the Duchy of Aquitaine."

Paxton nodded, his smile slight. "As your proxy, I would be delighted to journey to Avignon to bear faith and loyalty to the Valois."

"And your wife? From what I hear you dare not leave her alone to foment rebellion with that *routier* Bontemps against you."

This time Paxton's smile twisted into a grimace. "I dare anything, *Monseigneur*," he said, leaving off the address of "your Majesty." "Even dealing with the sorceress of Montlimoux."

Edward leaned forward. "Paxton, of all my commanders I trust you most. So be warned, your wife cannot get in the way of our—"

"I shall take care of my wife."

CHAPTER XVI

"As a representative of the Duke of Aquitaine, it is required that I pay homage to King Philip."

Dominique might love Paxton, but that did not alleviate her suspicions of him. She had absolutely no desire to leave her fiefdom, much less participate in the political affairs of the French, who for centuries had laid claim to Languedoc and her county. Her county was one of the precious few not within the French fold.

"Montlimoux needs someone to administer its affairs," she said. "I prefer to remain here." Resuming her rule of her county would no doubt restore some of the loss of identity she had felt at Paxton's usurpation.

"John is quite capable of administering the county's affairs for a few months' time." Paxton did not even glance up from the sheet of parchment he was scanning.

If only the fire of his love would burn as deeply for her during the day as it did in the unguarded and abandoned hours of the night. "I see." If only he would reach out and touch her hand, smooth the hair from her brow, wrap his arm around her waist, splay his hand across her stomach, once more flat. Some gesture that demonstrated she meant something more to him than merely a chatelaine.

"Paxton, is your insistence on my accompanying you to Avignon some sort of revenge for the loss of our child?" She leaned her hands on the escritoire. "Do you still blame me for the unborn babe's death?"

He settled back in his chair and stared up at her with measuring eyes. "Revenge? Why, Dominique, I thought you would enjoy associating with the most learned minds of the world."

Clearly, he would continue to circumvent the issue. "How thoughtful of you."

His gaze narrowed on her, his mouth took on a stringent curve. "Besides, your Francis will be there."

"He is not *my* Francis."

He picked up the quill pen with which he had been writing. For him, the work was laborious, but he preferred doing his own writing to dictating. "You are quite correct, of course. The Bishop of Beauvais is the Pope's man."

He resumed penning his missive. How easily he dismissed her from his mind as well as his presence! She snatched up the oxhorn of ink and hurled it at him.

"God take your—" Before he could even finish the oath, he was out of the chair and around the desk. Ink splattered his doublet, and a few drops flecked his face, wild now with fury.

She whirled to flee, but her skirts were too heavy. She barely made it to the door when his hand slammed it shut. Surely, the thud resounded throughout the chateau.

He jerked her around to face him. He looked as if he wanted to throttle her. She was pressed between him and the door. "'Tis the right and privilege of the husband to discipline an errant wife," he gritted.

Her tilted chin, her flashing eyes, taunted him. "And what is it you wish to do to me?"

His anger matched hers. Blood pounded in his temples, and his teeth clenched. "By Christ's thorns, I do not know what to do with—"

She leaned her head close to his, and with her veil gently wiped away the drop of ink sliding down his jaw.

The resulting quiver crept all the way through to the hands that gripped her. His eyes, as brown as stones beneath deep waters, glazed with the sudden heat that seized him.

"I do not understand you, Dominique," he rasped.

His mouth claimed hers in a kiss rapacious with anger and passion and the need to subjugate. She was the embodiment of his fears. She did not let his mouth master hers but responded kiss for kiss, her teeth catching his bottom lip, her tongue dueling with his. Her breathing was heavy in her ears, her thoughts cloudy. She was rapidly losing her centeredness.

His hands deserted her shoulders to tear open the laces binding her corseted breasts. They burst free to fill his kneading hands. "You burn me, witch," he muttered against her hardening nipple. "Set me afire. So that I no longer know what is true or false. Right or wrong."

She cradled his head against her. "Is it wrong to love me, Paxton?"

"Aye." He tore away her bodice and pushed up her skirts about her thighs. "Aye, 'tis wrong to love a woman who bewitches as you do."

She laughed hysterically at this indirect declaration of love. Her laughter goaded him on, and, pulling her down onto the floor with him, his hands pushed her skirts high on her thighs.

Her laughter turned to tears of rage. She would not let him dominate her. She rolled atop him and had to smile. Her breasts swaying gently above him captured his immediate attention. "Perhaps, my Lord Lieutenant, I can persuade you that this time, at least, my position is best."

An abashed half grin eased the strain of his expression. "Aye, I think you can."

Avignon was called a "sink of vice," where luxury, pomp, and loose morals ruled. Francis had once told Dominique that there was a church brothel in Avignon where girls spent part of their time in religious duties and prayers and the rest of their time in servicing customers, Christians only. So Dominique had not been relishing the journey toward this illustrious city on the Rhone River.

Day after day, the journey was monotonous, with the redundant creaking of ox-cart wheels, the thudding of hooves, and soldiers' voices filling the air.

With Denys still raiding and ravaging the countryside, Paxton had taken the precaution of doubling the guards that flanked the procession of soldiers, wayfarers, and the female pilgrims who had taken the opportunity to escape the bondage of domesticity. In addition, the cavalcade included Dominique's entourage of cooks, ladies-in-waiting, seamstresses, laundresses, and maids.

At the head of the procession, Paxton rode, sitting tall in a high-pommeled saddle studded with Bertrand's handicraft of silver. Paxton's arrogant bearing singled him out from the various country squires and their own pages, riding at his side.

As usual, Hugh was never far from Paxton. She knew the boy had dreams of one day becoming a squire, then being knighted himself in the traditional ceremony, when the chatelaine of Montlimoux would dub him on the shoulder with a sword blessed by a priest. But first, Hugh as an acolyte would be required to earn his sword.

Dominique was able to endure the long days of travel that left her saddle-sore by focusing on the evenings to come. After the meals, she and Paxton would retreat into the privacy of their tent or, on warmer nights, would retire beneath a sheltering tree on a spread sheepskin blanket. She was close to rapture, just lying there with him, gazing up at the stars.

Occasionally, they would talk, but only of the commonplace. Vital issues such as feelings, values, beliefs were avoided. "There are weapons that have fire power to kill," he told her in an offhand manner one night.

She did not believe him, even after he described what he had seen. "The Italian mercenaries have used them with mild success."

Sometimes she would tell him one of her favorite *fabliaux* and would be pleased when one of those short, often bawdy stories would bring him to full laughter. At those relaxed moments, she was closest to him.

Today, she rode just ahead of the pack mules and heavier wagons, weighted with not only clothing needed for the next several months but, also, with camping equipment for the nights spent along the old Roman road, the Domitian Way.

On this particular afternoon, the road crawled through a narrow river valley with sharp, thickly wooded peaks. With Dominique rode her maids-in-waiting and Iolande and Baldwyn, whom Dominique insisted upon accompanying her or else she would not go at all. Hour after hour, the caravan lumbered on toward the coast, where the traffic would increase, offering safety in numbers.

She turned to Iolande and said, "One more day on horseback, and I swear by all the pope's relics I shall take the veil and decamp in the nearest convent."

Iolande was cackling. "Paxton would not let a nun's cell stand in his way. He would be excommunicated for consorting with a—"

Iolande's cackle turned to a choked gasp at the apparition that appeared on a rocky outcrop. It held its arms aloft, as if in succor, then toppled forward to flop near the nervously prancing hooves of Dominique's gray. She stared in disbelief at the body of one of Paxton's reconnoitering scouts. His eyes had been pierced and his lips and nose severed.

With shrill war cries, a horde of men slid down in a slither of shale from the rocky defiles to clash with Paxton's soldiers. Caught off guard, the men were forced step by step backwards. The woods rang with the clang of sword on shield and murderous shouts.

Along with the other females, she took shelter beneath one of the large wagons as the men engaged in a frenzy of killing. Paxton's voice could be heard, shouting directions to his men, disbursing some to cover the weaker ground defenses, others to protect the women. Hugh, he specifically charged with her safety. The boy's eyes were as round as walnuts, but he quickly obeyed Paxton's order.

In the melee, she glimpsed Denys, deftly using his left hand to hack with his sword a way through the throng of combatants. One man was pierced through, another's throat was severed, as Denys fought his way toward Paxton, himself beseiged by three men with maces and axes.

Despite the surprise of the attack, Paxton's men held their own. Training, discipline, and skillful leadership gave them the mental and emotional advantage.

Denys muscular torso, even more developed since last she had seen him, was blood-streaked and still he battled. Time and again, Denys was obstructed from his target by an opponent. Paxton, likewise, sought to dispatch each foe like a pesky fly because his one goal was the one-handed *routier* who had dared touch his wife.

Such foolishness in the name of pride!

Her breath felt as if it were bottled in her throat by a cork. Her gaze whipped back and

forth between Denys and Paxton, encircled by
bodies of men he had slain. The soldiers'
shields dripped with blood. Tears at such
wanton savagery flooded her eyes, dimming
the two leaders who steadily inched closer
toward one another.

A blurred figure sprang up behind Paxton,
and she screamed. Perhaps he heard her, or
perhaps it was sheer instinct, but he whirled
to cut down the man with one powerful swipe
of his sword. At that moment Denys reached
the diverted Paxton. Denys's left hand hefted
his sword for a deadly downward slash.

This time the tears in her throat strangled
her warning outcry. Paxton's life would be
snatched from her! Even though time was
against her, she sprang from beneath the
wagon.

At that same instant, Baldwyn stepped between the two men. The red cross emblazoned on his white habit expanded to cover all
of Dominique's world. He raised his shield to
ward off Denys's blow. The blow was so violent that the shield shuddered and split. The
blade glanced off Baldwyn's helmet and angled downward to pierce his chest.

"Noooo!" Dominique screamed. A crazed
scream that was echoed and re-echoed by
Iolande.

Baldwyn swayed, and Paxton caught him,
lowering him to the ground. Denys took advantage of the diversion to withdraw his men
rapidly, many of whom were wounded. Their

own shields were broken and their swords notched and blunted. Backing away, lashing his sword indiscriminately at the few soldiers who still dared fight, Denys scarcely noticed Dominique as she hurried by him toward Baldwyn.

Some of Paxton's soldiers blocked her way. They leaned on their swords and halberds, recovering their breath. Pushing past them, she dropped to her knees at Baldwyn's side. She laid her hand along side the old giant's throat. The life force barely pulsed there. Wildly, she looked up to find Paxton standing over them. "Quick, Paxton! We need to get him to water—a stream or pond. Something. Oh, hurry, please!"

"We have been following a river for some time," he said, gently moving her aside. He knelt beside the Templar and pulled back his eyelid. "I do not think it will help. 'Tis too late."

"No!" Iolande said. Even to Dominique, the haggard old woman looked as fierce and forbidding as the storied witches. "There are herbs," the Jewess said. "Incantations. Do as my Lady Dominique says. Get him to the riverside!"

A camp of canvas tents was immediately pegged in a sheltering wood along a bend of the river where a steep cliff protected against further surprise attack.

While Dominique's maids-in-waiting and women pilgrims attended to the other wounded soldiers, she and Iolande worked feverishly over Baldwyn. At the old woman's bidding, men scurried through the woods and along the river's mossy banks, seeking a special type of lichen, bark from a lotus tree, truffles from the base of a white oak, and mushrooms of an exact variety.

Continuously, Dominique bathed Baldwyn's naked body with a sponge soaked in apple cider. Meanwhile, a grimly determined Iolande prepared the healing herbs with wagon grease, and Dominique implored the warrior/monk-soldier/mystic, "Hold on to your physical body, Baldwyn! Do not loose the tether. Listen to me! You are needed here. Hold on! Iolande and I, we love you, you old rogue." Her tears washed his leprosy-wasted face.

Her hands massaged the space bounding his body. She could sense his spirit straining to pull away, and she lovingly stroked that aura that dimmed and wavered. "You subscribe to the gift of healing, I know. Feel my intangible touch," she urged. "Let my energy complete its circuit from me through you and back."

Throughout the night she exhorted him and begged and cried. Curiously, Iolande remained stoically silent in the face of the Templar's subsiding spirit. "'Tis Paxton's fault," Dominique cried bitterly. "All of our misfortunes began with his arrival at Montlimoux!"

At dawn, she sprang up from the tent and hurried to the river. She ran along its bank, looking for a secluded spot to submerge herself. A small inlet concealed by reeds afforded her the opportunity to wade in unseen.

Her mind screamed for help but she knew that such inner turmoil was not conducive to communicating with the spirit world. Still she cried within, calling upon her inner resources. She needed help, now more than ever!

Drawing deep, restorative breaths, she quietened, while the water flowed around her shoulders, fanned out her hair, and tugged at her clothing. Her eyes closed, seeking the radiant white light. Seeking. Seeking. Waiting. She chilled and despaired. There was no inner signal that help was forthcoming.

She felt depleted, utterly drained. Her footsteps dragged as she left the river bank. She cursed Paxton of Wychchester with every step. The summer evening's heated breeze fanned her clothing almost dry by the time she reached camp. Fires pulsing before the tents looked like guiding stars.

When she entered her tent, Iolande glanced up from Baldwyn's bedside. Recently shed tears reddened her eyes. "The old leper is out of his head. Muttering, but I can tell not what. His ramblings make no sense."

Dominique circled to the far side of the makeshift cot. The fact that Baldwyn was no longer unconscious gave her hope until she drew near enough to perceive that he was dying. His lips were moving, and she leaned close. "Tell Iolande . . . tell her I owe her a great apology."

She looked up and beckoned the Jewess to kneel with her. Baldwyn continued, "A terrible misdeed . . . I did not realize. I was indifferent with the arrogance of youth to the sufferings of others."

"Those early years at Montlimoux are past and done with," Iolande said, her hooked nose sniffling.

His big paw reached for her withered hand. "No, 'tis not the years . . . at Montlimoux of which . . . I speak. 'Tis of St. Jean d'Acre."

Iolande's eyes knitted in perplexed wrinkles. "You are daft, old man."

"I was there. I helped beseige the fortress . . . helped murder your father and brothers . . . helped. . . ."

The Jewess's face was strained to the point of breaking into a thousand cracks. Her outcry was of an animal in extreme pain. "No . . . no . . . no! It cannot be so! It cannot be!"

"I was not . . . one of the ones who raped you. But I looked away while the . . . others took their . . . did so. That I did not . . . participate was due to no knightly honor. Only that you stirred no desire in me. I was one of the knights set to guard you. I took . . . no pity on your pleas . . . your weeping. God help me . . . old woman, I need your forgiveness!"

Iolande laid her gnarled hand, trembling, across his sweat-beaded forehead. Tears dropped like spilled gold. "I would still tell you, leper, that those early years—at St. Jean d'Acre—are past and done with. But then you would selfishly depart, leaving me to spend the rest of my years on earth without your churlish gests to vex me. No, old man, you owe it to stay here with me. Do you hear me!"

But it appeared he could not. He was fast slipping away. From the entrance of the tent, Paxton asked, "How does the Templar fare?"

Wordlessly, Dominique shook her head.

Paxton dropped the canvas flap and crossed to the cot. He took one glance at the scene. His mouth set in a hard line. He placed his hand on her shoulder. "Dominique . . . he is dead."

Iolande covered her face with her hands and wept in great, agonizing gasps. Dominique stiffened. She would not give up, even though it was obvious Baldwyn Rainbaut of the Knight Templars was dead. She knew that when one changed energy, one changed reality.

She looked to Paxton. "Order a man to draw in the dirt a circle around the tent."

He stared at her as if she were little better than a performing monkey. "What?"

"For defense and protection. Please, just have it done. Please."

He gave into her, but not without rolling his eyes as he left the tent. Feverishly, her hands worked with her energy. Once more, she caressed and fondled the space bordering Baldwyn's body, but this time she did so with a determination that would not reckon with any outcome but life returning to this physical body.

Paxton reentered the tent and watched, horror and fascination warring for dominance in his expression.

In an altered state of consciousness, she transmuted her breathing, her body temperature, her heart rate so that the Light within her, that same Light within everyone, was allowed to move into her outer consciousness.

She was the first to detect the pulsating of Baldwyn's life forces and knew that he was reentering this dimension. Paxton and, yes, even old Iolande, were astonished when the Templar's lids quivered. His foam-spittled lips barely moved. Only Dominique heard his ragged whisper, "Manifest what is good for the whole . . . not just what is good for the individual . . . then you will move permanently back into the light, woman. Remember, only the heart that truly loves truly lives."

The statement, the tone, the form of address all jolted her. When Baldwyn's lids at last opened, she saw within his rheumy eyes another factor, something that had been added. She realized then his spirit had seeped through the cracks of this world to meet with that Greater Spirit of which it was a part.

She turned away, shaking with exhaustion,

and Iolande moved to take her place, to tend to her beloved Templar. Paxton put his arm around Dominique and guided her from the tent into one next to it that had been set up as his headquarters. "Come rest," he said gently. He pressed her down upon his cot and covered her with a woolen blanket. With guarded eyes, he stared down at her.

"You mistrust me more than ever, do you not?" she asked so weakly she could barely lift her hand. "You think me a sorceress, for certain." The last was not a question but a weary statement.

"I do not know what to think." He plopped down onto a three-legged stool. "You confound me at every turn, Dominique. I know not what I shall do with you."

Her eyes had closed but at this last they snapped open. "What do you mean by that?"

He rubbed the bridge of his nose. "Simply that I have never dealt with a woman—or man—like you. I do not know what action is wisest for everyone concerned."

She was too exhausted to try and divine his words for deeper meaning. She sank into a restless sleep that was disturbed when Paxton shook her shoulder minutes—or was it hours?—later. "The Templar calls for you."

She roused herself enough to understand Paxton tell her he was making a round of the camp to check on his soldiers. His face was grim. "I have to tell you that this seeming miracle-healing has alienated many. The people in the caravan might have considered you merely fey before, but now there is open talk of you being a sorceress.''

"Then they are fools," she said with a shrug, but she was concerned more than she wanted Paxton to know. She splashed some water from a basin on her face, then made her way back to the other tent. Baldwyn was sitting up, while Iolande put a fresh dressing on his wound. He appeared as white as the strips of bandaging, and still looked as if he tottered on the brink of life and death.

"I told the leper to let you rest," Iolande grumbled. Though her tone was waspish, Dominique sensed some kind of refined thread had been woven between the Jewess and the Templar.

"I have something important to say," he said. "Something to tell you should I still not . . . make it."

She flashed him an encouraging smile. "You will make it. You are too knavish to leave this world yet."

He did not return her attempt at joviality. "In my journey between here and to another life, I was told to return to you, that my time here wasn't finished."

Her mouth opened in astonishment. "Who . . . What was said?"

"I think you are both out of your minds," Iolande said, fussing with Baldwyn's bandaging.

He made a face. "I know I sound crazy." He

looked up at Dominique. "But I know you, if no one else, understands. It was only a warm, loving voice that coaxed me to return here. That's all I know. Except one other thing."

"Which is?" she asked, greatly interested in this phenomenon she had long believed to be possible.

Baldwyn fixed her with a hollowed gaze. "There is something else you should know, my Lady Dominique. There is another who, even before the runes were inscribed, has been orchestrating events through another close to you in order to gain your soul."

"Do what was best for the whole" Baldwyn had said. The phrase lingered in Paxton's mind.

Beside him, Dominique tossed in a restless sleep. He had more than Dominique to consider. He had the whole. Not just his own men, but the whole English army, the whole of England.

Then there was the whole of France. For which side did God lend His support?

On Francis de Beauvais's side?

Was the bishop an agent provocateur? He had the Pope's ear, but he appeared not the type to be politically interested in mere feuds between countries. Something grander, something more personal beckoned Dominique's confidant.

CHAPTER XVII

Though ramparts built centuries before by the Romans ringed Avignon, the city itself was dominated by a giant, fortress-like palace considered Europe's greatest building, the palace of Pope Benedict XII.

Construction on both the papal palace, which had been combined with an old bishop's castle, and on the city itself was continual. Night and day, stonecutters and carpenters, woodcarvers, and glassmakers labored to keep up with the demand for dwelling from the swelling numbers of people immigrating to the international capital.

How Denys would have loved to be a part of this creation, Dominique thought wistfully. Sawdust scented the air, and the sound of hammering throbbed in the ears and the blood. The sophisticated and lively Avignonese possessed an air of youthful *joie de vivre*.

Here, next to a licensed salt shop, a rich burgess's houses was going up; over there on the Place de L'Horloge a chapel to Saint Pierre was under way; and fronting the Rhone river was the remodeled countinghouse of the Lombard Companies. Of course, everywhere were palaces of prelates and princes, but new ones were being erected in the suburbs where vineyards had predominated.

Located near the Comtat Venaissin, a papal territory, Avignon was virtually neutral, neither French nor Italian but more Provencal. Because of its site near the confluence of the Rhone and Durance, the holy city was also a thriving commercial port. Foreigners from all over the world crowded its narrow streets.

When Paxton's party passed the forbidding commandery of the Hospitallers of Saint John of Jerusalem near Rue Rouge, Baldwyn spit from his perch on one of the equipment wagons. "Bah. Sons of Lucifer!"

Iolande, who watched the Templar like a falcon for any signs of relapse, found no humor in the remark, but Dominique had to chuckle. The Knights of Saint John had been bitter rivals of the Knights Templars during the Crusades, but when the order of the Templars was abolished, the Hospitallers took over almost all the order's property and had since become rich and powerful.

Past the prostitutes' quarters, a stone bridge, the Pont St.-Bénézet spanned the Rhone. On its far side rose the imposing tower that garrisoned King Philip's soldiers. It had been built to counterbalance the stronghold of the papacy.

With a raised hand, Paxton halted the procession at the bridge to stare broodingly across at the fort and its tower. For a fleeting second his expression was forbidding, so much so that she shivered and bumps raised on her flesh. Then the wind from the Rhone ruffled his hair and he appeared almost a boy.

So that was what Paxton of the village of Wychchester had looked like as a child, working the earth, plowing it and planting it and fertilizing it. Did he not realize this was a tremendous love they both shared? At that moment, she wanted to kiss his brow and hold him and love him with all the love that overflowed her heart.

But the moment quickly passed, and he signaled for the procession to continue on to a bourg that was the residential quarter of the rich. Ancient patrician families had built rambling mansions reminiscent of the aristocratic towers of Italian cities. Here, the entourage had to move to the far side of the street for two red-hatted cardinals. Even though it was still daylight, torchbearers preceded them.

At last, they reached the abode Paxton had rented for their stay. The Hôtel de la Prefecture, built by a Florentine banker, was a squat

mansion with a wrought iron gate opening
onto its outer courtyard. Moss grew between
the courtyard's cobblestones, which were
hard on the ankles. Statuary was artfully
placed amidst the greenery where, incredibly,
peacocks strolled in the peaceful coolness of
the afternoon. Moss-sheathed blades of a water wheel creaked over a stream meandering
through the grounds.

Inside, the mansion was a labyrinth of frescoed corridors, chambers, and halls, all fur-
nished lavishly. The ornament over the
fireplace was a chevron of gold, no less. For
their arrival, the tiled floors had recently been
covered with fresh grass and rosemary. So,
Paxton had planned ahead for everything.

Like a boy, he grabbed Dominique's hand
and pulled her along with him up the flight of
marble stairs to inspect the rooms. She was
delighted with the water from a well that was
piped into the garderobes. No more need for
chamber pots.

Paxton was pleased with the multitude of
bedchambers on the upper floor. He threw
open the triple doors to the main one. A bed
canopied in red damask dominated the warmly paneled room. The bed was so enormous
that a long stick had been provided for the
maid to use in straightening the bed linens.

"Had I known that the post of Grand Seneschal included such benefits as this, I would
have insisted on coming sooner."

Recalling Baldwyn's warning, she felt uncomfortable both here at the Hôtel and in Avignon itself. She knew not what to guard against, but she trusted her inner signals. She tugged at Paxton's grip. "Do we have to stay here for the remainder of the year?"

He turned to give her an appraising stare. "I do not know yet just what turn events will take. Does it matter? We are together. Is that not enough?"

She held his gaze. "Enough would be for you to tell me you love me."

His eyes released hers. He tunneled his fingers through his hair, growing longer now that he was not soldiering. "I do not know how to love you, Dominique. You are not like—like other women."

Her laugh was short. "Like other women? Or like Elizabeth? Look at me."

When he did not, she said, "Look at me! I have a womb for you to implant your children." Her hand splayed across her stomach. "I have two breasts to nourish them." She cupped her breasts then put her hand to her chest. "I have a heart with which to love them. And I have a mind to teach them what they will need to know."

"'Tis your mind that I cannot grapple with."

"Oh, since I have a mind, I cannot be a woman? Is that it?"

He threw up his hands, and his mouth pulled taut in a frustrated expression. "Why can you just not be—"

"Be what?"

"Like other women."

With a provocative walk she crossed the room to stand before him. She laid her hand on his chest. "Would you want me as you do, Paxton, if I were like other women?"

He wrapped an arm about her waist and caught her tresses in one hand to draw her head back so that she was forced to meet his gaze. Anger blazed there, but it was directed at himself. "If you were like other women, I would have left you back at the chateau, Dominique."

Her eyes sparked. "And doubtless girdled my loins with a chastity belt."

"Like a knight on a crusade, I would have abandoned you without another thought."

Her lips parted, and she found herself hungry for his strong mouth loving hers. "But you could not. I tell you, Paxton, you will never rid your mind of me. Never!"

His mouth tightened. "I know that. If I could have, I would have. But I find a certain pleasure in trying to satiate myself with your love, though I have yet to succeed." He bent his head over hers, murmuring, "Shall we try out our bed?"

Dominique had to admit to a measure of excitement about calling on the pope. Certainly not because she felt he was any divine source of guidance for the human spirit. Far from that, for amoral deeds of the popes had been the rule rather than the exception for centuries.

Nevertheless, the mental stimulation she anticipated encountering in that cosmopolitan court was as tempting an apple as lust was to self-gratification.

The palace itself bore witness to the fabulous wealth of the papacy. Its high, honey-colored walls were pierced by narrow windows but for the Indulgence Window from which the pope gave his blessing to the congregation in the courtyard below.

The Pope's Tower jutted out like a prow of a ship, dwarfing the city with its high, thick walls. Massive pointed arches rhythmically punctuated those walls, and huge machicolations made the castle practically unconquerable.

Dust from the pope's ambitious construction project flurried in the air. Followed by their requisite retinue of servants, she and Paxton passed under scaffolding and through the Great Gateway, surmounted by Benedict XII's coat of arms. A vaulted passage led them into a cloistered courtyard and the Pope's Tower, guarded by twelve sergeants at arms.

In that apostolic fortress-like palace, the Pope's Tower safeguarded the Holy See's most valuable possessions—the sacred person of the pope himself, who had his bedchamber there, the Great Treasury, and his library, replete with manuscripts.

The hall was packed with theologians,

princes, cardinals, clergymen, and eminences of the Sacred College, Italian and French artists, not to mention the courtesans. Judging by their tall, gilded cone-shaped headdress, from which diaphanous veils floated, Dominique realized her clothing was sadly dated. How on earth did these women avoid knocking off their headdresses when passing under low lintels?

The men wore clothing that was shorter and tighter than that of the women. Scandalously, the male hosiery conformed boldly to the most private parts. A law had recently been passed in France, prohibiting such flagrant flaunting of these sexual parts by those below the title of a knight's rank.

Even more scandalously, the monks combed their hair over their tonsures and openly dallied with the courtesans, according to gossip the most beautiful women in the world. Dominique had to agree.

She glanced about the milling crowd for sight of Francis, but he was not among the prelates, clerics, deacons, and novices.

After a Florentine ambassador was admitted into the presence of the pope, Paxton's papers, bearing the royal stamp of King Edward of England, Duke of Aquitaine, gained them entry at once. The Salle du Consistoire was where the pope conferred with his cardinals and received with great pomp and circumstance distinguished visitors—sovereigns, ambassadors, and legates who had accomplished missions on his behalf.

The ceiling was covered with a blue fabric simulating the heavens, with stars of lapis lazuli. Four casement windows were placed just so in order to throw light on the Universal Shepherd. No one could possibly overlook the pope. Jacques Fournier, for all his humble origins—the frail Cistercian was the son of a baker from Foix—possessed a charisma that netted every eye in his presence. He was the Fisherman on earth.

Before being elected pope, he had been referred to as the White Cardinal because of the color of his habit. His habit was still white but was now embellished with sacerdotal jewels. The crook of the pope's crosier rested against his high-backed, pontifical platform chair, and his feet were propped on an embroidered stool. On his narrow head sat a tiara of three crowns. An emperor could wear a tiara of two crowns, and a mere king only one.

After a page announced them, the pope's wrinkled lids dropped halfway over eyes that regarded them closely. "Welcome, my children."

With Paxton, she proceeded to the chair and knelt on painted tiles to kiss the ring of the Vicar of Christ. When she rose, however, it was not the pope's scrutinizing gaze her own encountered but Francis's intense one. At once, her interest was captured completely. It had always been like that, the way he dominated her thoughts. Certainly, he had more of an aura of the supreme pontificate about him than Benedict XII. He smiled reassuringly and then leaned close to the pope and whispered something behind his hand.

Benedict nodded and then began to discuss with Paxton his role as proxy for the Duke of Aquitaine. She noted that the pope did not once refer to Edward as King of England but always as King Philip's vassal.

Not for nothing was the pope French. King Philip knew exactly what he was about when he had maneuvered for the majority of the cardinals to wear the French mitre. The power of the monarchy and the Church combined would be a formidable opponent against England.

Paxton responded adroitly to the pope's questioning, adding, "I shall eagerly be looking forward to King Philip's arrival next month so that I may personally do homage for my own fiefdom as well as that of the Duke's."

Under other conditions, Paxton's presence at the pope's palace might be questioned, but as Avignon was the intellectual center of Europe, he was but one of many foreigners in that court of intrigue. As it was, Benedict was more concerned about the ongoing conspiracy against him by the Roman patricians and princes. Because of this, Paxton was treated with nominal, though cautious, respect.

Later in the privacy of their bedchamber, Paxton explained to Dominique, "King Philip might not trust his English cousin, but he certain is not yet ready to go to war over Edward's legitimate claim to the French duchy of Aquitaine. In this one matter, Edward is at least King Philip's vassal, an arrangement I would imagine Philip finds immensely satisfying."

She paused in the midst of unknotting her girdle and smiled wistfully at her beloved. His features were so powerful. And so closed. "I find *you* immensely satisfying, my Lord Lieutenant." Forgetting her girdle, she went to him and slipped her arms around his neck.

Those long-lidded brown eyes grew wary.

"Paxton," she pleaded, "I want the intimacy and warmth between us that we once had." Beneath her palms, she could feel his neck tendons pull taut. "I want trust between us."

A muscle at the corner of his mouth ticked. "Can there be such a thing between any two humans?"

She kissed the end of his mouth, where the twitching had been. "Yes, with mutual work."

His mouth moved slightly so that her lips were beneath his. "Mmmmm," he murmured. "Is this mutual work?"

Her laugh was husky. Her head lolled back. Her eyes closed languorously. "Mutual pleasure, I would say."

He put his hands on her arms and set her away from him. Her lids snapped open. She did not mistake his forced smile. "A pleasure I must forego for the moment. Affairs at the pope's palace demand my attention."

With an aching hunger that she feared would have no end, she watched him take up his sword and knife and leave, dropping only the lightest of kisses on her cheek.

The departure was the first of many, and she did not know which she found more unbearable—the loneliness of the Hôtel de la Prefecture without Paxton's presence or the toadying of the courtiers those days she accompanied him to the pope's palace.

Paxton seemed most interested in attending the frivolous *appartements*. At these events, she had to witness the open flirtations of the women in attendance, among them, naturally, Esclarmonde. Was it possible . . . could Esclarmonde hate her enough to work evil against her? Admittedly, Francis's sister was little more than civil to her, which was not the case with Francis.

Despite the demand upon him by his service to Benedict, Francis found time to introduce her into the academic gatherings of the papal court. The lure of intellectuals and artisans like Andrea Pisano succeeded in drawing her often to these salons, so that she and Paxton occasionally passed each other coming and going. The majority of their exchanges, however, occurred in the privacy of their bedchamber late at night.

Piqued at his lack of attention, she associated more and more often with the learned minds while ignoring the flirtations of the other adepts in Avignon. One afternoon, as she was leaving the hôtel with Iolande and Manon, and Baldwyn as guard, she met Paxton just arriving at the courtyard gate. In court dress, he appeared devastatingly handsome. The sleeves of his doublet were split so as to show the fine white shirt, and he wore cordwain shoes of goatskin from Cordova.

"You look tired," she said, inflecting her voice with an insouciance she was far from feeling. Where had he been this time? He told her so little now that they were quartered in Avignon.

Holding the gate open for her, he stared down at her with a peculiar look in his eyes. Was it yearning? Suspicion? Why could she not read him as she did others? But then, even that gift seemed to have dimmed for a long time now. "Where are you going?" he asked.

"Only to the home of Cardinal della Provere." Perversity made her add, "Petrarch will be there." Despite the love poetry he wrote about an anonymous woman named Laura, the Italian evidenced a great deal of enjoyment in flirtatious conversation with Dominique. "You know how stimulating Francesco can be."

"Yes, I am aware of that."

Could she not even stir that impassive English face into jealousy?

As they made their way to the cardinal's house, Iolande grumbled continuously. "Outrageous, the morals of this city. Yet the law forbids a Jewess to touch the fruit in the market stalls. Bah. I spit upon it."

As a papal enclave, Avignon was a sanctuary. Jews, on payment of a small indemnity, were safe, as were escaped prisoners and adventurers fleeing litigation. Smuggling, forgery, and counterfeiting were rife, and brothels and bawdy houses flourished.

Dominique could sympathize with Iolande. After a short three weeks, she was restless to return to the familiarity of Montlimoux. "The time here will pass quickly, Iolande," was all she could offer.

Although dusk still provided enough light to see by, torchbearers guided Dominique's retinue to the cardinal's home just beyond the narrow Rue Peyrollerie. The mansion was richly appointed with gilded chests and cupboards, easily disassembled for traveling. Arras tapestries graced walls frescoed in yellow foliage on a blue background. Servants hovered at every staircase and screened passage.

Iolande was not impressed with the women who painted their faces and dusted them with fine white flour nor with the superficial discussions of the works of Ovid and Vergil, and least of all with Petrarch and his friend, Giovanni Boccaccio. Several couples were listening intently as Petrarch expounded. "The care of mortal things must be first in mortal minds," he told the painted woman nearest him.

"Bah, words," Iolande said beneath her

breath. "So many words. Where are their actions?"

Iolande was right, of course. But the afternoon was a diversion. An event to occupy Dominique's thoughts which were forever turned toward Paxton and the subtle change she could only vaguely perceive yet not specifically identify.

Tonight, Esclarmonde was not present, but Martine Blanchard was. A renowned court beauty, she was the wife of a portly Flemish merchant who specialized in cargo insurance. Martine specialized in seduction, so it was said, and Dominique suspected that Paxton was her prey. The Belgium woman's cold beauty chilled the length of the room, reaching its frosty tentacles even to Dominique.

Although she had been at the affair less than an hour, she was thinking of leaving. Only the knowledge that her early return would confirm her attachment to Paxton prevented her from doing so.

Then Francis was announced. Dominique noticed that all the women in the salon became alert, almost as if he were a lodestone, magnetizing their attention. And why not? With the shock of raven hair and those piercing black eyes, Francis was irresistible. The prohibition of his calling, the taboo of loving such a man, made him all that more desirable. In addition, he was most proficient at playing the political game, of navigating through the nuances of the papal court, a valuable asset for the courtesans among the crowd.

Like peacocks, those courtesans and the wives and daughters present preened. But after first pausing to discourse with a politician from Philip's court, then a diplomat from a foreign nation, and next another ecclesiastical, Francis wended his way directly toward her, bypassing even Martine.

Iolande gave an impudent snort, and he grinned. "I swear, Iolande, I am not here to course your charge into some indiscretion. Although I would have long ago if I thought I would have had a chance at succeeding."

He focused his attention on Dominique then and it was that very attentiveness, that sophistication, that made the rest of the evening pass all too quickly. "You know, Dominique," he said, as she prepared to leave, "the pope's palace has the most extensive alchemical laboratory outside of Islam. I suggest on your next visit to the palace I show you its wonders. You can become a pilgrim to a greater knowledge at which mere villeins scoff."

Why could Paxton not understand this quest for the path of enlightenment?

Rocher des Domes, just beyond the juxtaposition of the pope's palace and a smaller palace that was his official headquarters of the Avignon episcopate, was the highest point of Avignon. A windswept crag, the Rocher placed a seemingly endless view of the land-scape of the Rhone valley at Francis's feet, which never failed to send a thrill through him that was greater than any that came with sexual completion.

The north mistral lashed Francis's hair across his face, but he did not present his back to the wind. The stinging was just another sensation that reminded him he was alive, as did the Rhone's murmur, echoing off the surrounding hills.

So little and yet so much was required for that feat of feeling alive. So much when one was bonded to the remnants of malignancy lasting thousands of years—and hundreds of lifetimes.

"Francis!"

He turned and smiled at the lovely woman hurrying toward him up the sloping path that passed the orchard and garden well with its built-in sundial. Dominique was lovely with innocence yet to be initiated. For her, there could be another path, one to degradation lower than that reached by ordinary physical activities.

He took her outstretched hands, their flesh so soft, so alive with her extraordinary force-energy, force-energy generated by the soil and air and vegetation and water of Montlimoux, all of which she was a part. To possess both would be to possess life eternal and all its accompanying riches.

His smile contained centuries of calculation. "I was certain your scientific curiosity would get the best of you."

She laughed joyously. "I have been stifled for months now. Come, show me the delights you promised."

The wind whipped together his brocaded skirts with her silken ones, as, laughing, he led her back to the palace. He took her by way of the second-floor, a covered gallery to the vice legates' private apartments that because of their northern exposure were freezingly cold in the winter.

Only a few stairsteps and a gently sloping corridor separated those apartments from the bell tower. She hung back when he reached the barred door. "'Tis all right," he assured her. "People come and go constantly here, and nothing is thought of it."

"Women come and go?" she asked with a teasing smile that was familiar from their childhood. But at that time she had been a virgin.

"*Mais, oui!* Martine has paid me several visits." He crossed to the trap door in the floor and lifted it to expose the dark cavern below. "Martine has an intense interest in the concoction of poisons and the casting of spells, among other things." He took the torch from the wall socket to light the darkness. "One soon discovers that one can have many enemies at court."

"Then I must applaud your longevity here,

Francis. Your survival instincts must be at a peak pitch."

He held out his hand for her to kiss the cabochon of his ring. "Come with me," he said with a daring smile, "and I shall hear your confession."

She looked at him uncertainly, then, laughing again, kissed his ring.

The stairway descended three flights into a barrel-vaulted room that had once communicated with the lower gallery of the cloister. Just as he expected, Dominique's eyes lit like twin torches when she saw the array of alchemical apparatus in the room. "Come, I shall you show you more than you ever imagined."

Her hands caressed appreciatively the various flasks and vials and burners. "How fortunate you are, Francis. All this knowledge at your disposal."

"Much of what I learned in the last few years has come from a manuscript by Simon Magus who was a magician and Jew and who eventually became sorcerer to Nero."

She tilted her head. "Like what?"

"Like the mystical jugglery with numbers and letters, the writing of amulets, and such. It was Simon who pointed out the close relation between gold and execrement, the importance of dew as a solvent of gold, the value of menstrum and virgin's milk."

He detected an uneasiness in her laugh.

"Virgin's milk? Francis, isn't that a contradictory term?"

"Not at all." He clasped her upper arms, turning her toward him. "The more one studies and experiments, the more one perceives that all is the opposite of what it appears."

Her eyes glistened with the opportunity of increasing her knowledge. "Will you teach me, Francis?"

"It would be very much my pleasure. Very much."

Francis's knowledge of the hidden enthralled Dominique. Even his voice held that power to enthrall. "It has previously been thought that semen must rot in order to impregnate, for rotting is procreating. The corruption or breaking up of one form is the beginning of another. Can you understand this, Dominique?"

Chengke had taught her that death was not an end but a beginning. Francis's statement had a sensible point, yet the pull of life, not death, was too strong in her to accept fully his viewpoint. Not yet anyway.

Perceiving her confusion, he said, "With further lessons, you will come to see what I am trying to teach you. Tell me, have you heard of the Basilisk?"

She shook her head.

"'Tis a monster that grows in the greatest impurity of woman, her menstrua, and from the seed of man, putrified in horse's dung. Its glance is fatal, but one can protect oneself if clothed in mirrors. With the knowledge I teach you, Dominique, I shall clothe you in mirrors that will defeat the ignorant."

She accepted the hand warming her shoulder and said, "I am forever indebted for your friendship, Francis."

He smiled benignly. "Your love is enough, Dominique. By the way, do you realize that *amor* spelled backwards is Roma, or the Roman Catholic Church?"

CHAPTER XVIII

The alchemical laboratory at the pope's palace and Francis's friendship and guidance were the only two things that enabled Dominique to get through each day. Eagerly, she descended with the bishop to the laboratory, where she could immerse herself in scientific studies to which she had never been exposed.

But even this once-consuming interest was not enough to totally distract her from the anguish she felt at Paxton's emotional distancing from her. It was not only that Paxton seemed to have shut down his emotions since coming to Avignon, it was his disinterest in everything beyond his own amusement. He fluttered from *fête* to *fête*, from chateau to chateau. He neglected even Esclarmonde's amorous advances in favor of the court beauties, of whom Martine was the acknowledged queen.

The few *fêtes* Dominique attended found her with her choice of partners if she so desired. The ambassadors at the papal court, as soon as they had discharged their duties, sought her out. Her ardor for knowledge, her familiarity with myriad subjects, her growing fondness for the Italian *novel-lieri,* made her most sought after.

Yet her spirits lagged. At one such gala, dwarfs, and buffoons, and rope dancers entertained, while the ecclesiastical guests degenerated into a loud, rambunctuous, and immoral lot. Noble pages handed round ewers and basins and were pouring water over the diners' fingers, while noble knights stood behind diners' chairs to catch inebriated guests who toppled out of their chairs.

In the midst of this revelry, death presided in the form of various poisons—from food to incense, a result of any one of numerous monks' plots. After these galas, an orgy of contrition usually ensued, with four hundred bishops singing *Veni Creator Spiritus.* It was fast becoming her opinion, the higher the birth, the lesser the piety.

The dross, the base desires, the dregs drained her. So, after a while her attendance at the galas declined, and she focused more on those afternoons spent at the laboratory with Francis.

Among other things, her friend claimed to have a formula that, once divined, would lead to the secret of transmutation: iron to gold. Gold, that metal sought after by mankind not merely for its rarity and glitter but for its wonderful malleability.

With limitless gold, she could buy Montlimoux from the king of England, from all the kings of all the countries for that matter! And she could restore her cherished countryside to the splendid grandeur it knew in the days of her mother, the mistress of alchemists.

"You are putting yourself in peril," Baldwyn told her one morning after she had requested his accompanying her to the palace. "The bishop is alienated from nature." When she looked askance at him, he added with an uncomfortable shrug, "A bit of spiritual knowledge I gained from my near-death experience."

"I heed the warning," she sighed, "but my own force-energies have always been equal to those of others. Francis cannot harm me without my permission."

Little by little all her force-energies were being directed toward preserving the tenuous relationship between herself and Paxton. And, too, there was the growing knowledge that more than ever she wanted his child. This time the conception would not be happenstance—although Chengke would have argued that nothing, not any single thing, was happenstance—but would be a planned event.

With that in mind, she spent an entire afternoon in the hôtel's lead bathtub. The tented bath was spiced with herbs and provided with sponges.

Marté and Beatrix, who pined for her English captain, drew her bath and took great delight in the tub, because it was equipped with two gilt-bronzed keys in the shape of leopards for cold *and* hot water, no less! Perfume and body creams procured by Iolande scented and smoothed Dominique's body. Manon brushed her hair until it glowed with a fiery sheen. A lavender silk tunic that clung to her womanly curves was laid out by Jacotte.

The young maid appeared to have gotten over her infatuation with Denys, because she had recently become betrothed to a saddler and within the year would be leaving Dominique's household.

The wait for Paxton seemed eternal. When he at last returned to the hôtel, dinnertime was well past. He looked distracted, scarcely noticing her. In the privacy of their bedchamber, he stretched and rubbed his beard-shadowed jaw. "By my oath, I am tired."

"Your day was busy?" she asked, taking the cape he shrugged off. Clad only in his hose and short tunic, his physique was so perfectly masculine that it was difficult to turn her gaze away.

"Philip arrives on the morrow. That means a confrontation of wills. Wills disguised in the utmost diplomacy."

He seemed distant, reserved. Forcing her uneasiness away, she drew him to the great bed. "Then you will need your rest for the meeting."

Lovingly, her hands divested him of his tunic. When they reached for the points and laces of his hose, he eyed her curiously. His gaze finally absorbed her efforts at setting herself off to her best advantage. "You mean to seduce me, my lady?"

She laughed at his directness. "No, I mean to instruct you in a much-neglected science, my Lord Lieutenant."

She commenced with a single-minded intent: pleasuring Paxton until no coherent thought remained in his mind. All her energy was concentrated into her hands, into caressing and fondling and stroking him.

At one point, he groaned and said, "That is enough. I need you now. I need to pour my seed into you."

She smiled. "You will. I promise you will."

Her hands lovingly traced the scars on his back. She realized that it was Paxton's unseen scars that had never healed properly—his bitterness; his lack of trust in the opposite sex;

317

his feelings of inferiority, despite all that he had accomplished, toward the ranks above him.

Then she did something that sent him sitting bolt upright. He grasped her hair and tugged at her head. "What is it you think you are doing?"

She shook free his grasp and repressed her levity as she attempted to explain. "Your power is focused in the area between your legs, Paxton. When I place my forehead there, that power is transmitted to me. And when you empty your seed into my mouth—"

"Enough!"

"'Tis never enough," she rejoined with light laughter.

Before he could stop her, she knelt again and began to love him with her mouth.

With a moan, he hauled her atop him. "I surrender, maiden. Give me surcease. Ease this pain."

She rode him then like the Amazon women of old rode their stallions. Exulting and always loving, loving. How she loved him, this man of hers.

If she had felt Paxton's neglect, he too must have sensed her own distancing or, at least, been curious about the increasing amount of time she spent with Francis, because one sunny afternoon as she and Francis sat deep in conversation in the seclusion of the garden east of the palace, Paxton came in search of her.

"I was told I might find you here," he said with an easy charm that was more characteristic of Francis. Her husband dropped down in the grass beside the stone bench where she sat opposite Francis. "We have been invited to a feast tonight given in honor of the newly appointed Pisan ambassador."

"Another one?"

"No, the last was a Turkish—"

"No, I mean another dinner. I am weary of them, Paxton."

"I confess I am, also," Francis said, his smile congenial. "The summer festivities become tedious, and one looks forward to the autumn court in Paris. A much more diverting city."

Paxton draped one arm over an upraised knee and said to Francis, "Tell me, why did you give up law practice to become a priest?"

Her husband's question appeared totally sincere, and Francis surprised her by replying in a totally sincere manner. "The Inquisition, my good son. The Dominicans tortured my parents."

"I would have thought that would have driven you away from the Church."

Francis's dark eyes glowed. "For a while it did. I was forced to watch first my mother subjected to the rack and then my father." He paused, and a tic twitched in his cheek. "I

319

cried. And cried. Hour upon hour. Their screams burst in my ears. But at some point in their terrible ordeal I began to perceive that their sacrifice was to a greater glory."

Dominique shook her head, and her veil fluttered around her shoulders. "I do not understand that line of reasoning, Francis."

He spread his well-formed hands. "My parents became wonderful symbols of the same glorious suffering and ultimate sacrifice as Jesus Christ made."

"That is what I am talking about," she said, her brows knitting. She leaned forward and said earnestly, "Christ's message was not about sacrifice but about unconditional love and the spiritual laws of transmutation—the very same as the physical laws of transmutation of iron to gold, Francis!"

"Ah, but we can know no transmutation because we are impure. We must experience hell's fires. That is the purification, do you not see?"

Paxton sprang to his feet with a grace unusual for a man his size. He took her hand and drew her up beside him. "I see that you both entertain ideas vastly different than the pope's spiritual ideology. I would rather expound on political idealogy myself, Francis. What say you and I engage in a more worthy discussion in the near future?"

Francis rose also, his hands tucked into the wide sleeves of his robe. "I will anticipate the encounter with great pleasure, my son."

Paxton tugged her along the tree-shaded path. "Your choice of friends, Dominique, may well land you in trouble."

She jerked on his hand and came to an abrupt halt. "What do you mean?"

He caught her by her arms. His tight lips clearly expressed his vexation. "I mean that you would do well to curtail your visits with the priest."

"I might suggest that you curtail your visits to the various *appartements* you find so fascinating, my Lord Lieutenant," she snapped back.

Exasperation drew a sigh from him. He ran his fingers through his hair. "This is getting us nowhere. Come along, we have a dinner to attend."

She watched him stride away, his back a symbol of the wall between them.

Dominique tried to avoid the obvious, the moments when she was at court and would catch Paxton and Martine deep in conversation or sharing an intimate moment of laughter. Then, when Jacotte came to her one afternoon, Dominique was forced to heed the whispers.

Jacotte could not meet her gaze. With a trembling hand, she handed Dominique one of those scandalous broadsheets that circulated around Avignon. "My betroth found this."

Dominique glanced at the broadsheet. Her

eye was caught by the script tucked away in one corner. "Higamous, hogamous, the Lady Dominique is monogamous. Hogamous, higamous, her husband is polygamous."

She wadded up the broadsheet. With a shrug, she said, "The work of gossip-mongers."

Her pain was more difficult to shrug off. Wherever she went, she felt as if people were talking about her and Paxton. Humiliation became her companion. She wanted to believe in Paxton and refused to discuss the subject with anyone.

Then Manon approached her. The maid chewed her bottom lip in an effort to find the right words. "Yes?" Dominique asked, dreading what she suspected was coming.

"I . . . er . . . Martine's maid-in-waiting . . . ah, oh, my Lady Dominique, she says that my Lord Lieutenant has been—ah—that her mistress is his lover."

Pride, the millstone of the ego, lashed Dominique with anguish at this confirmation of his deception. She hardly heard, nor even cared, that a rumor was also circulating concerning his previous wife.

Manon stared down at her pattens, as her words rushed on, "A French legate here at court knew Paxton's first wife, my Lady Dominique. He says stories abounded for years about Paxton murdering her in a fit of rage."

Tasting the nausea that welled inside her,

Dominique turned from Manon and hurried to the garderobe to throw up. Trust, respect, honesty . . . these were the cornerstones of a solid marital foundation. Like a priceless Oriental vase, their relationship had been shattered and it would never be put back together in the same, flawless way it had been. The cracks would devalue its one-time perfection.

Day after day her stomach wrenched in knots. A metallic taste coated her tongue. She could not eat. She lost weight. She paced, constantly walking the perimeters of her chamber, unconscious of her surroundings, forgetful of things she had said or done only moments before. Her sleep was restless. Unflattering shadows appeared beneath her eyes. Over the succeeding days, she could not bring herself to go out, even to see Francis, and the trellis work of iron over the hôtel's windows became her prison bars.

At last, even a preoccupied Paxton noticed her decline. Late one night, he raised on one elbow to stare down at her. "What is it, *ma migonne*? What ails you these last few days?"

Remembering her maid's revelation of the deadly gossip, Dominique could not meet his heavy-lidded gaze. She turned her head to stare at the darkness above. "'Tis nothing. Merely the heat. I am used to the mountain coolness."

After a long moment, he turned on his side and went back to sleep. They were so close physically. She had only to move her hand and

323

she could touch that muscle-striated back, yet so distant emotionally and spiritually.

Was it possible that she was making more of this than was validated by mere rumor? After all, had anyone actually seen Paxton and Martine in bed with each other? There was no sin in being attracted to another.

Why did she not just ask him if he were being unfaithful to her?

Because he might confirm her worst nightmare?

Was it better not to know? Was pain the unavoidable price of love?

She was tempted to confront him with the information several times over the next few days. Instead, forcing herself to resume some of her former activities, she sought out the comforting solace of Francis's presence and walked to the wind-swept loneliness of the Rocher des Domes where she would scream her agony in an animalistic howl that raised goosebumps on the people who heard the howl carried by the wind.

Why? she cried to herself. *I only loved him. I never hurt anyone! Why did I deserve this? Why had I to fall in love with this man? Where, Divine Force, is the lesson to all this pain?*

And she wept, she who rarely wept, felt the hot sting of silent tears stealing down her face at the most unexpected times. She was an empty shell, so empty that if one could hold her to the ear, the sound of the sea would have been heard.

Then one morning, as Paxton was being shaved, he suggested, almost too casually, that they hold a reception at the hôtel for King Philip. "'Tis said Martine was once the Frenchman's favorite. I think it would be interesting to invite her, also."

She stared back at him, her eyes searching his soul, but she could not get beyond his eyes. Those dispassionate eyes were a wall as thick as the four-foot ones at the pope's palace. "I shall attend to the reception details," she said tonelessly.

They both looked at each other across a chasm that would forever be unbridgeable. She lowered her gaze and turned back to Manon, who was lacing her up. How could one's heart cease to beat and yet beat so fast and hard that pain swamped the body?

By rote, she oversaw the myriad details of the coming reception, a duty for which life as chatelaine had aptly prepared her. But she moved through the maze of the hôtel's corridors like a legendary ghost.

When both a king and a pope were to be one's guests, no expense or effort was to be spared. A host of servants and extra cooks were hired from Avignon and its suburbs. The day before the event, hunters were sent out to comb the forests for game and fishermen to trawl the ponds for pike. Iolande made several trips to the markets with Baldwyn in attendance, since as a Jewess she was forbidden to touch the produce. All the candles were bought from the city's chandlers. The mansion's staff scoured the hôtel to a pristine cleanness.

Dominique immersed herself in this preparation with a feverish intensity that made the hôtel's inhabitants gape—all except Paxton, who seemed to be engrossed in his own projects. With a collective sigh of relief, the mansion's staff welcomed the arrival of the evening's reception and its first guests.

The French king arrived late. Studying him, Dominique had to admit he was Edward's equal in handsomeness. Yet it was an effete handsomeness, with not even a modicum of Paxton's virile masculinity. Throughout the elaborate dinner, the guests talked and joked without once politics entering the discussion. Paxton was affable without being obsequious, and midway through the dinner Philip appeared to relax his stiff manner.

With the commencement of the carols and other dancing, the guests more readily mingled. At one point, Dominique found herself conversing with the king, and realized he had actually maneuvered through the press of his sycophants to reach her side. "You are the most lovely and charming of women to have ever graced Avignon, Comtessa."

Despite his short beard and mustache, his jaw-long hair made him look surprisingly young for forty-five or so. "Your compliment is appreciated, your Majesty." Around them, the guests listened with differential silence as they discoursed on everything from flying the hawk to the merits of Languedoc wine.

She should have felt highly honored to have been singled out by His Majesty, but the entire time her eye was searching among the guests for Paxton. She found neither him nor Martine.

Extracting herself from Philip's attention, she went in search of her husband. Her hands were sweaty and her heart thudded. Her breathing was shallow and rapid. It was that moment when night meets the raging dawn, when the tides reach their zenith and with a mighty backwash reverse their direction. When one knows her world is about to change irrevocably.

The hôtel might have a maze of corridors and numerous antechambers, pantries, and alcoves but it was as if she were following an invisible cord which linked her to Paxton.

Torchlight silhouetted him at the end of a short hall, his back to her. At first, she thought he was alone and strangely still. Then the noises of two people in the throes of passion, those raspy murmurings and short-breathed kisses, reached her. They were killing noises for the observer. She did not need to find out the identity of the woman Paxton pressed against the tapestried wall.

She would have backed away, but from the staircase came the sound of people ascending. Pride would not countenance anyone seeing her with the tears streaming down her face.

She was forced to take refuge in the nearest chamber, Paxton's interim office.

Her back pressed against the door, she waited for the voices to fade. The footsteps of the guests departed and then, even Paxton's and his mistress's footsteps wandered off down the corridor. For long moments, Dominique stood there, quaffing deep breaths, feeling the door's splintery wood piercing her palms.

Moonlight from the trefoil window spilled over Paxton's secretarial desk. She crossed to stand before it, and her tears splashed onto the moonlit-covered surface. How she detested the weakness of tears, she who had always thought she was strong. But she was the weakest of humans!

Her fist thudded on the desk once, then again and again and again. "No . . . no . . . noooo!" The words were but soft, mewling cries of which she was totally unaware making.

Eventually, the pain of injury reached through her dazed mind, and she realized she had hurt herself. A small slice on the side of her hand. Her gaze found the culprit, a tiny knife used for quill sharpening. Stoically, she watched the droplets of her blood mingle on a parchment with her tears. Something took her over. She seated herself and picked up the quill. Dipping it in her blood, she began to write on the sheet of parchment held in place on the writing board by a deerskin thong.

"I truly believed that in you I would find my counterpart, that lock that would fit my key. As you would in me, the lock that would fit your key."

She refreshened the quill tip with her blood and continued in a rush of penned words:

"I suppose I should feel humiliation that I surrendered myself to you. I feel none. The possibility of achieving something so perfect was worth the pain of the humiliation. Worth the chance. Worth your child that I bear. Good-bye. Dominique"

Trembling, she folded the missive. She meant to leave it in the desk drawer where he would not discover it until long after she had fled Avignon, but she found in the drawer a document with a royal seal, that of the king of England. Swiftly and disbelievingly, her eyes perused the broadly stroked words. Among other things, the letter hinted that Paxton was involved in a plot to overthrow Philip.

". . . two kings. Both claim France. As my cat, you must corner the French mouse after he scurries to his tower."

The knowledge of the evidence she held in her hand took her breath away. Because Paxton was a vassal of the French king, this was treason and punishable by death.

The door opened suddenly, shafting candle-light across the desk—and her. She whirled, and her own letter floated like a feather to the floor behind her. She recognized the massive shadow. Paxton set the candle in its wall sconce and crossed to her in what was almost a leisurely stride. His face chiseled of marble, he stared down at her. "You have been meddling, Dominique?"

A fury ripped through her. "I saw the royal missive! Knowing what I do about you and Martine, it would give me great pleasure to expose you as a traitor and watch your execution."

He listened with a deadly calm as she continued in a furious whisper. "As it is, Paxton, I shall repay your kindness you once did me in letting me remain at Montlimoux. I give you forty-eight hours to leave France ahead of Philip's soldiers."

Watching the play of his expression, she suddenly realized he could just as easily murder her, dispose of her body in such a way it would appear that she had been set upon by brigands, and resume his place in court. Had he not murdered Elizabeth?

His pulse hammered at his throat, and his temples were a road map of throbbing veins. A weakness that was relief washed over her when, after a long moment, he bowed curtly. "As you would have it—mistress."

Mustering the shreds of her dignity, she swept pass him and out of the room—and out of his life.

Autumn at Montlimoux triggered restless peregrinations in Dominique. Heavy with child as she was, riding had lost some of its pleasure. But then, everything even the sunlight had lost its pleasure for her. Was autumn's sunlight hazier with that last rendezvous with summer? And was this pain in her chest, was that what was meant by an attack of the heart?

The court at Avignon had adjourned in favor of Paris, and Esclarmonde and Francis had recently taken up residence at a stately home in the village of Montlimoux. Curiously, Dominique was reluctant to seek out Francis. Like a hermit, she avoided society, wanting only the healing balm of nature.

During her excursions into the countryside, as on this day, she was unfailingly accompanied by Baldwyn and several guards, at his insistence, because the month before, King Edward, Duke of Aquitaine, had formally claimed the French crown and had launched a war against northern France.

Somewhere on French soil was Paxton with his army. Apparently, Martine was not with him but had followed King Philip's court to Paris. Paxton had used her for information just as he had used Dominique herself.

For his part, King Philip had sent troops to southern France to raid the Duchy of Aquitaine. Lighting brands, the soldiers had set fire to every house suspected of English sympathies.

"Word is even about," Baldwyn said, "that the French are disrupting the main lines of transport and communications in and out of the duchy, as well as laying waste to the rich vineyards. Being this close to Aquitaine, I think it wise we ride no further today, my Lady Dominique."

With a sigh, she reined in her palfrey near a salt pan in a closeby marsh. "'Tis always the innocent people and the land that suffer the consequences of war."

"The Albigensian Crusade all over again. As the peasant says, 'What cannot be cured must be endu—'"

He broke off, sawing in on the reins of his mount. On the crest of the next hill was silhouetted a line of horsemen. Immediately, they moved out, with one unmistakably in the lead. "Christ's thorns!" Baldwyn said, and reached out to haul in Dominique's reins.

"The English?" she asked.

He shook his head. "I do not know, but 'tis trouble that is coming, that I am certain!"

As a unit, she, Baldwyn, and the three guards pivoted their horses around, flurrying dust. Frantically, she urged her palfrey into a gallop. Their party streaked for Montlimoux's ramparts. Their pennants waved in the far distance. Too far.

She strove to keep her seat, but her ungainly form made it difficult. She bounced more than rode as part of the animal. Baldwyn kept a worried eye on her. The jolting was sending small waves of pain through her. The babe. She could not lose this one!

She spared a quick glance behind. Their pursuers were gaining on them. Baldwyn saw this also, and saw the wrenching pain reflected in her face. "We shall not outrun them, my Lady Dominique!" he shouted. "We face them and fight?"

Grim-faced, she nodded.

The old Templar chose well their battleground, a plateau backed by a dense growth of trees. The heavily armored horsemen would have to scramble up the rocky slope in order to reach them. Baldwyn, with the three guards, formed a wall of blades to protect Dominique.

When their pursuers were close enough to make out, Baldwyn spit into the dirt, and said, "'Tis the French!" The French were almost as formidable and as destructive an enemy to the people of Languedoc as the English, and he cast Dominique an inquiring glance. His rheumy black eyes were full of his abiding love for her and his intentions, should she accede to his unspoken question.

Knowing what lay in that question, she nodded. She would accept his sword as a death instrument.

The clanging of armor and swords unsheathed recaptured her attention. Sunight glinted off the French soldiers' armor and conical helmets, for a moment blinding Dominique. Then a maniacal laughter reached her. Chills crawled up her arms and spine. "Denys Bontemps!" she breathed.

"Baldwyn Rainbaut!" he shouted. "Surrender my fair maiden Dominique to me."

"A Templar never surrenders, Denys. You know that."

"I know that we shall chop all of you down like withered grapevines to get to her, so stand aside, old man."

Mayhaps she knew that Baldwyn could not hold out forever, mayhaps she was merely tired of the warring—the warring in the countryside, the warring within herself—but she cried, "Enough!" and slipped between her defenders to confront Denys just below her.

His gaze fastened on her extended belly. "'Tis true then, what Esclarmonde says. You carry the English bastard's child!"

Esclarmonde? "Since when do you murder for the French, Denys?"

Bitterness had left its ravages on his once-handsome face. His sunlit smile was now little more than a sneer. "I could run that unborn babe through with my sword, Dominique, but 'tis not you I wish to kill."

The malice in his tone made her shiver.

"Guard your time closely," he continued. "I shall return for the life of Paxton's child."

CHAPTER XIX

"Paxton has deserted you, my dear. You should have the marriage annulled."

"I carry his child, Francis!"

He tried to keep his smile gentle. Despite her girth, her face was thin and drawn, with shadows darkening her eye sockets. "A small detail for the pope."

Her mouth crimped in annoyance. "Our child is no small detail."

She was concentrating on embroidering the laying-in pillowcase for the coming childbirth and so missed the way his own mouth curled downward. He reached down and placed his hand over hers, stilling it. "Dominique, let me care for you."

She stared at his hand then raised her

puzzled gaze to his. "What do you mean by that, Francis?"

"Let me take care of you."

"I have always been able to take care of myself, you know that."

"But now with the child coming. . . ."

"Baldwyn and Iolande are like my own parents. They will care for—"

"They are old. Who knows when they might die?"

"Francis, I enjoy my independence. I do not think your suggestion would work. Besides. . . ."

"Yes?"

A tiny smile curved her lips. "Besides, I do not think it would be wise to subject your vows to such temptation."

"Are you implying I might finally succeed in seducing you?"

Her laugh was short. "I am implying the temptation of riches. You know, those legendery Albigensian treasures buried here and all that."

"*Touché*," he said, smiling. "Now, I must take my leave, but think on what I have said, will you not?"

She nodded toward the window. "The rain is turning to snow. Why not stay the night?"

"Esclarmonde will be expecting my return."

She rose and crossed with an awkward grace to the portable iron brazier used for heating. He could tell she was choosing her words carefully. "I am told that your sister spends more nights away now than at your residence."

The muscles in his jaws tightened, and he forced them to relax in an easy smile. "'Tis time she found herself a mate. I just would not have chosen a *routier* for her."

"Denys is a soldier now, Francis, not a brigand."

"That may be so, but it does not ease my trepidations." His sister was a part of him. As she strained away, so, too, could he feel part of himself straining away. He would remedy that, anon. "But that is beside the point I wished to make. I ask you give consideration to my suggestion, Dominique. You and I, we are Montlimoux. The blood of my afterbirth nourished its soil, as yours did. 'Tis time we reunited with Montlimoux. Your child is Montlimoux."

She rubbed her temples. "When you speak such, I—I have trouble following your meaning."

He stared hard at her. "You did not use to."

"That was before. . . ."

When she did not finish, he said, "Before the foreigner possessed you. Anon, the snow will make traveling difficult. I must go."

He took his leave, and, entering the protection of his litter, pulled the curtain closed against the blowing snow. From his cloak, he withdrew the missive he had been carrying with him for months now. He waited until his litter bearers had steadied their gait, then unfolded the letter.

The dim, afternoon light made reading the blood-red words difficult. Besides, he knew them by heart. In his mind's eye, he could see all the alchemical and astrological signs and their conjoining.

He smiled, his lips thin and bloodless. At last, the time was propitious for using her missive. Mixed with sulfer, ash, and a child's urine, the shreds of the letter would draw all the characters, as if in a Mystery Play, to center stage.

From Edward's flagship, Paxton surveyed the enemy invasion. It was dauntingly large, including not French but also Castilian and Genoese vessels, as well as Saracen corsairs.

Most of Edward's vessels were cogs, merchant ships designed for carrying cargoes which ranged from wool to wine and from livestock to passengers.

The Mediterranean galleys of the French possessed oars which gave them superior speed and maneuverability, and placed Edward at a considerable tactical disadvantage. The one thing in favor of the English cog was that, while it was hardly a warship, it made an excellent troop transport, a boat for all kinds of weather and especially suitable for plowing the North Sea.

"There are so many ships, their masts look like a great forest," Edward grumbled.

"'Tis not the ships that will decide the battle, *Monseignor*." Paxton said softly, "'tis the people."

Dominique would have said the same. He had learned much from her. She was a mermaid, a sylph, an undine, a nymph, a charlatan healer.

Abruptly, he put her from his mind. "Philip's twenty thousand men on board are largely press-ganged, and few of them have even seen a battle. They are frightened fisherfolk, bargees, and longshoremen. Our soldiers will make the difference when all 'tis said and done."

His prediction appeared shaky, because once the two fleets clashed, the first casualty was a fine English cog, which was carrying a great number of countesses, ladies, knights' wives, and other damsels who were going to see the queen at Ghent. With the sinking of the cog, the screams of the drowning ladies in their heavy skirts was maddening. In every cry, he heard an echo of Dominique's voice, its pain that tore apart his dreams every night.

The battles by sea were fiercer than those by land. Here, there was no fleeing, no remedy but to fight and abide fortune and prove one's prowess. He feared not death but Dominique and her magnificent feminine power. Ultimately, he knew he feared most that surrender of self.

An iron cloud of quarrels from crossbows and arrows from long bows darkened the sky.

When the king's flagship hauled alongside a Castillian ship, the English soldiers had difficulty in boarding safely because the sides were so tall. The battle aboard the Castillian ship rang from morning until noon, and Paxton was in the thick of the melée. His white boots were covered with blood.

His anger, his fear, all were channeled into the act of destruction. "Dogs of unbelievers," he cursed his enemy, swinging his bloodied sword along its murderous path. "Whelp of a she-wolf," he cursed himself.

Eventually, his prediction proved true, with the English archers shooting two and even three arrows for every one crossbow quarrel fired by the French. The French squadron was overwhelmed, and the corpse of its admiral was swung from the yardarm of the king's flagship. Many of the enemy jumped overboard, their wounded being thrown after them. The sea was so full of bodies that the water appeared blood-red to Paxton.

The coming of dusk went unnoticed, so bright was the light of the burning ships. The victory was a great one for the English. Yet, when darkness fell Paxton was not among the celebrants. In his quarters, he sat ill and wretching. The violence of the day had turned his mind.

As the witch had turned his mind. By the body of Christ, he missed her and, aye, loved her. But he was relieved to be away from her.

She would do anything to keep Montlimoux.

The sorceress.

Esclarmonde snuggled against Denys's side, trying to absorb the warmth of his big body. His ruffians and free-booters slept not far away in a field of charred stubble. The night air was chilled, the ground on which they lay was chilled, and her heart was chilled. Would she never know warmth?

She had thought by running to Denys he would protect her. From what? From herself? She knew now she would never find that protection.

She stared up at the full moon. Thin streamers of black drifted across it. A full moon was said to expose misdeeds. Was Francis accountable for his? The brother she had loved so consummately, so completely, appeared to be two different men. No, not two men. Man —and beast. One loving. One fiend. Would he let her come back home? Would he take her into the safety of his arms again once she had accomplished what he demanded of her?

The ravages of war began to intrude on Montlimoux's pastoral beauty, its flowered hills and tree-sprinkled meadows.

These days Baldwyn made certain that guards patrolled the chateau's watchwalk night and day. From the north came occasion al news of the English forays of heavy cavalry that left the land and its people devasted. English forays often under the brilliant and incisive generalship of Paxton of Wychchester.

Here, on the boundaries of Edward's principality of Aquitaine, a farm was burned out, its corn ricks and wine vats smashed; there, on the river road, a trade caravan was ambushed; a village church plundered, its priest beheaded, his head used as shot in a catapult.

Death and rebirth.

Dominique felt that with the birth of her child would come her own rebirth; that somehow she would take joy in life once again. The birthing of this child was ravaging her body worse than any war. Once her *accouchement* began, she concentrated solely on surrendering to the pain.

Again and again, she left her bed to seek out the birthing stool, but her stomach's contractions were not enough to force the babe out.

"A syrup of the red poppy will ease your pain," Iolande said, stroking Dominique's sweat-dampened hair.

"No. No, I want to be fully . . ." She paused and caught her breath at the sharpness of the next pain. Her hand twisted the bed sheets until the veins stood out like a road map. ". . . fully conscious, all of me partaking . . . in this welcoming."

The hours of labor faded one into another, each moment passing and stealing with it her strength. Her thoughts could not push beyond the fog closing around her.

"Will she die?" she heard Baldwyn ask but could not detect Iolande's reply.

What she did hear was her own inner voice. *Soon, you will cross the bridge from birth, to death, reaching all selflessness.*

At the earliest hour of morning, the first squawl of a newborn pierced the chateau's stillness.

Iolande and Baldwyn stared at each other in unspoken horror. Baldwyn was the first to break the dead-calm of the silence. He spoke in a hoarse whisper. "Twins! What will happen?"

His question galvanized the old Jewess into action. "What you are thinking is nothing but an old wife's tale!" she said, taking a swaddling cloth to the first babe, who cried lustily. "You and I both know Dominique. These boys did not have two separate fathers."

"I know Paxton. He would be merciless if he even thought Dominique had betrayed him with another man."

She passed him the first infant and began cleaning the mucus from the second. "What would you do, leper? Kill one before word gets out?"

The big man winced from the blow of her words. "You know I could not—"

"Or mayhaps select one to give away to a peasant's wife to raise to manhood? Are you daft?" Her gnarled hands worked rapidly. There was still Dominique to be cared for. The birthing had gone hard for the slender-hipped young woman, and she slept, soothed by the hand of the poppy drug Iolande had given her after the birthing.

"Listen to me, old woman!" he thundered.

"Hush, you will frighten the babes!" She thrust the second infant in his other arm. The sight of the giant cradling the two tiny bundles brought a smile to her prunish lips. Her mouth twisted. "You make a respectable grandfather, Baldwyn."

He glared down at her. "That is the first time in thirty years or more you have addressed me by my given name."

"Well, then 'tis time I did so." She busied herself with the cleanup of the bloodied linens and afterbirth.

"Then 'tis time we make ourselves official grandparents. What say you?"

She darted him a gruff look. "What are you talking about?"

"Marriage, old woman."

Her eyes softened. "My name is Iolande."

The suckling of Chretien produced a most pleasurably aching sensation in Dominique's engorged breast. She smiled down at her infant son. His skin was as fresh as dew, his eyes as dark brown as . . . as spring's sparrow, perched on the stone windowsill. Outside, one would never know that spring was imminent. The grass was white and withered, as she often felt.

Except when she gazed upon her sons. Her sons and Paxton's. She pressed her nipple to free it of the tiny mouth and passed Chretien to a waiting Iolande, who grumbled, "You would be better changing yourself to a cow if you mean to nurse both."

After Iolande left with Chretien, Dominique bent over the second cradle and lifted out Rainbaut. He was a rainbow, with the fat, rosy cheeks and the endless blue eyes. They met hers so artlessly and acceptingly. She studied the tiny hand that curled around her finger and the fine wisps of hair that crowned his head.

Such a tenderness, a total selfless love, would well inside her that she wondered how she had ever felt her life was complete. The villagers were distressed that she had chosen no nurse from among them to suckle her children, but the earth mother in her demanded this privilege for herself.

Chretien and Rainbaut slept more hours than they were awake, and she was left with her memories of their father too much of that time. If it were not for Francis's diverting visits, she suspected she would go crazy. Some said she already was, because she did not accept Church doctrine and believed in supernatural powers, benign though she believed they might be and available to anyone.

The crazy chatelaine of Montlimoux.

She was anticipating a visit from the bishop this very afternoon for the twins' baptism on the morrow, so when she heard the noises in the corridor outside her chamber her face lit up. Her pleased expression faded when Esclarmonde opened the door first, with Francis behind her.

Dominique could not control her resentment nor her tongue. "Your visit is unexpected, Esclarmonde. Doubtlessly, you have come to see Paxton's children, but I—"

Her words faltered when the bishop closed the door and lowered the hood of his cassock to reveal—not Francis—but Denys. "What are you doing here?" she demanded. But by the sudden icing of her veins, she knew exactly why he had come.

He pushed past Esclarmonde and, before Dominique realized his intent, snatched Rainbaut from her arms. The infant cried out in protest at the separation from his mother.

She started to scream for help, and he snarled, "Do so, and I will have Esclarmonde baptize the babe with my dagger."

She stared up into the face of her friend, not even recognizing it, so distorted was it by hate. "Denys, you cannot mean this!"

Her expression gloating, Francis's sister reached to unsheath the Italian dagger. "This should silence your scream, Dominique— and the howling cur Denys holds."

"No," Denys ordered. "The babes come with us. Sooner or later, Paxton will have to come on bended knee to me—if he wants his infants alive and whole."

Overwhelming fear for her children hammered at Dominique's heart. The fear swelled in her chest and burst upward through her head, blinding her and filling her throat so that it was like a dream where one tries to scream and cannot. "Please—oh, dear heaven, Denys—please, have mercy on my sons!"

"Paxton's sons."

"You cannot take my babies! What has happened to you, Denys, to destroy all the goodness within you?"

"This!" He held up his stump, pitifully scarred and reddened. His cruel smile held the bitterness of one who has suffered greatly and not learned why from the experience. "But, mayhaps, we can arrange an exchange. Do you think Paxton might lay down his life for those of his sons'?"

The infant was crying lustily, and Dominique could only hope the cries would bring someone. "He cares naught for his children." Or he would not have deserted her, her heart cried out, while another voice reminded her she was the one who had ordered him to leave.

"He *knows* naught of his children," Esclarmonde said. Her smile was as sharp-edged as the dagger she held near Rainbaut.

"You are wrong, Esclarmonde. I penned him a missive about—"

"My brother has the missive. You see, I

found it after you and Paxton left the office that night of the reception." Her mouth formed a spiteful curl. "From what I witnessed that evening, it would seem that you and I have something in common after all, Dominique—rejection by Paxton of Wychchester. Do you think Martine keeps his camp bed warm these days?"

The demented gleam in Esclarmonde's eyes spurred Dominique into action. She sprang from her chair, screaming, "Give me my baby!"

She would have wrenched Rainbaut from Denys, but Esclarmonde got there first. Her knife plunged downward, and she shrieked, "I baptize the bastard!"

In that heartstopping moment, all seemed to slow down to Dominique: the knife plunging, Rainbaut crying, Denys's mouth angrily shouting something at Esclarmonde.

Next Denys veered away, taking Rainbaut out of the knife's reach. The knife continued its journey all the way to Denys heart. He staggered, and Dominique tried to support both him and her baby, between them. As she lowered them to the floor, Esclarmonde watched, transfixed by the scene. Then she whirled and ran from the room.

"Denys!" Dominique begged. "Look at me." His eyes were open but they would not meet hers. She had encountered that resistance often in the ill, especially the elderly, who were bent on dying. "Do not give up, Denys, my own. Fight the darkness!"

At his side, Rainbaut wailed, but she ignored her baby and begin tearing away at Denys's doublet and blood-wet shirt. Bubbles of blood pumped from the wound, a small one to inflict such a horrible result. She pressed her hand over it, feeling the blood seep between her fingers. She pressed and encanted and affirmed, knowing all the while that her efforts were useless.

Her childhood friend did not want to remain in this form.

CHAPTER XX

Paris court life was said to be the most glittering pageant in years, with all of Avignon's courtiers retreating to the royal city on the Seine.

At the same time, tales were passed from tongue to tongue of wolves entering Paris to eat the corpses. For the French, unlike the English, the war between them was turning out to be a dreadful experience. The English were systematically plundering the French countryside.

The late summer days that saw Rainbaut and Chretien taking their first steps also saw the county of Montlimoux in chaos. Thanks to the firepower of the English longbow, the

English enjoyed a military superiority and the French soldiers were routed at every turn. Forests and fields were burned, corn and cattle destroyed, graineries raided, the innocent tortured and murdered. A pall of smoke hung constantly over the land, and everywhere peasants and noblemen alike were starving.

Within the fortress walls of Montlimoux's chateau were crowded more than forty families, refugees from King Edward's mercilessly cruel *chevauchée*. Dominique moved among them, rationing food, administering aid and tending the wounded. Water, also, was in short supply since the chateau well could not sustain the increase of so many people on a continual basis.

Beyond the ramparts bands of *routiers*, English troops, and French forces battled for control of the county. Peasant rebellions and civil wars had altered family sinecures, and Dominique's was no longer as secure. Word of her seeming resurrection of Baldwyn Rainbaut the summer before had spread among the peasants, and she was now openly regarded as a sorceress. Her wisdom used in the Justice Room was interpreted as heretical dogma.

Occasionally, a wayfarer would wander into the chateau with news of the outside world. One wayfarer, a Marseilles parchment maker, brought news of a dreaded death, much like the smallpox but worse. Dominique knew it was the inevitable pestilence that accompanies wars and death.

Then one day, Francis and Esclarmonde arrived, along with their entourage, seeking asylum from the war as well as from the pestilence. Dominique met the two at the portcullis, and whatever joy she felt at beholding Francis was muted by the sight of his sister, dressed in a sequined royal-blue gown, as if she had just left a *fête*.

Rage exploded inside Dominique, the rage for revenge for Denys's death, but she tried to blot it from her mind. Esclarmonde had unintentionally killed him—but she would have killed Rainbaut.

"I cannot welcome your sister, Francis." Ice crystalized her words. "I presume you know why."

He dismounted his horse and took her hands. His were cold, despite the summer heat. "As chatelaine, you have always offered hospitality even to the most beggarly. I ask you not to turn my sister away now. We need the haven and security of Montlimoux."

Dominique remained resolute. "Nonetheless, I will give your sister alms and food, then she must be on her way. Where, I care not."

Esclarmonde spit on her. "I will not take your alms, I will take your county!" She whirled on Francis. "Destroy the woman!"

Francis laid a brotherly hand on her shoulder. "You do not know what you say, Esclarmonde." He glanced at Dominique.

"She has been ill with fever since eve'tide."

Indeed, Esclarmonde's lovely face was flushed by more than rage or hate. She reached out a clinging hand to her brother's robe. "Francis!" she breathed.

"'T'will be all right," he reassured her. He looked to Dominique. "My sister needs your mercy."

"Mercy?" Dominique repeated, wiping the spittle from her cheek with the back of her hand. "Would your sister have shown my son mercy?"

Francis laid a hand on her arm. "Do this for the sake of an old friendship, Dominique."

She sighed then, losing the strength of her anger. She had no recourse. "Come along then." She installed them in separate chambers on the north wing of the chateau, a suite of rooms not much larger than the chateau larder.

At the chamber door, she asked Francis, "What of your parishioners? Who will care for their souls and administer the Last Rites?"

A peculiarly sad half-smile touched his beautiful mouth. "They are lost sheep, Dominique."

She had no time to dwell on his statement, nor the way he was keeping to his rooms, remaining aloof wheretofore he had been gregarious.

Within hours, a pestilence invaded the chateau itself.

She had never encountered its symptoms

before: ugly black knots beneath the skin, most often at the neck and the base of the armpits.

Esclarmonde showed the first signs. Her perfect skin gradually became marred with splotches. As the second night wore on, her swollen face turned into a grotesque mask. When Dominique tried to administer medicine, Esclarmonde shouted, "Do not touch me! 'Tis you who have cursed me so!"

Her ravings continued throughout that night. At one point, she was lucid enough to demand a looking glass. "I would see this hideous thing you have made of me!"

But Dominique denied her even so much as a glance. The sight of her face was enough to make any who had known the beautious maiden wretch. Francis was horrified by the knots protruding from his sister's malodorous body and kept a safe distance.

Finally, Esclarmonde fell silent in a stupor in which she intermittently awoke over the following days to recognize her surroundings. Piteously, she cried out for Francis, but he would not come. She refused to eat, and by the end of the week she was little more than a skeleton on her bed. Dominique was with her childhood friend at the last.

Esclarmonde clutched her hand tightly. A wild look glazed her eyes. "Dominique, I am so afraid! I see—oh, God, it is awful, the beast that awaits me!"

With a shriek, she threw up bony hands to cover her face. And then it was over. The breath of life left her.

Dominique did not have time to grieve. The pestilence was already fast at play within the chateau. Bodies were piling up in the outer ward, awaiting burial. Harried by the demands of the dying, she began to work ceaselessly in her laboratory.

Various urine samples from the stricken were sniffed and studied for discoloration, as was the blood that oozed from those knots that had become open sores. But she could discover nothing of note in the variations of experiments she carried out.

Discouraged, she went in search of the pestilence, confronting it at the bedsides of the dying. She resorted to a compress of boiled beetles and leeches for bloodletting. She tried Iolande's suggestion of newly baked bread applied to the lips to soak up the poison, then fires that were made to smoke abundantly to purify the air. Sponges were drenched with opium, mandrake, dried, then soaked in hot water and inhaled but nothing seemed to defeat this unseen enemy.

She feared naught for her own health. About her person, she knew, was an aura as protective as any knight's shield against the talons of death. But she worried incessantly for Chretien and Rainbaut and made sure they were kept away from the others. Daily, she saw to it that they received a concoction of milk of pulverized almonds, barley water mixed with honey, figs, and licorice.

Meanwhile, the inhabitants of the chateau sang and danced frantically until they fainted or fell dead themselves.

"They believe such acts will drive away demons and keep the dead from escaping their graves to infect the living," Iolande said contemptuously one afternoon as she brought wine and cheeses on a tray for her mistress.

The wine was among the last of the bottles left in the cellar, and the Brie cheese a portion Iolande had rescued from being distributed. The tray of food appeared incongruous among Dominique's array of lancets, needles, scalpels, scissors, and speculum.

Although she continued to try to save those afflicted with the plague, she was eyed with an increasing hostility that pained her. Whispers were rampant, some of which reached her. A witch, she was.

Fewer and fewer among her people would submit to her ministrations. She was tired, drained of all her force-energy and without hope. Over the chateau hung the odor of death, a sickly sweet smell that made wretching an ever-present possibility.

In the early hours of morning when she would seek out her bed at last, she would tell herself how foolish she was to work at concocting various elixirs or attempt to nurse her people through the plague. Not only was there little hope that any of them would survive, but there was that very great possibility she would pass the deadly disease on to Chretien or Rainbaut, who glowed with rosy health in the midst of death.

Nevertheless, the stricken people were just that—her people. Just as her female forebears were committed to the county, so, too, was she. And so, there were more endless hours spent in her laboratory, although mostly she resorted to common sense in her remedies for this black death.

As weary as she was, sleep would not come. It was not yet time to rise to nurse her sons, and sunrise was still another two hours away, so she lay there, remembering. Remembering Paxton and wanting, wanting, wanting. Wanting so badly the ache was worse than any wound. An endless ache. A hunger that would never go away.

She knew that thoughts had more power than deeds, and it appeared this morning she was correct, because at dawn Baldwyn knocked at her door. The gentle giant appeared as exhausted as she, and his usual merry black eyes were troubled. "My Lady Dominique, the sunrise silhouettes Paxton of Wychchester's standards against the northern horizon."

She rushed Beatrix and Marté with her robing. Beatrix's heightened color betrayed her excitement at being reunited with her English captain.

358

Dominique was not certain if excitement was what she herself was feeling. A part of her wanted to lash Paxton with her anger at his betrayal, another part of her wanted to withdraw so as to block any future pain, and still another part, a greater part—her heart— wanted to forget the past. People could change. Could she and Paxton change enough to rediscover that invisible, intangible cord that bound them as soulmates?

By midmorning, astride his giant war horse, Paxton and his troops of Flemish pikemen and archers crossed the drawbridge and through the portcullis that she had ordered opened. Dressed in her best, she awaited him in the Justice Room, fittingly presiding from the justice chair. Her heart was pounding so forcefully she thought it would surely split asunder. She heard his heavy mailed tred before she saw his tall body darken the doorway.

"Welcome, my Lord Lieutenant."

He advanced, taking off his metal gauntlets. His cloak was thrown over his shoulder to reveal a brigadine, that cheap, lighter leather jacket sewn with thin overlapping metal plates. When he was close enough, she could see that the lines in his face had hardened. He had not laughed nor found amusement for his soul during their separation. She supposed she should take pleasure in that, but his stringent expression told her that the reason for his return to Montlimoux did not bode well.

"My men will be quartered within the chateau," he said briskly without a trace of warmth or compassion, "so that they can sally out to protect nearby Aquitaine from French raids. To ensure your cooperation, Baldwyn Rainbaut has been taken hostage."

Her heart ceased its pumping. She sought out to strike back at this detested foreigner, this man she loved so bitterly. Into the dark silence of the chamber, she said, "Why not take your sons hostage as well, Paxton?"

His tanned skin yielded to a pallor. The hand that held his gauntlets trembled, the other tightened on his sheathed sword. When he spoke, his voice was ragged. "You speak—"

"The truth. Come with me, my Lord Lieutenant." The last was laced with vinegar.

As she led the way up the corkscrew staircase to the bedchambers, she could feel him so close behind her it was as if his breath stirred her veil. She reached their old chamber and opened the door. Iolande sat on a stool before the twins, who giggled at the tops with which they played.

"The Lord Lieutenant wishes to see his sons," Dominique said tonelessly.

Iolande nodded. Her hooded eyes flared then communicated a message of wary acquiescence. With her mouth pressed tightly in unspoken remonstrance, she passed the babies to Dominique but obstinately stayed close.

"This is Chretien," Dominique said, pressing one son forward, "and this is Rainbaut."

His laughter held the edge of iron. "Twins!"

What did Paxton mean to do? She broke the strained silence, saying, "Rainbaut is the oldest by a few moments."

Paxton tossed his gauntlets on the bed and took Chretien, holding him up beneath the tiny armpits to stare at the face with round, unblinking pebble-brown eyes. They stared back at him with solemn, but fascinated, interest. Paxton cleared his throat. "Why did you not tell me?"

"Pray tell, where would I find you to deliver news of the blessed event?"

He spared her a piercing glance. "It was you who sent me away."

She forced a curl of utter contempt to her lips. "You would have gone away, regardless, once your deceitful and despicable deed was done." Then she feigned a shudder of disgust at the sight of him.

He passed Chretien to Iolande. "I wish to be alone with your mistress," he told the old woman without looking at her. His heavy gaze held Dominique fast. She saw that time and weather had chisled their story on his face. After they were alone, he said, "When I leave Montlimoux, Baldwyn will be released as hostage but my sons come with me."

She sprang at him, her fingers arched like a cat's claws. "I shall see your soul destroyed first!"

He caught her arms and yanked her across the bed. In retribution, he took her mouth in a violent kiss, despite her mumbled protests. "You forget your pledge, Dominique. My will is your will."

She shook her head from side to side, but he repossessed her lips. His tongue was his sword, and he plundered and ravished her mouth. She answered his challenge with a kiss as fierce and demanding as his. She ceased to breathe, locked in that duel of passion.

At last, his mouth released hers. "The rumors across the land are right," he told her, taking the caution to capture her wrists above her head with his manacled grip. "You are a sorceress."

She glared up at him, not even attempting a rebuttal. Her lips were sore from his rapacious kiss, and somehow her tunic and camisole had gotten torn.

"All this time, I have tried to deny it, to refuse the spell you have cast on me. But I have come to break it, Dominique. And break you and Montlimoux, before I return to my country."

There were no tears in her left to cry at this ultimate rejection of her. She turned her head away. "You will leave an empty man, Paxton of

Wychchester," she whispered. "The rest of your life you will know only emptiness."

That night they slept with their backs to one another, but she sensed he was awake when she took first Chretien and then Rainbaut into bed with her to nurse them.

He found her in her chapel. She was sitting with her legs crossed and pondering God knew what. He broke in upon her meditation, as she called what she was doing. "I ride out today. Word has come that a French encampment has been erected as closeby as Albi."

She rose, her expression carefully controlled. "Do you know when you will return, my Lord Lieutenant?"

Or if he would return at all. She would doubtlessly be pleased to learn he suffered the same fate as his war horse, which emerged from the last fray bristling with arrows like a pincushion. "I have no idea. John will oversee any problems that may arise in my absence."

He started to turn away but was reluctant to leave with such hostility between them. His hand made a sweeping gesture of the chapel. "The room does not seem like a place of worship without the cross." He had meant to say something of a conciliatory nature, but his words affronted her, he could tell.

Her lips tightened. "I told you once, the cross for me symbolizes self-sacrifice instead of selflessness."

He faced her fully. "You know, Dominique, you are unlike even my wildest imaginations. You are like something out of the *Arabian Tales*, with animals changing into humans and magical happenings. I cannot understand you."

She clasped her hands demurely. "You can understand the Scriptures?"

"Certainly."

"Then reflect on the wild, incredible and impossible things that happen in their stories."

"But the stories have an underlying meaning."

"And as for magic," she continued, "think back on the Book of Numbers. A very great mystery is hidden there. By means of numbers, Paxton, one can perform all the operations for friendship, riches, honor, and all sorts of things—good and evil. But, as a Chinese sage once warned me, 'Only the worthy will find the key to the whole work.'"

With an exasperated sigh, he took his leave. He was no closer to understanding her than before. An image of her stayed with him throughout the duration of the maneuver: her face, her smile, with its piquant space between her teeth. Then there was her indomitable pride and resolution. He had to admit to himself that his will could never easily resist hers. He could not resist her, period.

She had spent an inordinate amount of time with Francis. Intimate hours, possibly. Had she cuckolded him with the priest?

Whether she had was not what plagued Paxton. It was the certain knowledge that he could not, could never, reconcile himself to this strange woman. He was surprised at the heaviness of his heart.

CHAPTER XXI

Dominique watched from the ramparts each afternoon for a sign of Paxton's return from the sally on the French encampment. She waited with foolish hope that she would see a relenting in his cold behavior toward her. Only toward Chretien and Rainbaut had his attitude softened. The little time Paxton had spent at the chateau before he had left was spent mostly with his sons.

Their sons, she amended.

As for Francis, he avoided her and the others at the chateau, almost as completely as he had avoided his sister at the last. Did he feel no remorse? She was too preoccupied with fighting the pestilence and fighting her weakening feelings for Paxton to give more than a fleeting thought to the bishop.

One afternoon, she spotted a calvacade and felt the first stirrings of joy, but by dusk the calvacade turned out to be little more than a peddlar with his packs of mules. Because of the plague, the gnome of a man would not enter the chateau walls, but spread his gew-gaws for all to examine at a safe distance.

Listlessly, she surveyed the hats, ribbons, gloves, pots, goose quills, and nappery and listened to his patter. "If 'tis not the French killing good folk, then 'tis the English. And if not the English, then the plague. Why I saw in Albi hills of bodies waiting for the funeral pyre."

Her heart contracted. "Was there any skirmishing between the English and the French?"

"That, too. But the damned plague, by the Virgin Mary, is the most accurate archer of all."

After the peddlar left, she retired to her room. A multitude of feelings assailed her. She did not know whether to be angry, throw up, or cry. True, she was angry at Paxton's cavalier treatment of her, but her fear he would be killed in a raid made her stomach sink the way it did when her gray jumped a gully. At last, she found it easier just to cry.

Paxton returned the next day. His countenance was as forbidding as ever. Blood smeared his armor-plate mail.

"Your raid was successful?" she asked in an indifferent voice.

"Aye." He pushed the fold of his cloak over one shoulder as if the act required great effort.

She tried to watch his aura and caught the red rage of violence before the color of dark gray slowed down the vibrations. Black, the absence of colors, the absence of the body's energy, lingered close. Alarmed, she crossed the chamber to him, but before she could reach him, he put a hand to his visor, swayed, and collapsed at her feet.

"Paxton!" She knelt beside him to pull off his chain mail. Under this, his tunic was sweat-dampened. Tearing it away, she beheld with a gasp the ugly black knots beneath his skin. She realized his soul was hovering in the clutches of the black pestilence.

"John!" she screamed. Panic beat at her throat like bat wings. "Someone! Help!"

Marté came running and, at the sight of Paxton sprawled on the floor, she turned back. With relief, Dominique heard her summoning help. While waiting, Dominique poured all her energy through her hands to Paxton's chest. It barely rose and fell. Concentrating, she could perceive the miasma of his breathing. It was the grayish-black of a swamp vapor.

That night, and on into the following days, she worked ceaselessly over Paxton, but his body's energies ebbed hourly. His body ap-

369

peared as ravaged by the plague as Baldwyn's was by leprosy.

This man had betrayed her time and again, yet she was fighting for his life, even to the point of breathing her own breath into him when once his breathing appeared to have stopped. Near dawn of another morning, she knew not how many mornings since his collapse, she faced the truth as she gazed upon his drawn face. Whatever this man was, however his male nature may threaten her, she loved him wholly. Fire could not burn her love, water could not drown it, old age could not diminish it. Her love may have seemed to be suppressed, but it could not be extinguished.

In those bleak, wrenching hours, others often came to Paxton's bedside to spell her, but rarely did she take the opportunity to sleep. Her gaze remain locked on her beloved's battle-scarred face.

One evening, in the hush of twilight, John came up behind where she and Iolande sat, keeping watch, and put his hand on her shoulder in a comforting gesture. "How is he, my Lady Dominique?"

She did not take her eyes off Paxton's face. "He raves. About Elizabeth." Bitterness ripped a ragged edge along her words.

John pulled up a stool and sat opposite her. In a low voice, he said, "My lady, ye must know that Paxton did not love Elizabeth. Obsessed with her initially, but loved her, no. In fact, he refused to share her bed once he learned she had willfully chosen to rid herself of his child, 'debased by serf's blood!' was the way she had told him."

"But to have murdered her for—"

"Nay, he did not. When he refused to bed her, she went to her father with a concocted charge that Paxton was conspiring to overthrow the old earl. When confronted, Paxton chose honor rather than explanation. He felt his conduct spoke for itself."

"What happened?"

"The earl, of course, believed his daughter and ordered Paxton flogged. Left for dead, he was hidden away and restored to health by his old tutor, the abbot."

Dominique closed her eyes. "Oh, John! Then Elizabeth's heartless actions must have confirmed in the most painful way the abbot's teachings of the perfidy of the female sex."

"While still recovering, Paxton discovered one afternoon that the tutor had left with the intention of secretly poisoning Elizabeth. As weak as Paxton was, I think he felt he could have made an effort to prevent Elizabeth's death. If he raves about her, it is because of the guilt he harbors, not because of his love for her."

So, the misogynous old abbot had had his triumph, but at what cost to his charge?

After John and Iolande took their leave, she smoothed the dampened hair back from Paxton's brow and laid a fresh cloth soaked in

Parris Afton Bonds

astringent on his forehead. His scars were
livid with the heat. On a nearby brazier she
burned a mixture of Indian root, myrrh, aloe,
olive oil, and tears. Her own.

Could she ever forgive Paxton the way he
had used her, forgive him his betrayal? Yes,
she knew that the capability was within her if
she but made the effort. But could he ever
love her as she did him? He did not countenance her free thinking. Besides. . . .

Besides, she loved him and that counted
everything else as nothing. In an instant of
dazzling foresight, she understood that her
English lieutenant also loved her. She understood that he had returned to Montlimoux not
to subjugate her but to protect her from the
warfare ravaging her county. She understood
that he had risked his life to come back.
Risking his life—that he did in every battle.
But he had risked for her something of far
more value to him—his pride.

With a heavy knock on her door, Baldwyn
entered the bedchamber. Since she was startled to see that he no longer wore the habit of
the Knight Templar, it was a moment before
she realized that his face was even more
mottled than usual. With him was John, his
mouth set in lines that had not been so grim
when he had taken his leave only moments
before.

In their wake, trailed a frightened Hugh.
Had the boy done something wrong? "What is
it, Baldwyn?"

He glanced at John. "The men and women camped in the outer ward are rioting, raiding the bakery. They claim you are hiding food from them. I have barred the keep and doubled the guards, but I do not know how long it will be before they try to storm our doors."

She looked to John. "What can be done?"

John's hand went to his sword. "The troop is out on reconnaissance, but I can muster the remaining guards."

After he hurried from the room, she rounded on Baldwyn and demanded, "But why? There is little food left to hide. They should know that, what with the hundreds of people crowded within the chateau grounds."

His mouth stretched thin. "They have been incited for a long time now."

"Incited? I do not understand, Baldwyn."

He took a deep breath and fixed her with eyes enflamed by rage. As the peasant says, 'An enemy who appears to be a friend is treacherous beyond all traitors.' Show her what you showed me, Hugh."

The boy shuffled forward, tugged at his hood respectfully so that his flaxen hair fell forward. His dirt-smudged little hand thrust out the scrap of parchment. His labored scrawl was difficult for her to decipher. "The bishop," she read, "sezs to the people that ye are a witch. For a long time, he sezs this to them."

She glanced from the parchment to Hugh. He nodded vigorously.

Baldwyn said, "They have been told you are responsible for the famine, for the plague, for their miseries."

Her mouth set in a determined line, she said, "I am going to find Francis."

"I am going with you," Baldwyn said.

With an anxious glance at Paxton, she knelt before Hugh. "Will you guard your liege lord until I can return?"

Self-importance nudged the beginnings of a smile onto the grimy face, and the boy nodded vigorously.

"Guard him with your life, Hugh, and when this is over, I shall present you with your own sword in preparation for becoming a knight!"

His round eyes widened, and his mouth broke into a full-fledged smile, revealing his missing front teeth.

Francis was not in his room. Feeling a pressure of time, she and Baldwyn hurried to the library but it, too, was empty. A questioning of the servants revealed little. "Mayhaps the chapel?" Manon offered.

The chapel, the Justice Room, the Great Hall, the kitchens—all empty. Then she knew. "The dungeon," she told Baldwyn.

The hinges of the dungeon's iron doors complained against being opened. Baldwyn held a taper aloft, lighting the spiraling staircase. For her, it was a descent into hell, because she realized whom Baldwyn had been trying to warn her against. The person seeking Montlimoux through her energy power, through her very soul, was none other than Francis de Beauvais! The knowledge struck her with horror.

Francis knew she knew, too. With a smile that she had once thought both warm and splendent, he turned from the laboratory counter to greet her and the Templar. His hair was dirty and unkempt, as was his soil-stained robe. She hardened her heart against this childhood love and fought the uncivilized urge to kill, to destroy this shell of a human before her. "For the sake of our old friendship, I will allow you to leave unharmed. But I want you out of the chateau and out of the county immediately!"

He remained sitting on the high stool, one arm casually draped on the counter, as if he had no fear of either of them. "I can save your Paxton, Dominique."

"I would never let you touch him. 'Twas you, was it not, who killed his cat and my falcon?"

He shrugged. "Necessary for my invocations. Through Paxton, I have access to your county, your energy power—your soul."

She shivered uncontrollably. "If you wanted my soul, then why did you declare me a witch to my people?"

"Because then you would be forced with the choice of burning at the stake or, with the blessing of the people, of delivering yourself into my priestly hands for safety. And the safety of your soul into my hands, as well."

"You wrestled for your sister's soul, too, didn't you?"

"I didn't have to. She loved me enough to do my will. Enough to unite with Denys in destroying all that was yours, even your sons, so there would be none left for you to love but me." In his narrow face, his eyes glowed like fiery coals. How could she ever have thought him handsome? "Join me, Dominique, in my quest for the ultimate power, and I will help you save your Paxton and deliver him back into England's hands."

Disgust welled in her. "You cannot even save yourself, Francis. Your magic will never wrought that miracle."

From the top of the stairs came Iolande's urgent cry, "Dominique, come quickly! Paxton is dying!"

"Begone from here today," Dominique flung at Francis, "or I shall see you quartered by four horses whipped to the four directions." Then she whirled to hurry up the staircase to Iolande—and to Paxton.

Bending over him, she saw the rosy blush of imminent death. She covered her face with her hands, weeping hot, angry tears. Rage at her beloved's needless death boiled over her. "I should have had Francis killed!"

Baldwyn said, "Is there nothing you can do for Paxton, my Lady Dominique?"

She hesitated, because the one hope lay in doing what for her had always been the unthinkable. "At the right moment, I can give all." She stressed the word "all." "All my energies, completely surrendering myself to Paxton."

Baldwyn's forehead knit in confusion, and she elaborated. "It is that liquid form, the female fluids, that carry the most powerful of energies."

"But Paxton's Church teaches the sin of carnality," Baldwyn responded in a frayed voice.

"His Church teaches also the gift of selflessness," she reminded him.

She knew that one's sexual energy was the closest energy to the Divine force because during lovemaking merging took place and the life force radiated and created life. It was the Divine reaching out through matter in order to experience Itself.

She understood what the nature of this sacrifice demanded of her. But was the coarser earthly love given by one physical and emotional body for another worth her soul? Was this what Divine love was?

The answer came to her in a small, still inner voice. *By losing, we find. By giving, we receive.*

She drew a steadying breath, then touched Baldwyn's shoulder. "I wish to be alone with Paxton for the next forty-eight hours."

Baldwyn rose from the stool. Iolande was there at his side at once. He said, "I can only hope John and his soldiers can keep the mob outside at bay for that long."

When she was alone with Paxton, she barred the door and opened the shutters to the fresh night air. Then she disrobed and went to his side. As never before, she devoted her complete self, every particle of her being, to focusing on his recovery. She used her energy in so many ways—in her hands to heal, in her throat to speak her love, in her flesh upon his.

Each hour she could see him growing stronger and each hour further debilitated her. She was like a sand glass, with time and life draining from her.

That hour between dark and dawn, a thunderous noise echoed along the corridors of the floor below. The mob had broken through the donjon door!

Even Paxton stirred at the roar of enraged voices. His lids opened. Confusion at their nakedness and the shouting outside narrowed his eyes. He made to rise and fell back weakly. "What. . . ."

"You have been very ill," she said, feeling it an effort even to speak. The moment had arrived, she knew, when she and Paxton were balanced, when even another hour would tip the scales of life's breath in the other direction. The time had come for her ultimate seduction of her lover.

She moved up over him. Bewildered, uncertain, his gaze roamed her face for answers.

Her kiss was her answer. His eyes took light, and she knew he understood.

She stroked the broad planes of his face, his chest where the hair whorled around his nipples, his groin, the base of his sex until it was turgid. Paxton's hands closed over her and drew her down under him. With the riotous mob thundering throughout the chateau, he took possession of her slowly, lovingly, while the moment crescendoed. She saw in his eyes the reflection of that wonder in her own, that recognition of souls who learn how to dance through each other. She felt she was drawing near a most exquistely powerful energy source.

Inside her, a voice, her Divine self, whispered, "You cannot merge until the heart opens."

She let her heart's chambers flood with her love for Paxton. A frightening feeling of traveling through the vortex of a tunnel of darkness clamped around her. "Love is a refining, sublimating force," her inner voice said, urging her forward.

She fought off her paralyzing fear and continued her solitary journey. She could feel the centrifugal force around her, spinning off that which did not have life. What was happening to her? An energy was seeking through her its own kind, gathering itself with a perfect pulsation until . . . it formed one law, one work, one vessel. Male activity from the gold, female from the silver, to get from the union that which perfects the mercury of both metals. Both fused into one symbol. She understood now the secret that alchemy held for the seeker of truth of knowledge: that the union of male and female form one powerful, indestructible whole!

She held the flicker to the flame and felt the flutter of the Divine. Waves of energy kept flooding over her. Around her and Paxton shimmered a radiance, that ineffable light that haloed them as they drew higher and nearer the well-spring of creation.

Between them the circuit at last closed, and a sudden joy surged through them with their transcendance. Their conjoined energy had created something entirely new.

At that penultimate moment, her finite mind crossed the threshhold to another dimension, and she recognized her soul's counterpart in Paxton!

The wind sang, the leaves clapped their hands, and the morning stars exploded their fireworks. In that instant, she realized that surrender brought not death nor the inability to survive, but always the birth of something new. By surrendering, everything changed, so that she and Paxton were a part of that grand flow.

As all moments must, this one, too, passed. The tumult in the chateau was gone, and all was quiet while the universe spun its cosmic web of pearls.

Gradually, a strange, orange glow filled the room, and Paxton rose to walk across to the window. Beyond the chateau, a fire raged. "What is it? he asked.

"A midsummer bonfire," she said from their bed. Later, much later, she would explain to him what her intuition told her with a certainty, that the fire was Francis de Beauvais's immolation on the faggots of a pyre. The mob had found its witch.

He returned to the bed, and drew her into the circle of his arms. She allowed her lips to curl in a lovely, subtle smile. As she had neared the moment of dying, laying down her body with grace and embracing death from the position of mastery and not fear, she knew that she was forever after the master. Or the mistress, she amended.

She snuggled within Paxton's embrace as he began to softly kiss that delicious area behind and beneath her ear, but he ceased this delightful pasttime to raise on one elbow. His big hand aligned itself with the contours of her cheek. "You are wonderous beyond all women," he breathed.

She reached up to trace his upper lip. There was such joy in her that she found it difficult to be serious. "Would you by any chance, sire, be needing an excellent alchemist at your castle in Pernbroke?"

He would not match her light mood. "Pernbroke is in the past."

She was afraid to hope. "Truly, you do not

intend to fight for England?"

"I am finished with violence." Then, with a solemn countenance, he drew her from the warmth of their coverlets to stand before him. Next, he astonished her by kneeling on one knee before her. Tears glistened in his eyes. "I am your liege man of life and limb and of earthly and eternal worship, my Lady Dominique, my love."

Addington, Jack Ensign. *The Secret of Healing*. Science of Mind Publications, 1979.

Allmand, Christopher. *The Hundred Years War*. Cambridge University Press, 1988.

Bach, Richard. *Bridge Across Forever*. Morrow, 1984.

Bentley, James. *Languedoc*. Salem House Publishers, 1987.

Bisson, Thomas. *N. Medieval France*. Hambledon Press, 1989.

Bondi, Julia. *Lovelight*. Pocket Books, 1989.

Bowden, Muriel. *A Commentary on the General Prologue to the Canterbury Tales*. The Macmillan Company, 1959.

Bracegirdle, Cyril. "High Life in Cold Castles." *In British Heritage.* Historical Times, Inc., 1987.

Burke, John. *The Castle in Medieval England*. British Heritage Press, 1987.

Campbell, Joseph. *The Power of Myth*. Doubleday, 1988.

Capra, Fritjof. *Tao of Physics*. Shambhala, 1983.

Clephan. *The Tournament.*

Clive, H. P. *Marguerite of Navarre*. Grant & Cutler, 1983.

Daraul, Arkon. *Secret Societies*. Octagon Press, 1983.

Gagnière, Sylvain. *The Palace of the Popes at Avignon*. Les Amis Du Palais Du Roure, 1985.

Gies, Joseph and Frances. *Life in a Medieval City*. Harper Colphon Books, 1969.

Grisom, Chris. *Time is an Illusion*. Fireside Book, 1986. *Ecstasy*. Fireside Book, 1987.

Huffines, LaUna. *Bridge of Light*. Simon & Schuster, Inc., 1989.

LaCroix, Paul. *France in the Middle Ages*. Frederich Ungar Publishing, 1963.

Mathers, S. L. Mac Gregor. *The Book of the Sacred Magic of Abramelin the Mage*. Dover Publications, 1975.

Munro, Dana Carleton. "A Period of New Life." *In The Twelfth Century Renaissance*. Robert E. Krieger Publishing, 1969.

Panouillé, Jean-Pierre, *The City of Carcassonne*. Ouest France, 1984.

Rowley, Sam R. *Discovering Falconry*. New Dawn, 1985.

Samson, Jack. *Modern Falconry*. Stackpole, 1984.

Shahar, Shulamith. *The Fourth Estate*. Methuen, Inc. 1983.

Silberer, Herbert. *Hidden Symbolism of Alchemy and the Occult Arts*. Dover Publications, 1971.

Skeat, Rev. Walter W. *Early English Proverbs*. Folcroft Library Edition, 1974.

Strayer, Joseph R. *Albigensian Crusade*. Doubleday, 1971.

Weber, Eugen. *The Western Tradition*. D. C. Heath & Co., 1965.

Wheeler, Sir Mortimer. *The English Medieval House*. Harper Colophon Books, 1983.

SPECIAL SNEAK PREVIEW!

PROUD PILLARS RISING

By Ana Leigh

"Ana Leigh's historical romances always captivate readers!"

—*Romantic Times*

Enjoy a selection from Ana Leigh's fabulous new historical romance, Proud Pillars Rising.

Fascinated by tales of the Wild West, Margaret Collingswood was thrilled to learn that she had inherited a ranch in the Dakota Territory from the father she'd never known. Traveling to Deadwood with her mother, stepfather, and sister, she longed to break away from the restraints imposed by her all too proper family . . . to discover real-life adventure . . . to finally meet the rugged Western hero she'd always dreamed of. . . .

**ON SALE IN DECEMBER—
AT BOOKSTORES AND NEWSTANDS
EVERYWHERE**

"Margaret, I insist you wear a dress," Katherine Collingswood demanded the following morning.

Maggie paused, jeans in hand. "But why do—"

"And I will not tolerate an argument," Katherine asserted. "My dear child, you were born a girl. It's high time you begin dressing and acting like one."

Diane's mouth curved into a vain smile. "What would be the purpose, Mother? She would still have a boy's haircut." She pulled a hair brush through her own long, golden strands. "Will you help me pin my hair, Mother?"

When Katherine turned away and began to

fuss with her younger daughter's curls, Maggie quickly slipped into her jeans and boots. "I'll be with Father." She sped from the room before her mother could voice any further objection.

Taylor Collingswood was not alone when Maggie paused in the door of the dining room. He rose to his feet and waved to her. "Here's Margaret now."

The man to whom Taylor spoke stood up and stared with curiosity at Maggie as she approached the table. Although he was as tall as Taylor, his body was heavier and more muscular. He had a thick thatch of gray hair, and bushy eyebrows dominated his face. Maggie guessed the man to be in his late fifties.

"Margaret, this gentleman is William Godfrey."

"How do you do, sir," Maggie said politely, feeling uncomfortable under the man's continued scrutiny.

"The pleasure is mine, Miss Harris . . . ah, Miss Collingswood."

"Mr. Godfrey is a local banker, dear," Taylor added as he drew a chair for her to be seated.

Maggie smiled nervously at the man, and after an awkward silence, Godfrey commented, "Your father and I were close friends, Miss Collingswood. Forgive me for staring, but you bear a remarkable resemblance to him."

Maggie had never seen a picture of her father. Intrigued, her interest in this man perked up considerably.

"I hope your trip to Deadwood was a pleasant one," Godfrey commented.

"Didn't Father tell you our stage got held up yesterday?"

"Good grief!" Godfrey exclaimed. "I hope no one was injured."

Taylor smiled cordially. "No, none of us are worse for the experience, and we even recovered all our valuables."

The conversation ended abruptly with the appearance of Katherine and Diane. As soon as Taylor dispensed introductions, William Godfrey donned his Stetson and shook hands with Taylor. "I will return shortly with a carriage to transport you and your trunks to Sam's ranch."

"A ranch! My father had a ranch?" Maggie's eyes gleamed with the excitement of this unexpected discovery, the fulfillment of her long-time dream—a ranch.

Godfrey nodded. "A horse ranch. Sam Harris ran the best horseflesh in the state." He paused momentarily and smiled down at Margaret. "I think you'll like the Lazy H, Maggie."

"My daughter's name is Margaret, Mr. Godfrey," Katherine sharply reminded him. "Sam Harris called her Maggie, that hideous name, to aggravate me."

"My apologies, Mrs. Collingswood."

Godfrey nodded politely. "Ladies, enjoy your breakfast."

Katherine cast a critical glance at the back of the departing banker. "He certainly doesn't look like any banker I've ever met, Taylor. And I think he was much too familiar with Margaret."

In an effort to appease her, Taylor patted Katherine's hand. "It was improper, Katherine, but Mr. Godfrey was a close friend of Sam Harris. Perhaps your late husband often spoke of Margaret with him."

"Well, he still had no business addressing Margaret so familiarly. And in public, too." She swung her disapproving glance toward her eldest daughter. "Of course, Margaret, your manner of dress invites such brash informality."

Maggie was only half listening to her mother's complaints. She had heard them often enough to recite the lamentations from memory. Maggie had to admit her mother might be right about William Godfrey. The way he stared at her was strange. And why would he call her Maggie? Or could Taylor be right? Possibly, Sam Harris *had* spoken of her so often to his friend that the nickname just slipped naturally through William Godfrey's lips. Maggie smiled with pleasure. Perhaps her father had cared for her, after all.

Anxiously awaiting the banker's return, Maggie barely touched her food. Her eyes remained riveted on the window. She jumped to her feet as soon as she saw William Godfrey approach in a shay. By the time they joined him outside the hostelry, Godfrey had a buckboard pulled up behind the carriage. "I'll drive the buckboard if you can handle the shay, Mr. Collingswood."

Taylor eyed the pair of spirited-looking black horses harnessed to the rig. "I don't see why not," he replied.

When the trunks had been loaded, Katherine and Diane seated themselves under the carriage's canopy, but Maggie climbed up onto the spring seat of the buckboard. With a flick of the reins, the wagon pulled away. Taylor followed behind with the shay.

Casting a grin at Maggie, Godfrey commented, "I can see what Sam meant. He told me you have a lot of mettle."

Her father's neglect of her still struck a sensitive nerve in Margaret Collingswood. "How would he know? He never knew me."

Her belligerent tone caused Godfrey to glance over at the girl. The man could see a lot of Sam Harris in the resentful expression on her face. She was a scrapper. This wasn't going to be as easy as he had hoped.

"I guess Sam figured a daughter of his couldn't be any other way," Godfrey responded lightly in reply to her feisty comment.

"Only he didn't think I was worth the effort to find out for himself, did he?"

Maggie fell into a brooding silence the rest of the way to the ranch, asking only an occasional question about the sights. After an hour's ride, they reached the ranch.

Her expectations had not prepared her for the size of the ranch house. Maggie's eyes widened in amazement when she spied the long, double-winged log house stretched out before them. "It's . . . so big," she stammered.

"Sam added another wing just before . . . he left," Godfrey said slowly.

A small building, which appeared to be a smokehouse, stood near a large barn and the bunkhouse. Several horses romped in a mammoth corral several hundred yards from the main house.

Katherine Collingswood, just as astounded, gushed forth. "This all belonged to Sam?" she gasped as her husband assisted her out of the carriage.

William Godfrey appeared to be well-known to the household staff. An Oriental servant opened the door, nodded politely to the banker, and after a few whispered instructions, scurried off.

Maggie loved the interior of the house on first sight. Roomy and masculine, a stone fireplace occupied one complete wall, and a long dining table framed by a dozen chairs stood at the other end of the large room. Several leather sofas and chairs were dispersed throughout.

Braided, oval-shaped rugs, scattered over a hardwood floor, which showed signs of a recent polishing with beeswax, added additional warmth.

William Godfrey motioned for them to sit down, then seated himself behind a large oak desk.

However, Maggie, attracted to a painting of an Indian hanging above the fireplace, walked over to have a closer look. The Indian's hair hung to his shoulders, and two eagle feathers dangled from a plait at the side of his strong, square jaw. The artist had captured wisdom in the dark eyes which seemed to focus on her, penetrating her very soul. Mesmerized, Maggie stared at the face in the painting.

"He's magnificent," she murmured. "Who is he?"

William Godfrey glanced up at the portrait. "Screaming Eagle. An Oglala chieftain."

"An Oglala?" Maggie asked.

"The Oglalas are a tribe of Dakota Sioux," Godfrey added as she returned her attention to the portrait.

The reappearance of the servant with a coffee tray interrupted the discussion. Godfrey quickly offered a cup to Katherine, then added a generous measure of whiskey to Taylor's cup, as well as to his own.

Unable to withdraw her gaze, Maggie remained entranced by the dignified face in the portrait.

William Godfrey settled down behind the

desk and took a deep draught of the liquid. "The ranch house is spacious, and I'm confident all of you will find it much more comfortable than the hotel," he declared. "I regret, however, you'll have to—" Suddenly, the words died in his throat, and the banker rose to his feet, his face creased in surprise.

All eyes shifted to the object of his attention. Maggie spun around, then gasped with pleasure at the sight of Dakota MacDonald framed in the doorway.

"Dakota!" Godfrey exclaimed.

"What in heaven's name is *he* doing here?" Katherine disparaged.

Ignoring her boorishness, Godfrey crossed to the door and shook hands with Dakota. Then forsaking formality, he pulled the younger man into his arms and hugged him. "When did you get back, son?"

"Last night," Dakota said succinctly.

Smiling sadly, Godfrey stepped back. "I can't tell you how badly I feel about Sam's . . ." His eyes shifted downward, unable to meet Dakota's pain-wracked stare. "He was my best friend."

"How did it happen, Will?" A deep huskiness edged the younger man's voice. "Yen Ching said you were with Sam when the accident happened."

Godfrey nodded. "Sam spied a herd of wild horses on the northern slope of Twin Buttes and took off after one of 'em. His horse stepped into a chuckhole and stumbled. They both went over the edge of the bluff."

"Was he riding Diablo?"

Godfrey nodded.

Dakota shook his head. "Can't understand it. That black of his was as sure-footed as a mule."

Katherine Collingswood's frigid voice shattered the exchange of grief. "Mr. Godfrey, may I ask why this . . . person . . . is being offered an explanation when my daughter and I are the two people directly affected by Mr. Harris's death?"

Anger flashed temporarily in Godfrey's eyes as he turned to the woman. "I beg your pardon, Mrs. Collingswood, forgive my oversight. This is Dakota MacDonald. Sam Harris's other heir."

"Other heir!" Katherine appeared to be on the verge of swooning. She drew out a handkerchief and began to fan and dab at her brow with the dainty piece of lacy linen. "Are you saying Sam fathered this . . . half-breed?"

Maggie was perplexed. She had heard the Army colonel refer to Dakota's father as a trapper, but Taylor had told her Sam Harris had been a soldier in the Army.

Her gaze lingered on Dakota. If, in truth, this man was her brother, she could understand why she had felt such empathy for him from the first moment she saw him.

"I don't believe this . . . Indian . . . is Margaret's brother." Katherine fired another insult.

Maggie's heart ached for Dakota MacDonald. To learn of his father's death was a tragic homecoming for the soldier, and her mother's insensitivity to his grief was unforgivable.

Godfrey cleared up the confusion as he continued, "Madam, will you let me finish, please? Dakota's father was a Scottish trapper by the name of Angus MacDonald, and his mother, a Sioux Indian named White Dove. Seventeen years ago, they found Sam severely wounded and they nursed him back to health. The next year, when Angus and White Dove were killed, Sam took their boy, Dakota, and raised him as his own."

Dakota remained unflinching as he listened to Godfrey's explanation. Despite the inscrutable expression on the half-breed's face, Maggie sensed Dakota's scorn for these people who cared nothing about Sam's death, much less that of his parents. Sam's fortune had been their only purpose for coming to Deadwood.

Dakota's gaze scanned the room and came to rest on her. With a sickening awareness, Maggie realized his contempt included her. She shook her head in denial. *No. It's not true. I'm not like them,* she silently pleaded.

For a few breathless seconds, Dakota's gaze remained fixed on Maggie, then he turned his head away.

Godfrey called out to Dakota who had moved to depart. "Dakota, come in and sit down. Sam's will concerns you, too."

"I've got no claim on anything of Sam's," Dakota said. "I'll get my gear and clear out."

"I wholeheartedly concur with your decision, Mr. MacDonald," Katherine interjected, her face twisted in contempt.

Godfrey threw the woman an exasperated look. "Please stay, Dakota. Sam wanted it this way." He withdrew an envelope from his briefcase. "Sam instructed me to give this to you."

Reluctantly, Dakota walked over and accepted the sealed document. Maggie noticed the envelope was identical to the one she had received from Sam Harris.

Godfrey extracted another paper from his case. "Now that both heirs are present, I'll deliver the will." He cleared his throat nervously and began to read aloud.

"I, Samuel Houston Harris, being of sound mind, do hereby declare this document to be my last will and testament.

"To my daughter, Margaret Ann Harris, also known as Margaret Ann Collingswood, and to my ward, Dakota MacDonald, I leave my ranch, the Lazy H, and all possessions thereon.

"Furthermore, Margaret Harris and Dakota MacDonald are to share equally in the considerable fortune I have amassed in recent years due to a gold strike and shrewd investments. Each heir has been given one half of the map that will direct them to the site of the buried fortune. Should Maggie and Dakota seek the fortune together, I have no doubt they will experience heretofore undreamed of treasure.

"However, if one party chooses not to seek the fortune, then the entire inheritance, including the Lazy H, reverts to the other heir.

"In the event neither heir wishes to seek the fortune, then the Lazy H and all of my buried wealth reverts to my trusted colleague and executor, William Godfrey."

"Absurd. It cannot be!" Katherine screamed.

Godfrey paused momentarily to glower disapprovingly over the top of the document.

Utterly astonished, Maggie looked at Dakota whose face showed no emotion. His eyes stared far off into space as if he had not heard a word. In truth, the reading of Sam's will disgusted him, and his inheritance was of no significance to him. Dakota's thoughts were concentrated solely on Sam, his father and friend gone forever.

Godfrey continued to read.

"To my beloved wife, Katherine Harris, and former commanding officer, Taylor Collingswood, I leave my forgiveness—along with two return tickets to Washington D.C.

"Any interference on the part of Katherine or Taylor to prevent my heirs from receiving their inheritance will result in the release of a document which will be politically and socially damaging to Mrs. Harris and Mr. Collingswood.

"And now, having disposed of my earthly possessions, I shall muse from aloft on angels, coyotes and 'just desserts.' Samuel Houston Harris."

"Why, that's blackmail," Taylor blustered.

"How dare that hypocritical reprobate threaten us," Katherine added, her face pinched with anger. "Insanity! Just the sort of thing I'd expect from Sam Harris. He always had a flair for the dramatic," Katherine ranted. "Taylor, we'll hire a lawyer from the East to have this ridiculous document declared invalid."

The banker ignored her outburst and peered across the desk at Maggie and Dakota. "Are the conditions of the will clear to both of you? If either of you refuses to honor Sam's first request, the ranch reverts to the other. If both of you refuse the last request, the fortune reverts to me."

Dakota leaned back and grinned. "Sam must have been high on coyote juice when he concocted this one."

"He was as sober as a judge," Godfrey denied. "The will is legal and cannot be nullified."

By this time, Taylor Collingswood had regained his composure. "I'm inclined to agree with my wife, Mr. Godfrey. The will is too bizarre to be taken seriously."

Katherine rose to her feet and began to pace the floor. "I was the wife of Sam Harris at the time of his death. Legally, his wealth should revert to me."

Diane, who had uttered barely a word since their arrival, spoke out to contradict her mother. "How could you have been Mr. Harris's wife when you're married to my father?"

Irritated, Katherine turned on her daughter. "Just hush, Diane. This doesn't concern you."

The young girl broke into sobs. "It does too concern me if you and Father aren't married. That makes me a bas . . . illegitimate."

Taylor rushed to embrace his daughter. "Now, now, honey, this is all a mistake. Of course, your mother and I are legally married." However, he failed to confess to the distressed girl that the remarriage had transpired the day before they had departed for the Dakota Territory.

Maggie and Dakota were forgotten in the uproar of Katherine's shouting, Diane's bawling, and Taylor's officiousness, along with William Godfrey's efforts to placate them all.

The whole situation had become too over-whelming for Maggie to comprehend. She glanced at Dakota who had just opened the envelope and was studying a jagged piece of map.

She felt torn between crying and scream-ing. The whole affair was becoming a circus. Maggie surmised that Sam Harris must be laughing at all of them from his grave. Unable to bear the scene another moment, she dashed from the room.

Maggie raced across the yard to the corral. Breathless, she stopped by the fence and stared for several moments through unseeing eyes at the horses confined within the area.

"Are they always like that, kid?"

Startled, she looked up to discover Dakota MacDonald beside her, casually chewing on a piece of straw. Maggie, embarrassed by her family's actions, remained loyal to them and rallied to their defense. She raised her eyes with belligerent regard. "The trip has been very exhausting for my family, Mr. MacDon-ald. Being jostled about in a coach and threat-ened at gunpoint has been a shattering experience for us." Maggie purposefully in-cluded herself as one of them and lifted her head proudly. "I think we are conducting ourselves admirably, Mr. MacDonald."

Dakota hooked a booted foot over a rung of the fence. "Well, if you don't rein up, you're all gonna choke on each other's dust."

A lengthy silence ensued. Maggie stole several sideward glances at Dakota as he stared impassively at the grazing horses. She sensed he had said his piece and had put the matter out of his mind. Finally, she broached the subject foremost in her thoughts. "What do you intend to do?"

Dakota slowly straightened his tall frame. "Ride out to the north range."

"I mean what do you intend to do about Sam Harris's will?"

Dakota tossed aside the stalk of straw he was chewing. "Do about it? I've half a mind to go on a treasure hunt." The faint glimmer in his eyes revealed a side to his nature Maggie never suspected. Dakota MacDonald had a sense of humor.

Maggie squared her shoulders, cocked her hat, and thrust up a delicate, but determined, chin. "Well, if you do, you can bet your britches, Mr. Dakota MacDonald, I'm going with you."

For several seconds Dakota stared down at Maggie, torn between putting her over his knee or shaking the pesky girl until her brain rattled. Instead, he turned and headed toward the stable.

Determined not to be put off, Maggie followed, running to keep up with his rapid strides. "Remember, Mr. MacDonald, I have the other part of the map."

Dakota stopped and glowered down at her. "You know, kid, you're a real pain in the ass."

Maggie, not easily thwarted, returned the fire. "Please stop calling me 'kid.' Kids are baby goats. And another thing, watch your language in the presence of a lady."

"Lady? That's a laugh. Get smart, kid, take

some . . . lady lessons . . . from your older sister."

Older sister! Did he actually believe simpering, whiny Diane was older than she? Maggie thought, astonished. Just because Diane was prettier and dressed herself up like a peacock out for a Sunday stroll didn't make her sister smarter. *Oh, men are so . . . dumb!* How could she have thought he would be different?

Diplomacy was not one of Margaret Collingswood's redeeming qualities. Hands on hips, her emerald eyes flashed as her temper flared. "I want you to know I happen to be eighteen years old. If you'd bother to look beyond Diane's blond hair and fluttering eyes, you'd realize I'm two years older and ten times smarter than my sister. Boy, I declare, nothing that walks or crawls on this earth is as stupid as a man."

"That why do you run around dressed like one?" Dakota strode away, leaving Maggie sputtering for a retort.

Dakota could hardly believe the kid was eighteen; he had reckoned fourteen, fifteen at the most. But then, a gal dressed as a boy with most of her face hidden under the brim of a hat, well, her age would be anybody's guess.

By the time Maggie caught up with him, Dakota had already gone into the stable and had begun to saddle a horse. "Just where are you going?" she demanded to the broad width of his shoulders.

Dakota gritted his teeth, swung the saddle

over the horse's back, and turned around. He shoved his hat back on his forehead and glared down at her. "Let's get something squared away. I ain't planning on spending the next six months picking your straw out of my hair. So just ride wide of me, kid . . . ah, *lady.*"

Maggie understood the reason for his hostility. He had angered her and she had reacted as nastily as her mother. Feeling contrite, Maggie offered an apology. "I'm sorry, Dakota. I didn't mean to crowd you. I just want us to be friends." She turned and walked toward the house.

As he cinched the saddle girth, Dakota lifted his head and watched Maggie walk away. The kid looked pathetic, the picture of dejection. He could not understand why in hell he should feel guilty, but with a grimace of self-reproach, he called out to her. "Hey, kid."

Maggie stopped and turned her head.

"I'm heading up to the north range. Want to ride along?"

She grinned broadly. "Sure." Maggie ran back to the stable.

"Get me the roan mare. I'll saddle her for you."

Maggie looked helplessly at several horses in nearby stalls and wondered which one was the roan mare. Dakota eyed her quizzically. "You *can* ride?"

Unflinchingly, she answered, "Of course. I

just have trouble telling a roan mare from a . . ."—her mind groped desperately for a suitable word—". . . stallion."

Dakota grinned to himself and swallowed the obvious bawdy response. "The one in the last stall."

Maggie approached the tawny-colored horse, relieved to see the mare didn't appear as tall and formidable as the horse she had ridden in Washington. "We're going to be great friends, aren't we?" she whispered.

The mare snorted and regarded her through large black eyes. Maggie's quandary bordered on desperation. She did so want to ride with Dakota but would the horse be of the same mind?

Gingerly, she reached out to pat the animal. When the mare accepted the fondling, Maggie grew bolder. Soon she had forgotten her purpose for approaching the animal and stroked the horse with both hands while cooing affectionately in the mare's ear.

"You planning on riding that horse or just talking it to sleep?" Dakota asked, suddenly appearing beside her.

"She's so beautiful," Maggie enthused, stepping aside so Dakota could saddle the mare. "What's her name?"

"Last time I knew, she didn't have one."

"May I call her Tiger?" Maggie asked.

"Call her anything you want," Dakota said, shrugging his shoulders. "Sounds more like a cat than a horse, though," he added.

Maggie pressed her cheek against the horse. "I know, but she's the color of a big, tawny cat."

Dakota led the two horses out of the stable and handed Maggie the mare's reins. Her mind raced as she tried to recall the instructions in the textbook. Stand close to the horse . . . Face its tail . . . Gather all reins in the left hand . . . Grab a handful of withers . . . She cast her eyes heavenward and said a quick, silent prayer. With a show of bravado, she put her foot in the stirrup and swung herself onto the horse.

"Let me lengthen those stirrups," Dakota said. "Your legs are longer than I thought."

While he lowered each strap, Maggie adjusted to the feel of being in the saddle. She wished she would have had time for another riding lesson before coming to Deadwood. One lesson was not enough to give a person confidence. However, this time the ground did not appear to be so far away. When Dakota finished, Maggie grasped the reins. *Don't jerk them,* she warned herself. She planted each foot firmly in a stirrup and lightly pressed her knees into the horse.

To Maggie's immense relief, the horse stepped forward.

Fortunately, the terrain prevented any fast galloping. Within a short time, she found herself relaxing, and the thousand fluttering butterflies in her chest and stomach settled down.

Maggie became enthralled with the spectacular scenery. Even Dakota's silence did not disturb her. She felt a sense of companionship as they rode side by side.

When he finally reined up and climbed off his horse, Maggie remained in the saddle, watching intently as Dakota got down on bended knee to study the ground.

Dakota stood up and walked over to the edge of the butte. For several moments he stared down at the steep drop. "This is where it happened," he said somberly.

Maggie knew he was referring to Sam Harris's accident. She dismounted awkwardly and moved beside him. Scattered brush and trees dotted the steep sides of the declivity that ended in a dry gulch several hundred feet below.

Directly opposite and at a deceptively close distance, since the span gaped too wide for man or animal to leap, stood the face of another butte, similar in height and width. Buffeted by freezing blasts of the north wind sweeping across from Canada, the vegetation grew less dense there than on the twin slope.

Maggie stared down solemnly at the gulch between the buttes. A pall hung over the site; not a bird chirped nor a leaf stirred. The throb of her heartbeat seemed to clamor in her ears. Sadly, she turned away.

Dakota tied the horses' reins to nearby shrubs and grabbed a rope attached to his saddle.

"What are you going to do?" Maggie asked at the sight of his grim, determined face.

"I'm going down there."

"You mean climb down? Isn't there a way of approaching from below?"

Dakota shook his head. "Not from this side. We'd have to ride for hours to skirt the bluff." As he talked, Dakota tied the rope firmly to a tree. "I won't be gone long. I just have to drop about fifty feet, then I can make it to the bottom on foot."

Maggie was astonished. "You mean you've done this before?" She walked over for another look at the steep drop.

Dakota pulled his rifle out of the scabbard on his saddle. "Can you handle a rifle?"

Maggie shook her head.

He proceeded to show her how to cock the gun. "If you have a problem, point it in the air and pull the trigger to signal me."

Surprised at the weight of the gun, Maggie cocked the gun once and gave a hesitant response. "All right . . . I understand." Maggie felt uncomfortable being left alone. She had an uneasy feeling about the place, and the thousand butterflies began to flutter in her stomach again.

She held the rifle firmly as she watched Dakota climb over the side of the bluff and lower himself down the rope. When he reached the end, he grabbed a sapling and cautiously began a zigzag course from scrub to tree until he reached the bottom.

"Heck, it doesn't look hard at all," Maggie reasoned aloud. "He even went down standing up." That thought was all the incentive she needed to follow him. Laying the rifle on the ground, and without hesitation, she lowered herself over the side.

FOREVER GOLD

Catherine Hart's books are "Beautiful! Gorgeous! Magnificent!"
— Romantic Times

FOREVER GOLD. From the moment Blake Montgomery held up the westward-bound stagecoach carrying lovely Megan Coulston to her adoring fiance, she hated everything about the virile outlaw. How dare he drag her off to an isolated mountain cabin and hold her for ransom? How dare he kidnap her heart, when all he could offer were forbidden moments of burning, trembling ecstasy?

2600-7 $4.50 US/$5.50 CAN

A WANTED MAN.
AN INNOCENT WOMAN.
A WANTON LOVE!

Renegade Heart
Madeline Baker

When beautiful Rachel Halloran took Logan Tyree into her home, he was unconscious. A renegade Indian with a bullet wound in his side and a price on his head, he needed her help. But to Rachel he was nothing but trouble, a man whose dark sensuality made her long for forbidden pleasures; to her father he was the answer to a prayer, a gunslinger whose legendary skill could rid the ranch of a powerful enemy.

But Logan Tyree would answer to no man — and to no woman. If John Halloran wanted his services, he would have to pay dearly for them. And if Rachel wanted his loving, she would have to give up her innocence, her reputation, her very heart and soul.

____2744-5 $4.50